"I loved Mommy," she said. Shirley heard doubt in the words. Self-doubt.

Shirley gritted her teeth, bit her tongue, prayed for the right words. "I know you did, Allison. Because of the way you acted. You took care of her. You couldn't have done that unless you loved her."

Long silence. "I couldn't, could I?"

Shirley felt the small body in her arms relax, as though some tightly wound coil had been released. "No, you couldn't, honey. You did everything you were supposed to. You did even more than anyone could have expected. You were respectful, and you were kind." And I'm not going to let those bastards have you, she finished silently. She rocked the child, and the child let herself be rocked.

DEAD IN THE SCRUB

B.J. Oliphant

FAWCETT GOLD MEDAL • NEW YORK

Library of Congress Catalog Card Number: 89-91908

ISBN 0-449-14653-7

Manufactured in the United States of America

First Edition: March 1990

Author's Note

There is no Ridge County in Colorado, with or without a county seat called Columbine. And, though the fictional Columbine is near the urban sprawl of a very real Denver, the author chooses for the most part not to refer to real addresses. All characters, including those in police departments and sheriff's offices are fictional, housed in fictional locations.

1

MANY OF THE foothills of the Rocky Mountains are covered with low forests of scrub-oak. Often the oak is only brush: waist-high, head-high. Sometimes it grows into dwarf forests, fifteen to twenty feet tall, with enough space between the slender trunks that deer or cattle can push through and take shelter from the summer sun. Here and there a spearhead of juniper thrusts through the lower growth, or a lone ponderosa rears its massive top. On flatter lands the oak gives way to grassy clearings and meadows edged by chokecherry and currant and wild rose; along the meagre creeks, cottonwood and willow crowd one another at the waterside. But for the most part, the hills are only scrub-oak, gambrel-oak, sometimes called buck-brush, for the deer hide in its mazy depths, safe from any but the most stubborn and masochistic of hunters.

In late September the oak brush begins to lose its glossy green as it takes on a bronzy hue, an almost metallic shine from which the sun strikes hard, glittering shards of light to make the slopes seem forged rather than grown. If the days continue warm and there is no hard freeze, sections of the scrub change further, as though at random, here brightening to red, there to orange, here sinking from metallic bronze to sharper ochres and coppers, there flattening through shades of claret and burgundy to maroon. There are hints of melon and apricot, then carnival pink and bright orange, as rose and currant and chokecherry begin to flame at the foot of the scrub and along the roads.

From a distance, it could be a New England fall. All the colors are there except the brilliant scarlet of maples, though almost that red can be found where the dwarf sumac crouches at the roots of the trees. Up close, however, the scrub offers none of the exaltation of a hardwood forest in autumn. It does not welcome walkers or dreamers. No matter how colorful it may become, the scrub is hard and unforgiving still: mean, tenacious, and impenetrable.

At last a night comes, icy cold with a bitter wind, and by morning the oak forest is brown, all brown, wine brown and coffee brown and tobacco brown, the leaves curled and twisted and dull. Yesterday's multicolored hillsides are suddenly monochrome. Later they will fade to sullen gray, and then the leaves will fall.

The same cold that fades the oak challenges the river trees to glory! The green pours out the ends of willow and cottonwood branches, and only the gold remains, glittering lemon gold against a cloudless sky the color of jay feathers. Aspen and alder flicker their sequin leaves against the wind. Gold falls in shining showers. Gold carpets the red-graveled, trickling streams and lies in drifts along the banks, swirling gently at the rim of the clucking water.

And from the gold-edged stream come the young mule deer, their muzzles wet, tripping across the dun meadow toward the oak brush. They walk delicately, their slender feet set down like pegs, choreography on tiptoe, one following the other, one leaping where the one before has leapt, a single-file wave of soft tan bodies and white rumps lifting over the barriers in the trail: over the fallen tree beside the stream; over the piled stones in the meadow; over the body

2

that has lain dead in the scrub since early summer, food for the coyotes and the crows.

There is nothing much left of it now. Some bones, of course, the scattered ribs and leg bones, the tough spinal column, the few arm and foot bones that have not been carried away. A few shreds of cloth. A belt buckle. A shoe. And a skull staring up at the blue, blue sky.

A spider has built a web in one eye socket and caught a fly. The fly struggles and heaves, unwilling to die.

As the dead person had also done; had also been.

Shirley McClintock leaned against the trunk of a lone pine and tried to summon up some less-familiar expletives. Her usual cuss words were dull from repetition, like plowshares rounded off by being dragged through rocky ground. Both her arms had been deeply scratched through her canvas jacket. She had a wicked wound under one eye and had almost lost her glasses several times. The live scrub-oak was flexible and would bend out of the way, but among the living branches were many iron-hard dead ones that shattered into jagged dagger points as she pushed through them. No matter how she had crouched and swerved, holding her heavy-sleeved arms before her face, the oak had extracted its toll of blood. Adding to her discomfort, something small but implacable had worked through the lining of her boot to wear a throbbing blister on her left heel. Now the spattered red trail she had been following for the past two miles led down the hill into yet another thicket with enough brown-gray leaves hanging through it to make it impossible to peer into or through.

The only hopeful note was that there was more blood on the trail than there had been early in the chase. The poor little beast she was following might already be dead. If she could be sure of that, she could give up this painful, wearying trail and find her way home, but she could not be sure until she saw the body. Torturing animals was not what she had had in mind when she'd agreed to go bowhunting with Charles Maxwell. The farther she followed the bloody trail the less

3

sure she was exactly what she'd had in mind except that it had been a dumb-ass mistake.

Ridge County, Colorado, though unquestionably rural, with vast tracts of national forest covering wide areas of it, was nonetheless so densely populated that rifle fire was considered an unacceptable danger. Since hunters were an extremely vocal and politically active minority, however, the county achieved an annual compromise by allowing a brief deer season for bowhunters and muzzle-loading rifles. It was assumed that no muzzle loader could fire far enough to injure innocent bystanders or their livestock; and also that, no matter how strong the bow, arrows would not skewer victims the next valley over.

Though Shirley had fallen irremediably in love with Robin Hood (as played by Errol Flynn) at an impressionable age, bringing home a buck from Sherwood or any other forest was not essential to her self-image. She had not taken advantage of the bowhunting season for years. How she had found herself with the strange group she had recently left to follow the wounded deer was, if not a mystery, at least not readily explicable. Mike Carmichael she knew slightly, though only as an officer of the Columbine Savings and Loan, but she had never met his wife until today. She knew the Maxwells scarcely at all and had decided during the last couple of hours to take whatever steps might be necessary to prevent her from knowing them better. People who drank while they pretended to be hunting, people who wounded game but would not follow and kill it, were not her kind of people.

Of course, Charles Maxwell's hitting the doe at all had been a fluke, the wildest kind of accident. No sensible deer would have come within several hundred yards of the place the group had been ensconced, and any deer with normal hearing would have run in the opposite direction. Charles had simple gotten off a lucky shot at a curious, very young, and now-to-get-no-older doe. The Carmichaels, who could scarcely have been more unsuitably dressed if they'd been on their way to a formal dinner, had exclaimed insincerely over his prowess, and this fulsome blather evidently was to have

4

concluded the exercise. When Shirley mentioned that hunting etiquette required rather more than mere exclamation, Charles had popped another can of beer and refused absolutely to follow the deer into the scrub. Gloria, tottering on her high heels, had sputtered mindless agreement, while their eleven-year-old daughter, who had been crouched at the foot of a tree with a book, trying hard to be somewhere else, had resolutely kept her eyes on its pages. At which point Shirley told them she would go alone and had done so, trotting off in the direction the deer had gone without responding to the baffled remonstrances Charles had shouted after her.

Spattered blood had led her north through a long series of clearings and copses on a trail that eventually turned back on itself. She had come to her present location via a downhill diagonal that extended, so far as she could see, into the thicket before her.

She took an angry breath and limped toward the scrub, scanning for blood as she went. The spatters led toward a trail through the brush, which, like most trails, had been cleared by deer and cattle to a height of three or four feet and was almost impenetrable above that level. Deer trails were hell for persons who stood six-foot-two in their stocking feet. Not that this was any time to consider standing about in one's stockings.

Bird noise percolated through the thicket: jays shrieked, and a crow made a "somebody coming" noise, a croaked complaint accompanied by dramatic fluttering of black wings. Shirley pushed through a final screen and came up with her quarry. The little beast had started a leap, and the arrow had hung up between two forked branches. It was impaled in midair, struggling, its eyes already dim.

Shirley breathed out, an exhalation that combined pity with a certain satisfaction that the job was over. Her handgun slipped from its holster into her hand with a reassuring familiarity. She checked to be sure there was a live round coming up in the cylinder, braced her arm on a nearby trunk, and squeezed the trigger. The doe's body quivered in a brief spasm. Shirley walked forward and put another bullet through

5

its head, just to be sure, then reholstered her gun and fastened the flap securely. The body still hung on the steel-pointed arrow, its shaft stenciled with Maxwell's name and phone number. She considered withdrawing it and returning it to him—hunting arrows were expensive—but rejected the idea with a flash of hostility directed at the man personally. If he wanted to retrieve his arrows, let him damned well do it himself. Now all she wanted to do was find her way out of here and get home.

The thought of walking for several miles made the blister on her heel throb with sullen fury. She knelt to loosen her shoelaces, her eyes coming to rest upon the undergrowth at the roots of the scrub. From beneath the leaves the skull stared at her with its eyeholes, one empty, one full of spider web and old fly bodies.

"Oh, for the love of Mike!" said Shirley McClintock, retreating into childhood for a proper phrase. "Oh, shee-it."

The chopper pilot had no trouble finding three black circles, remains of the triangle of fires she had built in the meadow nearest her discovery. "Clever," he said, nodding at her with mixed humor and approval. Shirley appreciated the humor. Many men reacted to her with immediate hostility just because she was big. And ornery. And maybe for a few other reasons.

"Couldn't think of any other way to find it from the air," she shouted over the sound of the rotor. "I was lost."

"Not too lost," he smiled, pointing uphill. "Redstone Point picnic grounds is that way, about half a mile." In the direction of his extended hand she could see a red curve of road edging the ridge, a wider clearing at its side. Against the black of the forest, the concrete tables and silver-painted trash cans of the picnic ground showed up plainly. That was where Maxwell had parked the van before he shot the deer, but she could not see the van now. Probably they'd left, tired of waiting for her. The pilot reached for his radio and began talking, the static and the whup, whup, whup of the rotors covering what he was saying. She didn't need to hear it. He was telling the sheriff where to go. County Highway 57 to the junction with 42, up 42 four miles to the national forest picnic ground at Redstone Point. Just below the picnic area was the small clearing where Maxwell had shot the deer. To the north a stream bed was marked by the yellow of willows and cottonwoods. West the mountains loomed, dark and veiled in haze.

"Want to set down here and wait for them?" he shouted.

She nodded, yawning. She didn't want to walk through half a mile of scrub, she was sure of that. Even with a clean sock borrowed from a deputy plus a bandage and some antibiotic ointment out of the sheriff's first-aid kit, her left heel felt like somebody had set fire to it. It had been tempting to ignore the bones. At the moment, she didn't know whether she was pleased with herself for having done her duty or annoyed with herself for having caused herself and others more trouble than the matter might turn out to be worth. It was a dilemma she had experienced more and more frequently during the last few years. Life sometimes felt much like the scrub: tangled, tiring, painful, and unrewarding.

Of course, one could always get out of it, if one wanted to badly enough.

"How'd you come out?" the pilot asked, evidently for the second or third time, gesturing away from the meadow.

"Down." She pointed along the meadow toward a series of clearings extending through the scrub toward the south. "It would have been shorter north, but I didn't know that. So I went downslope south. There's a guest ranch down there about two miles. Belongs to some people called Mellot. I tried to call from there, but the phone was out, so Mrs. Mellot had one of her people drive me into Columbine."

"You're lucky those fires didn't get away from you."

"I cleared the ground first," she said. "And set them one at a time. Even so, I had to do a little war dance, stamping out the edges." Which hadn't helped her sore foot any.

He looked at her curiously, wondering at her, trying to

7

place her in his catalogue of people types. Big. Short gray hair under her battered Stetson. Whispery-deep voice, as though she had a cold. Broad, short-nailed hands, callused on the palms. He'd felt that when they'd shaken hands, back at the pad in Columbine. His first thought had been simply ranchwoman, lived here all her life. Now he wasn't so sure.

"You think somebody would see the smoke and come looking?" he asked.

"Hoped," she agreed. Not that it was likely, as understaffed as all the forest service offices were, but smoke might have brought somebody. It hadn't rained since sometime in August. Fire danger was supposed to be way up, which might have made the lookouts vigilant. Of course, her fires hadn't burned long. Just piled dried grass, enough to make a mark.

"Where's the body?" he asked.

She pointed uphill, sighting between two huge ponderosas and an outcropping of sandstone shaped like a bull's head. "Deep in there. What's left of it."

"It'll probably take the sheriff an hour or more to get out here from town. He was playing ball at some picnic or other, and he said he needed to pick up a couple of men, so it'll take him awhile. I'll fly up to Redstone Point to pick him up, but in the meantime I've got some sandwiches and a thermos. Share and share alike?"

"You're one of God's chosen," she said. He probably was, too. Anybody crazy enough to fly a chopper in these mountains had to be. Small planes went down every year, caught by the sudden downdrafts or the sheering winds the great canyons bred, lost so completely that no subsequent search, no matter how extended, brought them to light.

Over an hour later, when the pilot brought in the sheriff and his two men—borrowed, the sheriff said, from a neighboring county—she was able to lead them to the bones without hesitation. The sheriff stared at the impaled doe, and she said defensively, "I didn't put the arrow into it. I just chased it down and killed it when nobody else would, that's all.''

The sheriff made no comment. Fish and Wildlife might have made a fuss, but not him. Deer bodies were not his business. Human bodies were his business. He muttered about photos and how many bones were missing and how the hell they could find anything under all this leaf litter while the men made bored but competent noises. Shirley and the pilot walked back to the chopper, where she lay in its shade and went to sleep. By the time the investigators emerged from the brush with a plastic sack she felt somewhat rested and was no longer considering immediate suicide as an acceptable alternative to living another month or two.

"Wanna drop us over on the road?" the sheriff queried the pilot.

"Take two trips," the pilot said. "Like it did coming in. Plus that." He nodded meaningfully at the limp body bag.

Shirley waited with the sheriff while the two deputies or forensics people or whatever they were went out. The sheriff had not bothered to introduce them, though he had introduced himself. Shirley already knew his name was Botts Tempe. He was a heavy, square man with a military haircut, saggy bloodhound eyebrows, and a flat, humorless face that had received several painful-looking wounds from the scrub. He was less vocal about his injuries than he was at having his afternoon's enjoyment interrupted, however, for he complained, "Church softball game. Over-forties against the under-forties, and us old guys were winning." After a pause he grunted. "Hell of a thing on a Sunday afternoon."

"You think it was a man or a woman?" she asked when it became apparent he was going to offer no further comment.

"Man," he said. "Or . . ." He measured her with his eyes, running an invisible tape measure from her feet to the top of her head. "Or maybe a woman of your size. My guess is about six feet."

"Not many women my size," she said without emotion. "Not in Ridge County. Of course, you go to a women's basketball tournament, you see a lot of us."

He shrugged. "The pathologist will know. Maybe I should be able to tell from the pelvis, but I haven't seen that many. Most of the bodies I've seen still had meat on them."

"How'll you find out who?"

He considered this, then slowly ticked off what he would do, thinking his way through each step. "Check missing persons first. Then get a story in the city paper. If worst comes to worst, get one of those reconstruction people to build a face on that skull and run pictures of that. Trouble is, out here . . ." He looked around, scowling eyebrows half covering his eyes, gesturing in frustration at the scrub, the hills, the jagged horizon of mountains.

"Lots of strangers," she agreed. "Hunters. Hikers."

He became almost voluble. "People off on their own. Alone. Nobody knows where they are, where they were headed. La Plata county sheriff found two bodies down in the San Juans two years ago, and they still don't know who they are. And those were frozen under the snow, so they even had pictures. We spent quite a bit of time in there, and we looked around pretty good, but we couldn't find anything to tell us who he was. With only bones . . ." His voice trailed off.

She agreed with him. Too many people wandering around in the mountains without knowing where they were and without anyone else knowing they were there. People on vacation. People from Chicago and Detroit and New York. People who didn't know about hypothermia, or getting lost, or predators. People who went hiking alone, or cross-country skiing alone, and never came back. Here in the mountains death came more easily than in many places: more often in the cities, but more easily here, where nature helped, and there weren't any scurrying functionaries to stop it. Any hiker, any skier—well, the bones she had found hadn't worn hiking shoes. Or skis. She created a mental picture of a fox or crow making off with a pair of skis, then looked up at the sound of the chopper returning.

"You shouldn'ta been out here alone either," said the sheriff. "No matter how big you are. You come into the office tomorrow or the next day? Ask for me. Sheriff Tempe."

"What for, Botts?" He seemed to relax a little when he heard his first name. He hadn't known who she was before she told him, but he was willing to be known by her. She'd used his first name just to see how he reacted. Evidently he didn't mind. Maybe it even made him feel secure.

He said, "Just give me a statement, you know, how you found the bones. Names of the people you were hunting with."

Hunting with! Shirley sneered privately. Whatever that had been, it hadn't been hunting.

The chopper landed in a swirl of gray leaves and picked them up. Fifteen minutes later the pilot circled above the McClintock ranch, remarking as he did so that she'd found the body only about three miles from her own front door. He set down like a feather in the pasture and grinned at her as she fought her way out of the tight cabin. The muscles in her foot and leg had cramped and didn't want to move.

"Thanks for the ride. Have far to go yet?" she shouted at him.

"Back to Denver! That's home."

She waved him off and turned toward the house. If she was lucky, the damned-fool Maxwells would at least have brought her bow case home with them. Once she'd realized what was actually going on, she hadn't even taken the bow out of the case, so all they had to do was carry it back to the van. They should have it when they got home. If the damned-fool Maxwells had had the sense to go home. Though why anybody would want to go home when home was in town, cheek by jowl with hundreds of other people, Shirley didn't know.

The McClintock ranch was about fifteen miles away from any gathering of more than ten people. Sixteen hundred acres, inherited from Pa and Ma, who had been the third generation of McClintocks on the place. Shirley still kept registered cattle, a few horses, a few chickens, ducks and goats. The goats were just for fun. They weren't good for anything. A dog, naturally, who was now a welcoming brown blur headed across the pasture in her direction.

"Hallo, Dog," she said. Dog was half Australian shepherd, half Chow. Dog was built like a Spitz, short and fast with a curly tail, brown all over, with dirty-looking spots here and there. Dog's name was Freckles, which nobody ever called her, and she had more sense than Shirley did. You wouldn't have caught Dog being dragged off into the mountains to bowhunt for deer. If you were Dog, you just ran your prey down when you were hungry. Rabbits, mostly. Pocket gophers. Wood rats. The occasional unwary chicken. Well, that was all right. Survival of the fittest. Only fast, alert chickens would survive to propagate their kind. Come Armageddon there'd be a few survival-type chickens left, which was more than you could say for the fat, debeaked monstrosities sold to Colonel Sanders for his Kentucky Fried.

"Come on home, Dog," she advised. She wanted to be where it was warm and comfortable and wet, in her own big bathtub, a bathtub that was actually long enough for her. The elder McClintocks had had a dinky little tub, but after they had both died, Shirley had hired a decorator to redesign the bathroom along with the rest of the house. It had always looked like a bunkhouse when her Ma and Pa were alive, with boots everywhere, saddles on the dining room table, and saggy furniture that should have been retired to the Salvation Army decades before. The decorator had found Navajo rugs in a trunk in the storeroom, where

12

they'd been for fifty years, and had hung them on the re-finished, wood-paneled walls. He had taken out other walls to make a big kitchen and a big bedroom and had replaced dilapidated junk with Taos-style oak furniture. Now the house was full of bright colors and capacious cupboards, and it had a huge table in the kitchen to spread things out on. Sometimes it made her feel good, just see-ing it.

Dog stuck her nose in Shirley's hand and trailed along. Idiot Mare put her head over the fence and whickered. Idiot Mare hadn't the sense God gave a flea, but she was pretty. Zeke the gelding was ugly, but Zeke was all brains. Zeke did not waste a whicker because he could tell from two hundred yards away what kind of a mood she was in. If Zeke didn't whicker, neither did his lackey, Small Brown Horse.

At the house, J.Q. stood in the doorway, his pepper-and-salt hair on end, waving at her, the phone in one hand. Somebody. She made a pushing gesture at him, nodding approvingly as he turned away and made excuses. It was too late to talk to anybody. She was too hungry and tired to talk to anybody.

"That was Roger Fetting from Washington," J.Q. called, stumping out on his crutches to the top of the steps that led down into the driveway. "I told him you'd call him back, maybe tomorrow. How'd it go?"

She surprised herself by smiling at him, suddenly glad to see him, then stalked up the steps and hugged him, crutches and all, feeling the lean, string-bean length of him against her, like a strong old tree. Maybe everything wasn't dry bones after all.

He hugged her back, asking, "Did you kill anything?"

"Not decently, J.Q. Damn, not on purpose, but God I sure felt like it."

Along about eleven o'clock, the phone rang. Shirley cocked an eyebrow as J.Q. answered it to say yes, Shirley'd gotten home all right, sure, pretty late, after dark, right. Yes, well, it was nice of the Maxwells to ask.

"Eleven my god o'clock," Shirley rumbled. "If I'd broken a leg up there, I could've been torn to pieces by a cougar by now."

"You could have let them know you got home in one piece," J.Q. remarked calmly. "You didn't have to play the eccentric, taciturn recluse for their benefit."

"I don't play that for anybody's benefit but my own," she grunted. "I wanted them to suffer. Waste of effort. They've probably just sobered up enough to realize I didn't come back with them. Did they ask about the deer?"

"What deer?" asked J.Q. "She did say they had your bow."

"Small favors," she remarked, yawning. "I'm going to bed. What's on the agenda for tomorrow?"

"The vet's coming out around ten to check Idiot Mare, see if she's still pregnant and how she's coming. He said he'd take the stitches out of Dog while he's here, save us a trip. That man from Glenwood coming around noon to see if he wants some heifers. Other than that, not much."

"Thank God I'm retired," she said. "All this mad activity could get to me otherwise."

"Love, are you depressed?"

"How could you tell?"

"You sound like a kid on Christmas morning who got coal in his stocking."

"It wasn't one of my better days. When I saw that skull, first thing I thought of was Marty."

"Shirley, damn, I'm sorry."

"Second thing I thought was ignore the bones, let them alone. Chances were nobody else would go into that thicket."

"But you didn't."

"No. Habit. Take charge, get it done, call out the troops." She laughed at herself. "It was just a down day. Most days I'm fine."

14

"Most days you are fine," he agreed solemnly. "Except the days you pick to start a war."

"I haven't started a war for two or three weeks, J.Q. ! I've been peaceable."

"Peaceable," he snorted. "Well, in any case, your daddy did right by you, Shirl."

"My Pa was a nice man," she agreed. "My two husbands were nice men, too. Among what the three of 'em left me, we'll make it through to the end, J.Q. Only problem I've got is who I can leave it to if there's any left over when we're gone."

She got up and stared out at the moonlight, thinking of little Sal and young Marty. Little Sal who had been in the way of a drunk driver and had never lived to grow up. Young Marty who had become Marty the anthropologist, off on an exciting, much-anticipated trip into the Amazon from which he had never returned. When Sal went, Shirley and Martin had recovered, somehow. When Marty disappeared, it had seemed the world had ended. Losing all one's children was like being cut off at the roots. The thrust of life was lost along with them. Children were supposed to be there when the old folks went on, continuing the line, making life mean something. With children gone, meaning was gone.

Martin Fleschman, Shirley's first husband, hadn't survived the loss. His sap hadn't run strongly enough. During the two years after young Marty disappeared, Martin had turned gray and dry and quiet, and then one afternoon he had simply lain down and died. Heart, the doctors said. Grief, Shirley had thought. Pain and grief. He'd been twenty years older than she. By the time he died, she hardly felt the loss of a husband. He'd gone off into some other place when young Marty went. He hadn't really been with her for a long time.

A year and a half later, she'd married Bill. Bill was healthy and hearty and six-foot-four, built like a football player, with a heart that would never give out. Their life together had lasted a happy five years before the cancer took Bill. A lot of losses. And here she was at fifty-five with maybe twenty or thirty years left, most of it healthy, probably, knock on wood, and no one to follow her at all.

J.Q. said it was no different from having children grow up and go off to live in Connecticut. He saw his three kids about once in every three years, and they were like natives of some foreign country. "You spend most of your life looking forward to sharing your children's happiness," he said. "And then you learn they don't have any to share." Well.

"I'm going to bed, J.Q.," she said. "I'm tired."

"Don't grieve over it, Shirl," he said from behind her, his hand suddenly on her shoulder. "We agreed, remember? You did your grieving a long time ago."

"I know," she said. "It's just sometimes it all comes back, J.Q. And then for a while, it just seems . . ."

He hugged her, and she felt his heart, pounding against her. "I know," he said. "I know."

Monday's paper had a story about Shirley McClintock of the McClintock Ranch having been in a group of hunters, otherwise unnamed, who had found some unidentified but recently dead bones. Well, shit, she thought. Credit where credit is due. The paper gave the impression the whole group of them had found those bones.

She set the paper aside and called Washington. Roger Fetting was jovial but, as usual, in a hurry.

"You know, if I don't do this fast enough for you, Rog, you could get someone else," she said. "I don't need the work. I'm retired. My two husbands left me enough to live on the rest of my life." Especially, she thought, if I don't go dragging it out.

"Shirley, please. I don't want anybody else. I want you to write the report for me, and I'd love to give you all the time in the world. It's just that the Congressional hearings are next week."

She was somewhat mollified. It wasn't nice to be pushed, but it was pleasant to be valued. "It's almost finished," she told him. "I'll spend all day today on it, run it off in the morning, and send it Federal Express. You'll have it tomorrow, next day at the latest."

That took care of Monday, and she almost managed to forget the body.

Tuesday morning's paper added a bit to the story. No identification, said the reporter, no wallet, no tags in the clothing, nothing useful. But the bones, so opined the state pathologist, were of a man between the ages of thirty-five and forty-five, give or take a few years either way. He had been six foot one inch tall. He had a recent but well-healed break of two ribs on the left side. His teeth had been generally good. Scraps of scalp found near the body indicated that the person had had dark hair and a medium complexion. A shattered rib plus a bullet found under the bones suggested he'd been shot in the lung. Estimated time since death was four or five months. In answer to questions from the reporter, the pathologist agreed that the victim might have been shot somewhere other than where he'd been found. No way to tell when all you had was bones. There were no missing persons reported in Ridge County who matched the description. Other surrounding counties were being queried.

"Poor bastard," said Shirley. She could imagine him running away, wounded, just like that poor little deer. Finally he'd fallen, and then he'd died, lying there in the scrub, looking up through those glossy leaves at the distant sky. What had he been thinking? If he'd been lucky, he had gone fast, or at least he'd been unconscious for most of it.

"Poacher," J.Q. suggested. "Somebody poaching deer, shoots at somebody in the brush. Doesn't even know he's hit a human being."

That was possible. Last winter Shirley had found one of her Belted Galloways shot—a black cow with a white stripe around it, a veritable Oreo cookie of a cow, a cow that couldn't look less like a deer if it wore a red wig—rifle shot right behind the shoulder. Did the shooter know it was a cow? Did the shooter not care that it was a cow?

Did the shooter even see the cow? Or did he just fire at a noise?

"Damn fools," she said, feeling guiltily that she'd said that a lot lately. "Damn fools."

"Right," J.Q. agreed. "You want to talk to the vet?"

She shook her head. "I'm going to finish that report, then I'm going to make a grocery list."

In her office the word processor beeped and clucked at her as she cleaned up the final few paragraphs, checked Roger's original letter to be sure she'd included everything he'd asked for, then turned on the printer. Roger hired her to do certain reports because he had learned to depend upon her talent for synthesis and her ability to say things in clear, simple non-bureaucratese. The talent had emerged over the years she had worked for him at the Bureau, and he had come to value it. Shirley could take bits of this, bits of that, news articles, reports, television documentaries, polls, and from this disparate collection infer an inevitable direction. "It'll go this way," she had told Roger about this thing or that thing over the years, usually to be proven right later. "That's the way people are leaning," she had told him. "This is what they think."

Or, as in this case, "This is what's happening."

The report she had just finished for Roger, currently a member of a Presidential commission on foreign trade, claimed that American engineering was falling behind, that American education was, despite all the protestations of the educators, at the end of its rope, and that the country had no way to redress the balance of trade without massive infusions of money put into recruitment of talented youngsters followed by a decade and a half of expensive, demanding scientific and engineering education provided by a list (which she had had appended) of persons and institutions who still had some pride and creativity left. She had referred to the fact that these institutions were currently graduating classes that were approximately forty percent American, the other sixty percent being Taiwanese or Korean or Japanese or European.

Shirley had no expectations that the report would be acted upon or even accepted. There were many prestigious universities not on her list. Senators from those states would object. The report advocated recruiting talented kids and maintaining extremely high standards. Certain knee-jerk liberals would call it elitism and yell their heads off. The report came down hard on the side of science, including the biological sciences. The fundamentalists would scream bloody murder at that. Her report—Roger's report—would be attacked, then decried, then dismissed. Shirley already knew that. Chances were Roger knew it, too. Between the bleeding hearts and the fundamentalists, the country didn't have a chance.

Shirley's bet, which she often restated to J.Q., was that within fifty years America would be Japanized: managed by, controlled by, and paid by a people who understood the difference between reality and religion. Of course, Japan was a single-race, single-culture country, which made it all easy. And Japan achieved its educational excellence through the sacrifice both of the kids who couldn't cut it and generations of women who were allowed no career but that of maternal academic coach. . . .

"What are you doing!" demanded J.Q. from the door. "Sitting there like a broody hen with your mouth all pushed out."

"Doubting my convictions," she muttered. "As usual."

"I thought you were retired."

"Sometimes it catches up to me, J.Q. Even though I haven't turned on the TV for months, sometimes it catches up to me. But you're right. I'm retired."

She checked the paper cassette in the laser printer and then went to the kitchen to make a grocery list, J.Q. trailing along on his crutches, making soft *thump, thumps* on the quarry-tile floor. Tuesdays were shopping days. They'd drive in to Columbine together. J.Q. would see the doctor. Shirley would do the shopping. They'd splurge on a pizza and come on home.

"Think he'll take that cast off today?"

"Probably not for another week."

"You ever going to ride Idiot Mare again?"

"Never. From here on out, she's a foal factory, and that's all."

When Shirley went back to the office, the report had run out its fifty pages of text and its twenty pages of footnotes. She put the pages in order, covered them with a letter to Roger, put the stack into a nine-by-twelve brown envelope, and typed a label. Time was she'd have had a staff of fifteen to do all this scut work. Clipping. Filing. Research. Interviews. Editing. Typing. Time was she'd have been eager to see what each day would bring.

Time was she'd have had a stomachache all the time, too.

A horn honked out front. J.Q., in the truck, being impatient, wanting to stir her up. Well, she had been glooming around a lot today. Thinking about old times did that to her. Maybe it would be better to sever this last connection, refuse to write any more of these things. They made her think too much, care too much.

They kept her alive. She'd had that thought before.

She ran a comb through her short gray hair, tucked her shirt into her jeans, and picked up her coat as she went out the door. "All right, all right," she yelled to J.Q. "Hold the horses! It's only three-thirty."

A chilly wind whipped down the valley, shivering the gold of the cottonwoods into glittering lace. Sun spattered into her eyes. High above, at the dome of the sky, a prairie falcon called from its circle. She caught her breath at the perfection of the moment.

Despite everything—everything—there were still some things that made life seem well worth it.

They returned from town about half-past six. It was already getting dark, and Shirley dropped off at the chicken house to shut the poultry in. It wouldn't be long before it would be too cold for them to go out at all, at least some

20

days, and there were too many of them for this little house. She and J.Q. would have to get the other chicken house finished before it snowed.

She turned on the light inside the low-ceilinged room and stood aside as the Brown Leghorns poured past her feet, hackle feathers gleaming, their dark bronze flow interrupted by an occasional gray-speckled guinea hen. When all the chickens and guineas had gone in, the Muscovy ducks stalked after them, waddling to the far corner to flock together, united against the sometimes unpleasant attentions of the roosters. Muscovies didn't submit to the pecking order the roosters thought appropriate. The new poultry house would give them some space of their own.

She sprinkled a little corn in the trough, and the sound of the falling grain brought in the goats. She shut the gate in the cougar fence behind them, flicking on the switch to the hot wires at its top. Poultry had to be safe behind doors, goats safe behind eight feet of wire. There were still nighttime terrors in the world, still things with gripping talons or ripping teeth, things that ate cats and geese and goats. Nothing large enough to threaten the cattle or horses, though sometimes in the night one would hear them making uneasy noises in the dark, perhaps prey to ancestral memories of sabre-toothed tigers and gigantic cave bears. Shirley yawned hungrily as she strolled toward the house, followed by three stalking shadows: the barn cats, tails erect, coming in for dinner.

"You've been fooling with my coffee," J.Q. challenged when she came through the kitchen door with the cats behind her.

"I haven't touched your coffee," she bridled. "What do you mean, fooling with it?"

"I reached up there in the freezer where I always keep the decaf beans, left side of the shelf, and I got them down and ground them and made a pot before I saw it was regular. You can't drink regular or you'll be awake all night. Regular goes on the right end of the shelf, not the left."

"J.Q., I haven't touched it!"

"If you're going to fool with it, you make the coffee."

21

"Honest to God, I swear on a stack of bibles, I have not touched the coffee. I leave your arrangements strictly alone." She opened cat food and dumped it into bowls. At her feet a ravenous munching and chomping made more noise than seemed appropriate for such usually silent creatures.

He thumped his crutch angrily. "Waste of a whole pot."

"Put it in the thermos, I'll heat it up and drink it tomorrow morning." She leaned down to stroke a sleek back.

"Disgusting in the morning."

"Well, let me be disgusted."

"I already threw it out."

She sighed. If he'd already thrown it out, why fuss? "Pizza hot?"

"Give it another minute or two. It got pretty cool on the way back from town."

"Then there's time to change my boots."

From her bedroom, in the daytime, she could look across the deck through a wall of glass to see promontories of weather-worn stones and golden trees along the creek. Now there was only a chill vacancy across which she pulled the curtains before sitting down to take her boots off. Her lambskin slippers were not in their accustomed place at the edge of the bed. She felt for them with her feet, then knelt and discovered them pushed far back under the bed. She never put them there.

Grumpily she put them on, went to the bathroom, washed her face and hands, then returned to the kitchen complaining. "Somebody's been fiddling with my slippers. Dog, do you suppose? Did we leave her in?"

J.Q. muttered something.

She said, "Speak up, J.Q.!"

"No, we didn't leave her in," he shouted. "She's out at the garage barking at something right now."

"What? Raccoon?"

"Cat, more likely. I gave your mouse crew second helpings and let them out. That kitten is growing up to be a monster."

"Isn't he! That cat's going to weigh twenty pounds when

he's grown. I'm going to breed him, J.Q. I swear I am. We'll create a whole race of cats big enough the owls can't pick them off." The thought of owls made her remember Miguel, the orange-and-white cat, the one who sat at her toes and purred, begging for a sip of her coffee. An owl had taken Miguel.

"If you're going to breed him, you ought to name him."

"I should," she said, opening the oven door as she considered naming things. Naming things was a kind of commitment. Once things were named, they became yours, and you grieved when they died. Like Miguel, whose little body they had found where the owl had dropped it from a great height. She wasn't sure she wanted to grieve over the kitten. "This pizza is hot," she advised J.Q., sucking a singed finger.

"Well, put it on the table." He had made a green salad and was dishing it out for them. They sat at the table in the lamp glow, stuffing themselves on pizza, salad, coffee, listening to Dog barking at something. It wasn't Dog's "who goes there" bark, or her "stop or I'll bite your leg off" bark. It was more the happy "I see you" bark, and it probably signified she was playing hide and seek with the cats.

"If Dog didn't move my slippers, who did?" she asked.

"You probably kicked them without knowing it."

She subsided, mouth full of cheese, and reached for her coffee and the sugar bowl. "Sugar bowl's empty. I'll fill it."

She took it to the cannister in the corner, opened the cannister, fished out the full scoop and dumped it into the bowl without paying much attention to what she was doing. Then she scowled at the result, a powdery drift on the dark counter.

"What the hell is the flour cannister doing in the corner?"

J.Q. rose and came over to her. There were seven dark-blue glass cannisters in the row, two different sizes. The four large ones were supposed to hold sugar and corn meal and flour and breakfast grain, in that order. The smaller ones held brown sugar and tea and rice. Now the sugar bowl was full of flour with an additional untidy drift of it on the tiled counter.

"Did you rearrange them?" she asked him.

"Why would I do that?"

"Damned if I know, J.Q. I just thought maybe you did."

She left the kitchen hurriedly, plunging through the living room into her office. There were books she always kept in a certain order: dictionaries, books of synonyms, style and usage books, books of quotations. She ran her hand along the shelf, noting that several volumes were misplaced.

Back in her bedroom, she checked the closet. Shoes had been moved. In her dresser drawers someone had put her panties on top of her bras, rather than the other way around.

"Someone's been through the place," she told J.Q. as she returned to the table. "My room, the office. Better look in your room."

He departed to do so, returning to say, "The book I was reading isn't on top. I think somebody's been through my closet, but I can't be sure." He gave her a speculative look. "Not a thief?"

"TV's still here. Stereo's still here. I had a couple of hundred in an old wallet in the top drawer. It's still there."

"What the hell were they looking for?"

"Wouldn't I like to know? I haven't the remotest, not the remotest idea." It hadn't been an expert search, so much was obvious. Things had been put back neatly, but not by anyone who knew how to do a search without the searchee finding out about it. Either by someone who didn't realize the search would be noticed or by someone who didn't care. Someone naturally untidy, or someone who didn't give a damn.

"They were looking for something small," opined J.Q. out of the midst of silent thought. "Something little enough to be under a paperback book. They, he, she. Whatever."

Something small enough to be in or behind shoes. To be in or behind the sugar cannister. To be in the freezer, in or behind the coffee beans. "Haven't done any jewel robberies recently, have you, J.Q.?" she asked. "No stolen brooches worth millions?"

"Last one was in seventy-eight," he deadpanned. "Sold

it to live on the proceeds and turned the jewel robbery business over to my brother." J.Q. didn't have a brother. Or a sister.

She stared at the window, racking her brain, but nothing came to her. What were they looking for? Something valuable? Something missing? Or did somebody get the wrong house?

"Wrong house," she said. "Somebody got the wrong house."

"Sure," he agreed. "Your name's only on the mailbox and on the front door and on half the stuff in your office. The whole place spells out McClintock. Your family has only lived here for about a hundred years. Sure they got the wrong house."

"If somebody looked in here, chances are they looked in the garage, too. And maybe in the barn."

"Nothing in the barn but hay and manure."

"Garage, then."

"I'll look after supper," he said.

They had coffee, and ice cream out of the freezer, then Shirley washed the dishes while J.Q. went out into the dark. She watched him through the kitchen window as he opened the door at the rear of the big garage, the one that led to the shop and the tractor bay. Lights came on inside, and she could see him moving around. He returned in twenty minutes, shaking his head.

"Hard to tell, Shirl. If they were there, they didn't move anything big. But there's little stuff shifted. My crosscut saw's hanging wrong way, as though somebody took it down to look behind it, then couldn't remember which way it was facing. Stuff like that."

Something small. Something light, that could have been taped up behind a saw.

"What do you think, J.Q.?" she asked him, mystified, troubled.

"I don't think," he said shortly. "Not yet. I feel a mite uncomfortable, but I wouldn't go so far as to think." He

25

sipped at the last of his coffee. "Might be smart to lock the doors tonight, though. Just in case."

"Let's do that," she said. "And let's let Dog sleep inside, too."

During the night, something clicked in Shirley's mind. Over morning coffee she told J.Q. what she thought.

"The person or persons who searched our house, whoever they are, believe I found something when I found those bones."

"Now how did you arrive at that?"

"Finding the body is the only different thing that's happened lately, and the newspaper spread my name all over in connection with the incident."

"Someone thinks you found something and kept it? Something you didn't give to the sheriff?"

"They might think that either I have it or the sheriff has it, but it would be easier to search this place than to search the sheriff's office. They may have searched both."

"You going to ask him if he's been searched?"

"No. Not yet. First thing I want to do is ride out there where I found the skull and look around a little more. There might be something out there we didn't find the first time. Feel up to riding Small Brown Horse?"

"Just my ankle got broken, not my seat. But that's quite a ride, isn't it?"

"It was about three miles by helicopter, but I figure five on the ground. I got a good look at the site from above, so I could see where it lies in relation to the picnic ground. Then I figured out a ground route on the forest service map." She pulled the map from her jacket pocket and spread it on the table between them. "We can go down the creek here to Maudy Gulch, up the gulch to where it cuts off into the Starr place, down along their valley to Mitchell Creek."

"That's all fenced," he objected.

"No, there's a gate at Mitchell Creek. The hundred-mile endurance ride comes through there every year, so Wally Starr put in a gate three years ago. We go up the creek about half a mile, and then turn uphill to the place I found the bones. There are deer trails all through there. I went down the other side, south, into a whole different drainage basin, because I thought it was shorter. Actually the Starr place would have been closest.''

J.Q. looked out the window at the sky and thumped his crutch thoughtfully. ''It's going to rain cats and dogs pretty soon. Could take the truck.''

''If we take the truck it's half a mile to walk in from the nearest road, another half a mile out. Through scrub, on crutches? We can be back before it rains.''

''Why don't we have a horse trailer?'' It was a familiar plaint, with a familiar answer. A horse trailer would be an expensive luxury, and they only really needed one a couple of times a year. If they had to move the horses by road, really had to, they could use the big stock trailer.

''All right. I'll ride Small Brown Horse,'' he said.

J.Q.'s favorite mushroom-picker's guidebook had a category of mushrooms called Little Brown Mushrooms, LBMs for short, and the book strongly advised against eating any of them because they were difficult to tell apart and not really worth the trouble. In J.Q.'s lexicon, Small Brown Horses were of a similar nature. SBH looked like every other SBH in the county, and most of them weren't worth the trouble. *The* SBH had one great advantage, however. He was as steady on the trail as Idiot Mare was skittish, and he had a nice, easy walk.

The day was warm. It took them about a hour to reach Mitchell Creek and start upward along the flow. Though the streambed was flat and easy to follow along the valley, a mile farther on the banks became precipitous. Shirley referred to her mental map and pointed west along the slope of the hill. ''Through there,'' she said, and they turned the horses up the bank onto a steep meadow mottled with scrub, then southwest through the scrub wherever the horses could find a path. After fifteen minutes of this slow, winding, turning-back and trying-again travel, they came out into a clearing.

Shirley grinned and pointed at the three black scars on the grass. "Here," she said. "Am I an expert guide or not!"

They rode up the slope and into the scrub on the deer trail she had followed before. On horseback they were above the worst of the oak except for their booted legs. The dead deer lay to one side of the tiny clearing, bare rib bones arching palely over the blackened tatters beneath. The crows and the coyotes and the magpies had been at the carcass. The arrow was gone. Where the human bones had lain, the leaf litter was much disturbed, making the site easy for them to locate.

J.Q. dismounted and untied one crutch from the saddle, stared at the carcass of the deer, and shook his head. "How did you get involved with those crazy people?"

Shirley sighed. "It was while you were in the hospital with your leg, J.Q. I'd ordered a dozen stenciled target arrows from Bartons, six for each of Martin's nephews for their birthdays this fall. They're both bowshooters; they got their first bows from me when they were kids, and I thought it would make a nice gift. So, one bundle of six arrived with the right name on them—Neal's, he's the one who moved to California—but the other bundle had this Charles Maxwell's name on them. I called Bartons and they told me Maxwell had ordered a dozen at the same time, and the two orders must have been mixed in the shipping room, because we both have a Columbine zip code."

"So you called Maxwell and asked if he had your arrows?"

"Right. Next time I was in town, I dropped by to see if anyone was home so I could drop his arrows off and pick up mine. Well, Charles was home. He was so glad to meet me and all full of enthusiasm. He told me he and some friends were having a little gathering the first day of the bowhunting season, and it would be just great if I'd come along to give some pointers to these inexperienced hunters. It all sounded very smooth and plausible. It's only after you're around Maxwell for a while you figure out he always sounds plausible, but he doesn't know his ass from his left ear. He makes up life as he goes along."

J.Q. shook his head at her. "You're not usually that easy to talk into anything." He looked at the scrub and then at his crutch. "Well, I question whether I'll be much good scrambling around in there." He knotted his kerchief high around his neck and pulled his hat down in preparation for assaulting the thicket.

Shirley was already stooped, searching between the narrow trunks beside the disturbed leaves, brushing others aside with her hands. They moved off in separate directions.

Ater a quarter of an hour, Jim called from a distance, "Found a shoe!"

She moved toward his voice, ducking and thrusting branches aside. The dried leaves rustled on the branches, so perfect a curtain that she did not see J.Q. until she almost stepped on him. Somehow he'd managed to get into the center of a twiggy tangle, getting his chin scratched up some in the process. He pointed to the shoe lying on its side and half-covered by red creeper. She knelt to brush leaves away with her gloved hands, finding one bone and then another scattered on the soil. "Foot bones," she said, gathering them into her spread kerchief.

Jim had moved off, peering at the ground, moving leaves and fallen twigs with his crutch tip. "Here," he said. "Something else."

She followed and went down on her knees again. This time it was a wallet, or what was left of a wallet. It had been chewed, rained on, and half-buried. Some hoofed animal had stepped on it while it was soaking wet, leaving the print of the hoof along one side. Fastened to the stained leather by a sun-rotted rubber band was a wad of paper of roughly the same dimensions as the wallet. She tugged the tattered remnant onto the kerchief, along with the bones and the shoe.

"Why here?" she wondered aloud. They were at least fifty yards from the place the bones had been found.

J.Q. pointed at an occupied-looking hole under a nearby tree. "That looks like fox," he said. "Hungry animal dragged pieces home."

They spent another hour circling the site but found nothing

more. Going home was downhill, faster than coming up had been, which was fortunate, for they beat the rain only by minutes. As they entered the house it began to pour in a steady, gray curtain.

While J.Q. fixed soup and sandwiches, Shirley opened the wallet with a pair of needle-nosed pliers and pulled out the contents. Money. Quite a lot of money. Four thousand dollars in hundred-dollar bills. Chewed at the edges, but otherwise intact. No driver's license. No credit cards. Some ticket stubs, or what looked like ticket stubs. Beneath the wallet, one large, folded piece of paper. Thick.

She counted the layers of folded paper. There seemed to be about eight. One side showed no layers at all. Eight layers meant it had been folded three times. The mass was about five by six inches, so the sheet, unfolded, could be about one foot by one-and-a-half or two. Or perhaps ten inches by twenty-four. Something like that.

"Heavy paper," said J.Q., leaning over her shoulder. "Maybe blueprint paper? Like they do architectural plans on? Only they don't make them blue anymore."

The paper was grayish white, but J.Q. was right. It was thick, almost like light cardboard. "It looks like blotter," she replied. "I can't get it apart."

"More like papier-mâché. It's been wet and compressed. 9It'll take a lab to get it apart. Even then, they may not be able to decipher it."

She peeled back one edge, feeling it tear. Faded letters lined one edge. . . . *ill D* . . . Someone's name, perhaps. She pushed the piece back into the mass, returned the money to the wallet pocket, reinserted the bits and pieces of ticket or claim check into the slots she had removed them from, folded the wallet closed, and restored the fragile rubber band.

"Sheriff Tempe?" J.Q. wanted to know.

"Him, yes. And then the *Columbine Chronicle*. I want everyone to know what we found and that the Sheriff has it. I hope to God this is whatever he or they, whoever, were looking for."

"Want me to drive you to town?"

"No. I can do it. It'll give me a chance to think."

"Let the Sheriff think about it."

She smiled. "Well, I'm not stopping him, J.Q. It's just I've got this feeling I should know something, you know? Something I'm looking at here should tell me something, but I don't know what it is."

"Did you make copies?" he asked. "Of those scraps of paper. If you didn't, you'll wish you had. I know you."

Before she took the discovery to Sheriff Tempe, she drew facsimiles of the tickets on a sheet of typing paper, noting the numbers. After a moment's thought, she also recorded the serial numbers on the hundred-dollar bills.

The sheriff's office was in the new Justice Center, a pretentious title for a concrete-block pile at one end of Columbine's only shopping center. Shirley parked behind the building to avoid the abortion protesters outside the women's clinic. Last time she'd parked out front, her car had been plastered with religious propaganda from the Pro-life Brotherhood, including pictures of bloody fetuses. Shirley wasn't sure how she might have felt about abortion for herself, but she was damned sure it wasn't the business of some cultist to decide for somebody else. Between the Pro-life Brotherhood's stand on abortion and the Living Church of Jesus' stand on refuges for battered women (against them, because women were directed by the Bible to submit to their husbands) or child care (also against it because women ought to stay home with their children), women weren't safe in this town. Which was yet another reason not to live in town.

She went through the rear door and upstairs to the sheriff's office to deliver her find. Sheriff Tempe was not greatly pleased.

"You should have left this stuff where it was and called us."

"I could've," she admitted. "Of course, it might not have been there by the time I got to a phone and you got up there. Whoever searched my house has probably thought of searching the site by now."

31

"I told my men not to say where we found the body."

"You didn't tell *me* not to say where we found the body. Half of Columbine called me after they saw the paper, and I told anybody who asked. Why not?" Actually only three people had called, but she had mentioned the general location.

He scowled, trying to think of something cutting to say, finally deciding he had no justifiable cause. Shirley could follow his train of thought in the changing expressions on his face: anger, doubt, embarrassment.

"So your house was searched, huh?" he asked.

"Best I can figure out, yes. House and the shop in the garage. The searcher wasn't looking for anything very big, either. What I just gave you may be it."

The sheriff moved the contents of the kerchief about. "Not the money, you think?"

"There's four thousand something there. That could be very attractive to some people, I suppose, but I had stuff in the house worth at least that much, and nobody bothered it."

"Got to be this wad of paper, then. Or the ticket stubs."

Shirley nodded and told him she'd leave him to his puzzlement. She went out the front way, remembering only when she was in the middle of the protesters why she had used the rear entrance before. The picketers' umbrellas were like fat mushrooms, blocking the women's clinic entrance. Two men and a familiar-looking woman had one little girl surrounded while they shouted at her and dripped water on her from their umbrellas. The girl was shouting back at them, her face wet, either from rain or tears. Shirley assumed it was tears, got up a little speed, bulldozed her way into the group, took the little person by the arm, and delivered her inside the clinic door in one continuous rush.

The small woman behind the counter put her hand on what looked like an alarm button; a heavyset woman came out into the reception area, blocking the corridor she had just left, and Shirely heard locks snick into place behind her.

"Peace," Shirley said, raising her hands. "I'm friendly."

"She rescued me," said the girl cheerfully. "I didn't think they'd be out there today."

The receptionist nodded wearily, "Usually they only come on Saturdays. We do abortions on Saturdays, which is a good day for our patients who work, but also a good day for protesters. This coming Saturday they're having some kind of big anti-abortion meeting though, so they're getting their weekly nasties in today."

She turned to the colorfully labeled and racked patient records behind her, took one down, and said to the rescued girl, "Sorry you had trouble, Diane."

"And sorry we thought you were part of the lunatic fringe," the heavyset women said to Shirley. "I'm Bess Willison, the clinic manager."

"Shirley McClintock." Shirley offered her hand.

"We're a little paranoid around here, I guess. You probably saw in the newspapers about that break-in last spring. Since then we've become very security-conscious. Normally we have a volunteer to help patients get through the picketers, but we didn't expect a problem today."

The woman behind the desk said, "Good old Elise can show up anytime. Elise is a real nut case."

"You're not doing abortions today?" Shirley asked.

"Just regular women's health care, some prenatal visits, birth control, stuff like that. Oh, and there's a childbirth class at four. We only do abortions on Saturdays and Tuesdays."

"Are those people out there the same ones who broke in last spring?" Shirley stared through the rain-streaked window at the marchers.

"Elise Fish is. She chained herself to an examining table, and we had a hell of a time getting rid of her. That funny-looking guy with the crazy eyes was here, too, though I don't think he was arrested. Deitz. Somebody

Deitz. Deitz had this buddy that always came with him, and the buddy did get arrested. I guess he didn't like jail because he hasn't been back. Most of them spent the night in jail. The judge handed Elise one heck of a big fine, several thousand dollars, but her doctor husband paid it and, as you can see, she's still with us. Indefatigable, that's Elise.''

"Was there much damage?" Shirley asked. Another shouting match was in progress on the sidewalk. This time the two largely pregnant women being harrassed looked like they were doing well enough in their own defense.

"The patient records got thrown all over everything. It took us three days to get all the forms back in the right folders. Refiling wasn't bad, we use a color system that makes it quick. They also tried to burn the place, but we had extinguishers ready.''

"Elise was chained to a table, and they tried to burn the place?"

"Who says they're bright? Fanatical, yes. Bright, no.''

The door behind them opened, and two women came in, like Diane, cheerfully annoyed. "Damn bastards," said one of them to the receptionist.

The receptionist smiled. "Call them any thing you like. I'm not allowed to. Bess says I have to remain dignified.''

The wettest and more pregnant of the two went to the counter. "I'm here for my last prenatal and those idiots are yelling at me about abortion." She took off her scarf and unbuttoned her raincoat, her melon shape seeming to balloon before her. "They are so damned ignorant! You know that Fish woman's son was arrested for selling dope? And her fifteen-year-old unmarried daughter has a baby. You know that?" She turned and threw up her hands at Shirley. "Why doesn't she stay home and take care of her kids! Lets them run wild while she's here yelling at us!''

"No idea," Shirley responded, thinking that this was a question Elise ought to be asked.

The receptionist was getting the woman's name as Shirley shook the manager's hand again and went out onto the asphalt. Elise Fish contorted her rather pretty face into a mask of hatred and called Shirley a name.

"You people," Shirley thundered, "are beneath contempt. Especially you, Elise!" In Elise Fish she recognized a tireless anti-smut crusader; finder of satanic messages no one else could hear on rock records; crusader for cleaning up the school library to remove all references to sex or the supernatural; wife of Dr. Fish, a local obstetrician with quite a reputation among local women for always doing things the most painful way.

"All we wanted her to do was come to my husband's office," Elise screamed. "So he could show her the baby on the ultrasound. She wouldn't murder her own baby once she saw it!"

"Come off it, Elise," she said. "All you want to do is fatten hubby's pockets. With the birth rate down and malpractice insurance up, he's hurting, isn't he? Don't you have sense enough to know those two women are here for prenatal visits?"

"Murderer," one of the men sneered, poking his face into hers. He had fanatical eyes and a tight, humorless mouth.

"And who are you?" Shirley asked, laying a heavy hand on his sloping shoulder and gripping tightly so he couldn't get away.

Elise shook herself and assumed a quasi-social expression. "This is William Deitz," she said arrogantly. "And Henry Rizer. Workers with me in the *Say Yes to Life* campaign."

"My name is Shirley McClintock," she told the men in a loud voice, pitching it to carry. "I take offense when I am called a murderer on a public sidewalk. I know Elise here from way back, and I believe she ought to be home taking care of her children. I do not know you gentlemen. I would suggest, however, that you moderate your language, or you may make me mad enough to show up here every day to make your mission difficult. I know that your religious persuasion advocates the brutalizing of women in order to inflate your tiny male egos, and I assume this juvenile harassment is most gratifying to you . . ."

The men began edging away, and Shirley pursued them, holding on, raising her voice a little more. Outside the supermarket several people had stopped to listen.

". . . However, I do think it is unworthy of grown men. It is typical of boys who have not yet reached the age of puberty, which makes me wonder whether you gentlemen have, in fact, reached that stage of development, or whether your masculinity is in some question. Your need to dominate women and force pregnancy on them may be a symptom of lack of confidence in either your equipment or your methodology. I can recommend a good doctor, or, perhaps Elise's husband would look up a sex therapist for you."

Her last few words were delivered at a shout, since she was speaking to their retreating backs. Elise and the other female picketers had moved away from her to stand in a muttering huddle at one corner of the building. Shirley simply stood where she was for several minutes, enjoying the rain and the looks on their faces, feeling quite alive and pleased with herself. In front of the supermarket two women were waving and applauding her while their husbands scuttled off. Nothing like sowing a little family dissension to make one's day complete. She decided to give Elise's group the benefit of her attentions, but they fled as she came toward them. Stubbornly she waited until she was sure they had gone before she herself left.

After making a brief stop at the newspaper office to be sure they would report that she'd turned her find over to the sheriff, Shirley dropped by the Maxwell house to pick up her bow. The house was a small, one-story ranch-style in a subdivision of similar homes, each surrounded by a lawn of winter-dormant grass, each landscaped with a few staked saplings and small evergreens. Though people had been living in the area for several years, it still had a naked, unfinished look. There was nothing to break the wind that shrilled continually around the corners of the houses. Shirley had noticed the thin and irritating sound the other time she had stopped at the Maxwells, and the high-pitched whine was the same today.

Gloria Maxwell came to the door wearing a purple velour caftan and silver sandals. She waved purple fingernails like talons, the tips extending more than an inch past her fingers. Behind her stood a dwarf twin, also in purple caftan and silver sandals, the child, white-faced and expressionless, with pained and patient eyes.

"You remember Allison," Gloria bubbled at Shirley. "My pretty girl. Today's Allison's birthday, and she's eleven. Aren't you, love?"

Allison looked at Shirley without answering, without really seeming to see her. Gloria's eyes were made up with three colors of eye shadow, mascara, and liner. Allison's eyes were identically decorated. Gloria wore violet lipstick and so did Allison. Both seemed to be thoroughly foundationed, blushered, and shaded despite having, so far as Shirley could see, perfect skin to start with. Gloria was waving the ridiculously lengthy nails in Shirley's direction. "They're artificial," she bubbled. "Aren't they wonderful? They make a set with hands, too, so little girls can learn to put them on. Isn't that terrific. Mommy splurged and bought Allison a set for her birthday."

Shirley, seeing Allison's face become, if possible, even more expressionless, chose not to pursue the subject. "I came to pick up my bow, Gloria. If you'll tell me where it is, I'll be glad to get it myself so you don't spoil your manicure."

"It's here somewhere," she replied. "Come in and I'll look." She led the way to the kitchen where a half-empty glass, a coke can, and a display of plastic fingernails littered the counter. A pair of disembodied hands stood on the kitchen table, one hand fully equipped with purple talons.

Gloria wiggled her fingers again. "I'll find your bow and arrow thingummy just as soon as these dry. You want coffee?"

Shirley reluctantly agreed to a cup of coffee. Allison stood in the dining room, just outside the kitchen door. From where she sat, Shirley could see the child tossing a softball from hand to hand, her head bent broodingly over the ball.

"The same people who make the fingernail doll make a doll with hair you can do up in curlers. And the cutest makeup mirror! They never had anything like that when I was growing up. A Barbie doll was about it." Gloria touched her tongue to one fingernail, then another, testing for dryness. "If I'd taken enough cash with me, I'd have bought her one, but I only had enough for our outfits. I think it's just great little girls can learn all about personal grooming these days just by playing with toys."

"Personal grooming," murmured Shirley, sneaking a glance at Allison's lowered face. "Do you think personal grooming is terribly important to kids that age?"

"Oh, my, yes," Gloria bubbled. "Allison just loves to dress up, don't you darling? It's important to learn to look nice for the boys."

"When I was that age," Shirley said flatly, "playing ball and fishing were more important than anything. I wasn't ready for boys."

Allison's head came up, and she looked at Shirley with an attitude of alert interest.

"Oh, well," remarked Gloria, "I suppose you were very different as a child. I mean, you're different now, aren't you, so you must have been." She giggled and wagged her eyelashes at Shirley. "Charles says you're a strange bird."

"Really," murmured Shirley, feeling her neck get hot.

"Allison," Gloria called, "come in here, dear. Don't dawdle in the doorway."

The softball disappeared. Allison came into the room, her face merely patient once more.

"I'll find your bow," Gloria announced. "Charles was pretty pissed at you, you know. There for a while he wasn't even going to bring your bow back." She wagged a finger in Shirley's face and giggled as she left the room, letting it be known this was all in fun.

Shirley sipped at the lukewarm coffee and did not respond. Allison moved aside as her mother went by, then came back to stare at Shirley once more.

"Did you play softball when you were little?" she asked.

"All the time," said Shirley. "Softball and baseball and basketball, too. I also rode horses and camped out a lot. And I was not strange."

"Did you find the little deer?" The child's eyes were suddenly huge with remembered anxiety.

Shirley ached for her. "Yes, honey, I did. It's not in any pain. You don't need to worry about it."

The girl started to speak, then vanished like a mouse into a hole as her mother returned. Gloria carried the heavy case with the tips of her fingers, as though it were soiled, trying to keep from dislodging her nails. Behind her, Allison was playing with the softball once more, awkwardly. There was no question but that it was difficult to handle a softball with false fingernails on. Shirley wondered if Allison might not have preferred something other than purple plastic hand-decor as a birthday gift. Maybe she liked soccer. Allison had perhaps been hoping for a soccer ball for her birthday. Instead, she had received a cheap exercise in narcissism. Shirley did not believe for one moment that Allison had stuck the obscene plastic daggers on those ghostly hands on the counter. Gloria had done that. Gloria who loved such toys.

Gloria who was continuing her former comment insistently, as though there had been no interruption. "So here it

39

is, even though Charles really was pretty pissed at you, Shirley." She put the case on the kitchen table.

"That's too bad," Shirley remarked, trying to think of a subject that might interest Gloria besides how pissed Charles had been. The bow case was flatter than it should be. She prodded it, feeling for the quiver that she kept inside. "My arrows aren't here, Gloria. Did you or Charles remove them for some reason?"

"Well, he had to take out the arrows to get your phone number off them! You're not listed under your name, and Mike couldn't remember what listing the number was under."

Shirley had forgotten about Mike and his wife. The name reminded her of a question she had wanted to ask before. "Do you and the Carmichaels usually go out in the woods dressed the way you were the other day?"

Gloria posed prettily in the doorway, one hand spread against the wall, one splayed across her shoulder in a purple fan. "Well, actually, I don't think we knew we were going to be in the woods. I mean, I didn't know, so I guess Mike and Arlette didn't know either. Charles didn't say anything about hunting. I thought we were just going for a drive, you know, to look at some real estate you were interested in and then out to lunch so you could meet Mike."

Shirley shook her head. "I've been acquainted with Mike for years; I've done business with him at the savings and loan. I'd not met his wife before, but I know Carmichael a good deal better than I know your husband."

"Well, Charles could have gotten to know you better if you hadn't gone zooming off. He was really pissed. . . ."

At this repetition, something snapped. "He could not have been more pissed than I," Shirley said firmly. "I thought Charles's behavior was inexcusable. If you can find my arrows, I won't take up any more of your time."

Gloria's mouth came open and stayed open for a moment, as though put on hold. Then it snapped shut, and she almost scuttled from the room. Allison stared from the doorway, not speaking. Shirley wanted to apologize to the child but didn't know what to say. "I'm a crotchety old woman who gets more so the older I get." Admittedly she did not do well among people. The older she got, the worse she became. A simple trip to town, and she had already insulted almost everyone she had encountered. She chastised herself, resolving upon neutrality and passivity. She would be pleasant. She would be polite. She would suffer fools gladly or at least in silence. So long as Gloria did not tell her even one more time that Charles had been pissed. If Gloria repeated that particular phrase, Shirley could not guarantee a noninjurious result.

Gloria, however, returned with an olive branch. "Here's your arrows, Shirley. And I shouldn't have said that about Charles. I'm sure you thought you were doing the right thing when you went off that way."

In the doorway, Allison ducked, as though in anticipation of a storm. Shirley, however, gritted her teeth and managed a polite murmur as she inserted the quiver into the case and zipped it up once more. "Thank you very much for bringing the bow back to town with you. I know it was extra trouble, carrying it back to the van along with all the cans and stuff. . . ."

"No, that's all right," Gloria said with a forgiving smile. "We didn't bring the beer cans back."

Shirley's face went blank. She was afraid to ask, incapable of not asking. "What did you do with them?"

"We left them there. Charles says it's public forest, it's not like littering somebody's property or anything."

Later Shirley did not remember saying anything more. Her recollection was that she had simply walked out, frozen-faced, with no further attempt at civility. She could not remember that Gloria said anything either. Her only lastingly accurate recollections of the encounter were of a softball moving restlessly from hand to hand and of Allison's painted, patient, very worried face.

2

On Thursday morning Roger Fetting called from Washington to say thank you for the report; couldn't she have included at least one hopeful idea?

"I say it the way I see it, Rog," she told him. "Take it or leave it. At the moment I do not see hope."

At the moment she was still trying to recover from yesterday. Over breakfast, quivering with indignation, she had once more described the details of her various encounters to J.Q., who had finally poured her a double Glenfiddich and suggested she take the morning paper and go bask in the October sun until she calmed down. Morning drinking was, she had always felt, a sign that something was seriously wrong. When J.Q. suggested it, it meant she was unbearable. She would have to stop going to town, that was all there was to it. Dogs and cattle and codgers like J.Q. were all she was fit for.

In a chastened mood she ran up the patio umbrella and sat beneath it, alternately sipping Scotch and coffee, making her way through the labored syntax of the *Columbine Chronicle*. On page two, midway down the page, was the headline "Local Resident Found Slain." She started to skip over it, then caught the name of the victim: Charles Maxwell. "Oh, my God," she cried, unaware that her voice bellowed across the farmyard like that of a bawling cow. "Oh, my God."

J.Q. came stumping around the corner of the house, crutches flailing, his face white. "What?" he cried. "What's the matter!"

She pointed. J.Q. took up the paper to read it for himself. Charles Maxwell had been shot through the heart with a hunting arrow, his own hunting arrow, with his name on it. His wife had wakened at two o'clock in the morning to find he had not returned from a realtors' meeting he had attended the night before. She had gone downstairs to see if his car was back, only to find the car in the driveway, engine running and lights on, and the prone body of her husband in the middle of the open garage.

"You were here at the ranch all last night," said J.Q. "I can testify to that if need be."

"Don't joke, J.Q.," she snapped.

"Who's joking? I've seldom seen you as hot and shafty as you were last night and this morning. It was like old times! You were ready to do both the Maxwells in for littering, plus the whole anti-abortion crowd for being generally obnoxious."

"Only figuratively," she murmured, wondering at herself. Her first emotion on reading the article had been one of . . . what? Not grief, certainly. Shock. She hoped it had at least been shock and not something nastier. Like pleasure. She hadn't really disliked Charles Maxwell enough to want him dead, had she?

"I wouldn't have killed him, J.Q. Even though I'd be tempted, I wouldn't even kill Elise Fish, not really. I might want to injure her a little. . . ."

He hugged her. "I know you wouldn't, dear love. But you were mad as hell." For some reason he sounded glad about it.

She nodded, ashamed. She had been angry. Angry about women abusers and beer cans and shoddiness and American ingenuity, what little was left, wasted on false fingernails and

43

little girls who wanted to play softball instead of being dressed up like geisha dolls. And about men like Charles Maxwell who lied as easily as they breathed. She sighed. "I wonder if I should call the sheriff."

"Do you know anything that would help him?"

"The report says Charles had one of his own arrows in him. I may be the only one who knows how many stenciled arrows Maxwell had. He ordered twelve, six target, six hunting, and that's all he had. At least that's what he showed me when I picked mine up at his house. If he used one to shoot the deer, he should still have five. If some are missing, it might be a clue."

"Won't Maxwell's wife tell the sheriff that?"

"I doubt she even knows. I don't think she pays much attention to anything except her face and her fingernails."

"And figure," he remarked. "Face, figure, and fingernails. At least I thought so when I saw her."

"When did you see her?"

"When they picked you up to go off on that expedition. She gave me the eye, Shirley. Made my day. I thought that was the most unlikely vanload of critters I had seen in a long, long time. How about the woman with the high heels and all the hair?"

"Arlette," said Shirley. "Oh, yes. Arlette."

"Where was she off to, a dancing lesson?"

"Charles lied to them, J.Q. I think he must have been a constitutional liar, one of those who just says whatever comes into his head. When he invited me, he told me there'd be a group, and he asked me to come to 'give them some pointers.' There was no group, so he asked his wife and the Carmichaels along as audience. He knew the Carmichaels wouldn't be interested in hunting, so he spun some story about taking me to look at real estate—maybe some piece of property the savings and loan has foreclosed on. Carmichael would be very interested in that.

"Naturally, since I thought we were going hunting, I dressed for it and brought my bow. Gloria and the Carmichaels were dressed up to go to lunch with a real-estate cli-

44

ent. Each person in the group probably had heard a different story about our plans for the day.''

''Where did you say Maxwell was when he shot the deer?''

''We parked up at Redstone Point, in that picnic area. There shouldn't have been a deer within a mile of the place, and I wish to God there hadn't been. Oh, hell, I don't know, J.Q. Do you think I ought to call Sheriff Tempe?''

''Suit yourself,'' he said. ''You might conceivably be helpful. My mother always taught me to be helpful when I could.''

Shirley was reaching for the phone when it rang. Mike Carmichael.

''Shirley, I just wanted to touch base with you about the old Finley farm.''

Shirley's eyebrows went up into her hairline. ''Why's that, Mike?''

''Charles Maxwell said you were interested in buying it, but since we never got to look at it Sunday . . .''

''Mike, have you seen this morning's paper?''

A pause. ''No, why?''

''Take a look at the *Chronicle*, Mike. We can talk about property another time.''

She hung up and stood thoughtfully for a full minute before punching up the sheriff's number.

Sheriff Tempe was in no better mood than the last time she had seen him. When she said she wanted to tell him how many arrows Charles Maxwell had had, he remarked that he already knew, thank you. Charles Maxwell had six, and all six were there. Five hanging in the Maxwell basement in a quiver and one slightly dilapidated one through Charles Maxwell's heart.

''He couldn't,'' she blurted. ''One was in that deer, up in the scrub.''

''Well, he must have retrieved it, Mrs. McClintock. . . .''

''Ms.,'' she said. ''If you're going to call me McClintock, you'll have to say Ms. My husbands' names weren't Mc-Clintock, neither of them. Call me Shirley.''

Sigh. ''Maxwell must have retrieved it, Shirley, because

45

there are six at his house. Thank you very much.'' He hung up on her.

"Six," she said to J.Q. as she stared disbelievingly at the phone. "The bastard hung up on me."

"There was no arrow in the deer when we went up there and found the shoe," he reminded her. "We noticed that."

"But I thought the sheriff had taken it. And even though I told Botts I'd given other people the location, I really hadn't," she argued. "When people asked me, I just said, 'Up near Redstone Picnic grounds.' A description like that covers a few thousand acres."

"The newspaper said where the body was found."

"It really didn't, J.Q. It said about what I said. There was nothing in there about the fires I built to locate the place."

"You mean Maxwell couldn't have found it."

"That's what I mean, yes. He couldn't have found it from anything I said or from anything in the paper. Nobody could have. When you and I saw the arrow was gone, I sort of assumed the sheriff's men had taken it."

J.Q. ducked his head and peered at her over his glasses. "Even an elected law official might be supposed to be able to count to six. If Tempe had the arrow at his office, it wouldn't have been at Maxwell's. And if Tempe had retrieved it and given it to Maxwell, he'd have said so, wouldn't he?"

"I can't figure why he thinks Maxwell retrieved it. That's impossible, from what I know of Charles. It had to be someone else. . . .''

"Someone looking for whatever they were looking for here?"

"It's a nasty thought, J.Q., but I think it's true."

J.Q. didn't answer, but the quiver of his left nostril was answer enough. It was the expression he always got when he detected that something at least rat-sized had died in the cellar.

Shirley spent the rest of the morning among the cows, bringing six mamas with their heifer calves into the corral so she could ear-tag the babies and draw their pictures. Pure-bred calves could be registered only if their individual sires and dams were identified; Belted Galloway calves could be registered only if they had proper belts which went all the way around the animal with no interruptions. Each application for registration had to be accompanied by the names and numbers of the parents plus a clear sketch of the calf's markings. When Shirley had all the sketches in her notebook, with new calf ear-tag numbers double-checked against the ear-tag numbers of the mothers they were sucking from, she turned the pairs loose and went back to the house just in time to intercept a carload of evangelists, come to convert her or J.Q. or anyone else they could lay a bible verse on.

"No," she said firmly, pointing the way they had come, back down the mile-long driveway. There were two men and a fat woman. One of the men looked familiar, and all three of the visitors looked determined.

"No," she said again, more firmly, when they persevered. Maybe it was just that they weren't very perceptive.

"Can't you people understand English?" she asked at last, in a loud voice. "I do not wish to hear about your religion. Isn't that plain enough?" She handed the pamphlet about secular humanism and the one headlined *God, head of Man: Man, head of Woman*, back to the slope-shouldered man with the tight mouth. "Didn't I see you yesterday?" she asked him. "Bill Deitz, isn't it?"

"Reverend Patterson tells us to persevere for the Lord," the fat woman interrupted. Her loose, flowered dress and the single pink curler she had forgotten to remove made her look like a very large, mechanized Cabbage Patch doll, one that could be plugged in when the batteries ran down. At the moment she didn't need recharging, for she jiggled and nodded constantly as she said, "We must keep on, though we are reviled or persecuted for His sake."

It was unclear from her speech whether the pronoun referred to the deity or to the reverend. "Reverend Patterson," Shirley mused. "That'd be Orrin Patterson. He drives a Mercedes, doesn't he? And didn't I see something in the paper

47

about his buying the Kramer Winterburn place out at Palace Pines Country Club? That's quite a showplace.''

"Reverend Patterson works very hard for the faith,'' the weedy young man replied. He had innocent blue eyes and thick lashes, like a baby. He also had a forehead full of zits. "When the faithful receive worldly goods, it shows God's blessings.''

"Doesn't it say someplace in the bible that the rich should sell all that they have and give it to the poor?'' Shirley asked, directing her ire at the slope-shouldered man, Deitz, who so far had not said a word. "I used to know Kramer Winterburn. I've been in that house. It must have cost your reverend a bundle.''

"Oh, the car and the house aren't his,'' the fat woman objected. "Oh, my, no. They belong to the Living Church.'' Her voice was an intermittently grunting whine, like a small circular saw cutting chunks off a two-by-four.

"Then the church ought to sell them and give them to the poor,'' Shirley persisted. "Give the proceeds to some pregnant women who are having a rough time of it, and that should prevent a lot of abortions, and then Mr. Deitz can quit harassing clinics. I'll make a deal with you. When you've sold every car and every piece of real estate the Living Church of Jesus owns, then you call me and we'll make an appointment to talk. Until then, you people are trespassing. . . .''

"We must be willing to dare for His sake,'' the fat woman exclaimed, ducking and bobbing. "Willing to break man's laws in the keeping of God's . . .''

Shirley sighed. "You know, almost every morning I tell myself I'm not going to be rude that day. I hardly ever set out to be rude. I think people ought to be allowed to be damned fools if they want to. I think being a damned fool is a right guaranteed by the constitution, so long as they don't do it in my driveway. But private property is also guaranteed by the constitution, and if you three damned fools aren't off mine in three minutes flat—and by that, I mean all the way to the front gate—I am coming out here and shoot your tires full of buckshot so you can't get away, and then I'm going to call the sheriff and have you arrested. I am now going inside to get my shotgun.''

She left them gabbling to each other and went in. J.Q. had the shotgun off the rack and was replacing the shells when she came in. ''What are you doing,'' she muttered.

''Bird shot,' he said. ''I don't want you killing anybody.'' He handed her the gun, frowning reprovingly.

Hell, J.Q. would sit out there and talk to them all day. She returned to the driveway just in time to get hit on the knee by a rock kicked up by their tires.

''Why did we stop locking the gate?'' she asked the air as she rubbed her knee.

''Because when we locked the gate the UPS truck couldn't get in,'' replied J.Q. from behind her. ''And neither could the fire truck if we had a fire. Or the ambulance if you gave me a heart attack. Which some days you seem determined to do.''

''And neither could lightning-rod salesmen, or real-estate salesmen looking for listings, or people who are lost, or people who are looking for someone else who lives six miles from here,'' she murmured. ''Neither could people who think their mothers or grandmothers lived near here back in the nineteen-forties and wonder if we've ever heard of the Hefflemiers. Neither could illiterate hunters with camper shells on their pickups, gunracks in the back windows, and coolers full of canned beer, looking for a way through private property into the national forest so they can kill anything that moves.'' Her voice rose into a wail. ''Neither could top-heavy RVs driven by retired shoe salesmen from Indiana with the refrigerators stacked with strawberry wine coolers in disposable bottles. Neither could monstrous fat station wagons full of cub scouts, searching for a campsite while drinking cases of Pepsi and emptying dozens of fluorescent yellow plastic packs of corn chips.''

''I haven't found any cans or bottles on the place for three or four days,'' J.Q. remarked quietly.

''You haven't been out to the corral,'' she said. ''There's

three Bud cans and a potato-chip sack lying beside the squeeze chute. I left them because I wanted you to see them."

"You're kidding."

"I'm not. There's been only one person out there, J.Q., and that's the vet."

"He had his wife and in-laws with him. Showing them the country."

J.Q. sounded disillusioned, and for the moment she regretted telling him. The new vet had heretofore seemed acceptable. Well, he probably couldn't help it if his wife and her family were damned fools. Shirley put her arm around J.Q., and they went in to fix lunch.

It was late afternoon when the sheriff's car came zooming down the gravel road from the gate, skidding at the corner where the cattle guard was and plunging into the driveway near the house with reckless disregard for the lives of dogs, cats, or any other living thing that might have been out there. The young deputy who got out and patted his pockets didn't seem to care. He gave his gun a good hitch, too, before coming to the door.

"We got a complaint," he said after introducing himself. Deputy Bobby Jay Brett. Shirley thought that sounded like a TV actor. He looked like one, too. Dark curly hair. Bright eyes. Cute little bottom in his tight pants. "Sheriff got a complaint," he repeated.

"By religious folks?" asked J.Q. from the living room.

"Reverend Patterson," said the deputy, peering through the screen, trying to see who was talking. "Says you threatened some of his people."

"Threatened 'his' people, how?" asked Shirley in a dangerously soft voice.

"Threatened to shoot them."

"Threatened to shoot their tires if they didn't get out of here and leave me alone," she corrected.

"I loaded with bird shot," J.Q. remarked as he got up and joined them at the door. "She couldn't have done much damage, even if she'd missed."

"I wouldn't have missed," said Shirley.

50

"This your husband, Mrs. McClintock?" the deputy asked.

"No. Not my husband. Not my better half. Not my roommate. Not my . . ."

"I'm a friend of hers," said J.Q. "I live here."

"All Sheriff Tempe wanted me to do was get a statement from you so's he could tell whoever it was . . ." Bobby Jay's voice trailed away as he looked from unsympathetic face to unsympathetic face.

"Next time," said Shirley. "I will make a citizen's arrest and have Sheriff Tempe come out and pick them up. I do not want to be evangelized. Reverend Patterson has no right to evangelize me without my consent, and no right to send his people here without my invitation." At least not yet, she thought. Though the ACLU would probably soon figure out that trespassing for purposes of evangelizing was one of the civil liberties they needed to protect. They'd come close with that Nazi march business in Skokie. Not everybody could afford to own sixteen hundred acres. For most people, the street in front of their house was the only community space they had. To call it public and let the Nazis march down it was to deny the residents any privacy in their own community. Probably pretty soon all the fundamentalists would call a constitutional convention and rewrite it to include trespass rights for purposes of evangelizing. . . .

She came to herself to hear the young man repeating a question he'd obviously asked before.

"If I wrote it down, would you sign it?" Bobby Jay asked doubtfully. "I mean, if I wrote down what you said?"

He sounded rather like young Marty had, once upon a time, when he got himself in trouble over something that wasn't really his fault. Shirley found herself nodding. "Write it down," she said. "Come on in and sit down at the table. I'll give you something to drink while you compose. If you get it right, we'll sign it."

It took him about twenty laborious minutes, but he got it printed on his form eventually. Then the three of them had a lengthy chat about ranching and sheriffing and the state of the world, after which J.Q. and Shirley watched the car leave, Christmas tree flashing, back end fishtailing on the gravel.

"Should teach him how to drive," muttered J.Q.

"That's the least of his worries," Shirley commented. "Did you get a look at his spelling?" She rubbed her chin and forehead and started for the kitchen. "I'll bet sheriff's deputies in Japan don't misspell like that."

"I don't think they have sheriffs there. And I'm pretty sure you can't misspell in Japanese," J.Q. remarked as he followed her. "That's really why they're taking over the world."

On Friday morning it was Mike Carmichael on the phone once more, asking Shirley if he could drop out during the afternoon. Shirley told him she supposed so. She was hanging up the phone when it rang again, and she left it to J.Q. while she rescued the frying bacon.

It was the Reverend Patterson himself, calling, so he said, to apologize for his parishoners. As she turned the bacon, Shirley could hear J.Q. making excuses for her. She was out at the barn, J.Q. said. He would give her the message. Yes, he sure did understand how that could happen.

"He's coming out," said J.Q.

"Here?" Shirley thumped the counter with a wooden spatula. "Orrin Patterson, here? What in hell for?"

"Says he has to apologize in person. And he wouldn't be put off. Very strange."

They ate breakfast in silence. They were still lingering over coffee when the reverend's Mercedes growled to a stop outside. The driver got out and opened the rear door; not a uniformed chauffeur, just a stocky, short-haired man in a cheap blue sports coat, opening the door for a vision of silver-gray hair; a thousand-dollar, charcoal-gray, western-cut suit; leather gloves; and a silk kerchief knotted around his neck under a western shirt that looked suspiciously like silk. The outfit was finished off with handmade ostrich boots.

The reverend turned, stared around himself as though appraising the place, then strode lightly up the front steps, the boots and the hat adding to an already impressive height.

52

Orrin Patterson was a big, big man. He had a square, rugged face with authoritative eyebrows, and his mouth was pursed as though it had just spit out a sugar tit. Almost godlike, Shirley thought, looking him over head to toe. The only thing that made him seem halfway human was that he'd evidently cut himself shaving. Shirley rested her eyes on his boots. She had priced boots like that last time she was in Texas, astonishing herself by being slightly tempted to buy the fifteen-hundred-dollar footwear.

Shirley grabbed a sweater, put on her social face, and went out to enjoy the experience, however brief, of being looked down upon. She invited the reverend to sit down at the patio table. The wind was chilly, and she figured he probably wouldn't want to sit too long.

Reverend Patterson promptly outfoxed her by asking to use the bathroom. She countered the outfox by remaining on the patio. When he finished his ablutions, he had to come back out where she was waiting for him. Shirley had no intention of letting any evangelizer get comfortable inside.

"I wanted to apologize in person," he said as he looked doubtfully at the chair before sitting down. "Sometimes my people get very zealous and offend without realizing it."

"They were that," Shirley agreed. "Very zealous. Very offensive."

"I try to tell them there's a difference between sincere religiosity, even though it may not be our particular faith, or even well-informed agnosticism, and the ignorant, godless, humanistic kind of persuasion we seek to overcome."

"I'd say that's probably mine," said Shirley. "Ignorant, godless, and humanistic."

He laughed. "Oh, come now, Mrs. McClintock. . . ."

"Ms.," she smiled. "Not Mrs. Ms."

"But I understood you are a widow," he said.

"I am a widow. Twice. But it's still Ms. McClintock."

"Whatever you prefer. You and I both know that you are not ignorant. You are well known in Columbine and in the county, and everyone knows who you worked for and what kind of work you did. That isn't work done by ignorant persons. Running a ranch these days is not done by ignorant persons. What I've tried to teach our missionary workers is that they must go to people who need them, whether those people realize it or not, but not bother people who have had the opportunity to make informed and sincere decisions about their spiritual lives." He beamed at her. "As you have, Ms. McClintock. Persons like yourself can justifiably resent even well-meaning efforts."

"Yes," she agreed solemnly. "We can."

He breathed in, pausing, as though waiting for something more from her. She continued to regard him thoughtfully, giving him no opening.

"While I am here," he continued hastily, "I wanted to offer my sympathy for the unpleasant experience you had last week. Finding a body is certainly . . . well, not a pleasant thing to happen."

"No," she agreed.

He paused again. "My good friend and parishioner Botts Tempe told me about it. He was catching for the over-forties when the call came in."

"Oh, that was your church picnic he was at." The comment was surprised out of her, and she regretted it immediately.

Patterson nodded. "Botts said nothing found with the body helped identify it." He mused with a mournful expression. "Even the things you and your friend found later didn't help much, he said. That's sad. I can't help thinking of a family somewhere, wondering why they've never heard from a son or a husband. . . ."

She agreed it was sad.

"Botts thinks it's possible the man was a hunter or hiker. No one from around here."

"That does seem likely," Shirley said blandly.

A tiny muscle jumped repeatedly at the reverend's temple. "Does it bother you at all, Ms. McClintock?"

"Does what bother me?"

"Having discovered the body. Having no idea who he is?"

She gave him a long, weighing look, which he returned

with expectant eyes, as though her answer was sure to be freighted with spiritual significance.

"Reverend," she said, "I come on bones all the time out here. This isn't even the first time I've found human ones. I once found a small plane that had gone down a year before. It was buried in the trees at the bottom of a canyon west of here. Mother, father, three children, and a dog. That plane was full of bones and pity and sadness, my, yes, and gladness, too, that they'd evidently been killed right off, but I can't say it bothered me a great deal. Some, yes, because those poor children were cut off so young. But not more than that. As for the man and his wife: damn fools who fly a light plane over these mountains are simply asking for an early grave. As for not knowing who this man was, I didn't know who those folks in the plane were either. I don't think the death of strangers touches us very deeply, do you? If it did, with the number of people dying all the time, we'd be quivering wrecks, wouldn't we? John Donne notwithstanding."

"I'm afraid I don't know Mr. Dunn."

Shirley grinned quietly to herself. "He said no man is an island, Reverend, but out here lots of us pretty much are. At least at high tide."

At that moment J.Q. opened the front door and called, "Shirley, Washington phoned, and your man says it's important for you to call him back right away."

The reverend stood up, reached for her hand with his own gloved one, shook it with a mournful expression, and said, "I won't keep you. Please forgive my people. It won't happen again." She walked with him to the steps, returned his wave, and watched as the car growled its way through a turn and off down the drive. It left a puddle of oil in the gravel, and Shirley went down to kick gravel over the mess so it didn't get tracked into the house. The man who was acting as chauffeur was evidently new at the job, or he just didn't know much about auto maintenance.

Remembering with pleasure that the Reverend's bottom had picked up a good dusty stain from the patio chair, Shirley went into the house.

"There wasn't really a phone call," said J.Q. "I just couldn't stand to see you playing with him that way. Like the cat with a mouse."

"I was being nice," she protested, flexing her hand. The reverend didn't know his own strength.

"Um," he said. "Like the cats are nice. Nice not to kill right away. What were you doing? Saving him for lunch?"

She scowled at him. "That was one of the strangest conversations in my experience, J.Q. That man had absolutely no reason to come out here. You can't tell me he has ever before apologized to anyone for anything his missionary workers have done. He gave me a speech that was pretty smooth, considering, but it wasn't one he'd really worked on. It had little rough spots in it. He hadn't quite got the ignorant and godless humanism out of it, which he would have done if he'd used it very often with people like me, and he was determined it was my spiritual life I'd made decisions about, not just life itself. I'm sure godless humanism and spiritual decisions go down great with the Living Jesus people, but having him trespassing on my psyche kind of offends me."

"Then what was he here for?"

"Damned if I know, J.Q. Could have been just to get a look at me, or you."

J.Q. peered at her over his glasses, looking her up and down like a street-corner lout. "Do you think we're that interesting? To somebody besides us?"

"Maybe we are to him." She flexed her hand again, which still ached. Whatever else the reverend might or might not be, he was a very, very powerful man.

When Mike Carmichael showed up at about two o'clock, J.Q. was out fixing fence and Shirley was oiling the window-sills on the south side of the house where the sun and the wind conspired to make splinters out of solid wood. She wiped her hand on the rag hanging from her pocket and met Carmichael near the front door.

"You want coffee, beer, pop?" she asked him.

"I'd take a beer," he agreed, giving her the most charming grin. Shirley had always felt Mike Carmichael was a little over-charming, a little slick. He always looked as though he'd been gone over with a vacuum attachment and then buffed to a medium-high gloss.

They sat at the kitchen table, Shirley sprawling and Carmichael sitting with one ankle over his knee, "being casual" all too obviously. After one swallow of beer he pulled some papers out of his briefcase and set them on the table before her. She glanced at it. Descriptive stuff on the Finlay property. Six hundred acres, more or less, with some falling-down buildings on it.

"Maxwell told me you were interested in the Finlay farm," he said. "Which explains what Arlette and I were doing along on that expedition last Sunday. Charles told me you wanted to see the place and then go to lunch somewhere." He gave her the slick smile again, shaking his head slightly.

Bingo, she said to herself. "I kind of guessed that from something Gloria said, plus the way you were all dressed." She turned the papers over, wondering what he was really doing in her kitchen, drinking her beer. "As a matter of fact, I never mentioned the Finlay farm to Charles or he to me. Charles asked me to come along to give some beginning bowhunters some pointers."

He sighed and looked sincere. "Charles was like that, you know?"

"Not really, no. What was he like?"

"He . . . he got himself all tangled up. He'd start out to do one thing and then get all messed up doing something else. He could be fun. We had some good times, but he wasn't . . . well, he wasn't always truthful. He used to tell some real tall ones. Frankly I was surprised when he led me to believe you were a client of his. I wouldn't have said he was your kind of person."

"You'd have been right," she said mildly.

"On the other hand—" he smiled his little boy smile, "—he was right about one thing. If you were willing to pay cash, Ms. McClintock, you could snap up the Finlay farm for less than half its appraised value."

"Cash, hmm?" She gave him a skeptical smile. "Tell me, Mike, are your wife and Gloria close friends?"

He considered this. "I wouldn't say so, no. They're both homebodies, of course. According to Charles, Gloria never had any aspirations to be anything else, which is true of Arlette and which suits me, quite frankly. Present company excepted, I've never really liked career-type women. I like them frilly." He grinned. "Even when it isn't exactly appropriate to the occasion."

Shirley, keeping a poker face, made no comment about career-type women. "So our Sunday trip was just a mix-up," she commented.

"Just a mix-up, yes. Though I still think you'd be lucky to pick up the property for what the bank is willing to let it go for."

"I don't think so, Mike. I'm really not interested in more real estate, not at any price."

"Well, I wanted you to know that Arlette and I were as much innocent victims as you were last Sunday. It was just another one of Charles's . . . uh, inventions."

He gathered up his rejected papers and made small talk about Ridge County politics and the new house Carmichael's boss, John Fogg, was building.

"John's a great guy, isn't he?" Carmichael asked. "Great little wife, too."

Shirley gave the kind of grin that might be yes or no. Actually John Fogg was one of her oldest friends. She and John Fogg had grown up together, fought each other, made up with each other, decided they liked each other a lot but not in a boy-girl way (the first reasonably adult discussion of sex Shirley could ever remember having), and the two of them had always kept in touch, if only on an annual Christmas-letter basis. Last year John had surprised everyone by marrying a woman about half his age, but Shirley figured John had been a widower for ten years, and what he did was his business.

"We're very close, John and I," said Carmichael.

Shirley kept her face from showing what she thought, which was that Carmichael was a damned liar. She knew John Fogg better than that. "You're very fortunate, then," she said. "Having the boss's ear, as it were."

"I really feel that myself," he said in his sincere voice. "I'm always telling Arlette how fortunate I am to be working for such a great guy."

After Carmichael left, Shirley found herself reflecting that she had set a new record for visiting sidewinders today. So far as she could figure out, there had been no readily discernable reason for either visit. The reverend wanted to talk about bones. Mike Carmichael seemed to have been determined to let her know that Charles Maxwell was a bit of a crook, that she could buy real estate for half its value—for cash—and that he, Mike, was close to John Fogg. Whatever else Shirley believed or disbelieved, she was damned if she wanted to believe that John Fogg was at all intimate with Mike Carmichael.

Sitting at her desk in a pool of lamplight, Shirley worked on a list.

> Reverend Orrin Patterson
> The Corpse
> Charles Maxwell
> Gloria Maxwell (?)
> Mike and Arlette Carmichael.

After a moment's thought she put a question mark after Arlette's name, underlined Charles's name, and added:

> Elise Fish (Dr. Fish?)
> William Deitz
> Henry Rizer
> Fat woman
> Weedy young man.

"What are you doing?" asked J.Q.

"Wondering," she said, "whether certain things are connected."

It was ten o'clock that night when the phone rang. J.Q. answered it, mumbled, then brought it to her with a significant look.

"McClintock," she said sleepily.

"Shirley," gurgled a voice. "This is Gloria."

It took Shirley a moment. "Gloria Maxwell? I mean, yes, Gloria. I was so very sorry to hear about Charles."

"I'm . . ." the sound of weeping. The sound of a man's voice in the background. "They think I did it, Shirley. I didn't do it. They want me to go down to the station, and Allison would be all alone here. Could you keep her for me tonight? Please."

Shirley loosened her jaw and tried to think. Lord. An eleven-year-old girl? And it was half an hour into town. "Surely you've a neighbor who would keep her. A relative?"

"We don't know anybody here. Charles didn't want to get involved with people because he said they always borrow things. And we don't have any people here. I've got a sister in Albany, and she's the only one. . . ."

"Gloria, is there somebody there? A deputy? Put him on the phone."

"Deputy Brett," a young voice said.

"Well, Bobby Jay, this is Shirley McClintock. Do you remember where my place is?"

"On the old mill road off sixty-four, yes, ma'am."

"Can you bring that woman's daughter out here? Before or after you take her mother in or whatever you're doing. Can you bring the child here? It would save you and me some time. The child can't be left there alone."

A long silence. "I suppose there's no reason why not."

"And can you give, ah . . . Allison time to pack some clothes? And be sure she's got a key to her own house, in case we need to take her back there to get something?"

Muttering. "Yes, ma'am. Sheriff Tempe says that'll be all right."

So Tempe was there himself. Well, well.

Shirley hung up the phone and levered herself out of the deep chair she'd been sitting in, half-asleep since supper. "Did I make up the guest room after Martin's sister and the girls were here?"

J.Q. looked at her over the tops of his glasses. "How would I know, Shirley? I am not a mind reader."

"I thought you might have noticed my doing it."

"I didn't. But I'll help you do it now, if that's what you're hinting at."

She didn't answer him. On inspection it turned out the guest room bed had been made up after all. Shirley turned on the electric blanket. A warm bed wouldn't hurt the child. Probably feel more friendly that way. The guest room bath looked clean enough. Shirley took down the fancy towels she'd put out for Martin's sister Leah and put out some thick brown ones that matched the tile.

"Too good for her?" J.Q. asked, indicating the discarded towels.

"Not good enough," said Shirley. "All wrong for this kid. This kid likes softball, J.Q."

It was after eleven when the deputy arrived with Allison, a small suitcase, and a cardboard box. The cardboard box contained "toys," said the deputy. Allison flushed. Shirley, seeing that the toys included the disembodied hands, left the box on the porch when she carried the suitcase in.

Allison was wearing heels, a frilly dress, and makeup that made her eyes look bruised.

"Did you bring jeans?" Shirley asked her at the guest room door.

A frightened nod.

Shirley put the suitcase on the rack in the corner and opened it. "You get that dress off, wash your face in the bathroom next door, put on your jeans and a shirt and slippers, if you've got them, and come on back out to the living

61

room. We'll have some tea or cocoa or whatever you like, and you can tell me what's going on.''

It took about ten minutes for Allison to change. The jeans were designer jeans, with some idiot's name on the rear who'd never seen buck-brush or a cow. They were blue denim, however, and reasonably sturdy. The shirt was unsuitable, flimsy as to material, made cheaply, with the seams left raw. Still, it would do for tonight. Better than the girl would. Very pale, very quiet, the girl. A scattering of freckles across her nose glared orange against her pallor. With the makeup off her eyes were gentian blue, and her mouth was soft and childlike over a sweetly rounded and trembling chin.

"You got pajamas? Toothbrush? A bathrobe?''

Two nods and one shake, eyes fixed on the flames in the fireplace.

"Well, I'll give you an old flannel shirt of mine you can use for a bathrobe. That room and the bathroom have carpet in them, so your feet won't freeze. Now, what would you like for a bedtime snack?''

A headshake.

"Do you like cocoa?''

A quiver. Could be yes, could be no.

"I'll get it,'' said J.Q., his eyes concerned and watchful. "You sit down by the fire, Allison. You look a little chilly.''

"What happened?'' Shirley asked her. "Did those silly men think your mother killed your daddy?''

A tear, then another, accompanied by a dreadful dry gulping.

"She didn't,'' Shirley said firmly. "She didn't do any such thing. For heaven's sake. You know your mother! She wouldn't even let you play ball for fear you'd get dirty. Did she ever do anything messy or unpleasant? Did she ever garden or get sweaty or anything?''

Allison jerked in surprise. "No,'' she replied in a tiny, squeezed voice. "She never did. She took baths all the time and used perfume. She wouldn't even wash the car.''

"Well, then. I know about killing things. I've killed cattle and deer and chickens. Killing things is bloody and dirty and unpleasant, and you know perfectly well your mommy wouldn't do that. The sheriff just made a mistake." Shirley was cursing herself for not going in to fetch the child. Who knew what that fool Bobby Jay might have said to her on the way out.

"I heard him say, the old fat policeman say, that it's always husbands or wives," Allison blurted. "He said that."

"Well, he's wrong," J.Q. said, entering with a tray that held three cups, a pot, and a dish of cookies.

Sweet man, he must have had that all in readiness. Shirley gave him a grateful look, and he quirked an eyebrow at her as she went on. "The sheriff is just wrong. It is not always husbands or wives. Lots of time it's complete strangers, which is probably what happened to your poor daddy. And that's very sorrowful, what happened to him, but you know your mother had nothing to do with it."

"The funeral. Mommy said they were going to have a funeral. Will they let her out to go to it?"

The child seemed to be grieving more for her mother than for her father. Perhaps she had had little to do with him. "We'll find out first thing in the morning." Shirley handed her a cup, the frog cup, the one young Marty had had as a child. Now how had J.Q. thought of that? Shirley didn't even know where it had been kept.

"Is this your cup?" Allison asked, running a finger along the lily pads on the outside.

"My little boy's," said Shirley. "A long time ago."

"It's a nice cup."

"Thank you. He thought so, too. It has a surprise in the bottom." Marty had loved drinking the last gulp of milk or cocoa to disclose the frog squatted in the bottom of the cup, looking up with wide, bulbous eyes.

Allison stared at the cup, not drinking. "Does Mommy need a lawyer? They said if she didn't have one she could have one appointed, you know, like they do on TV. I wondered if I should call somebody. I don't know how to do that."

"First thing in the morning," said Shirley. "I have a very

good lawyer in Columbine, and if your mommy hasn't already called one, we'll arrange one for her. I'm afraid morning will be the earliest we can arrange that. It's almost midnight now."

"Why did my mommy call you?" Allison wanted to know. "And him?" Her chin indicated J.Q., sitting quietly at the end of the couch, hiding behind the western edition of the *Wall Street Journal*.

"Because your mommy wanted you to be safe and cared for and away from nasty or curious people," J.Q. replied, turning the page while Shirley was still trying to think of an answer. She, too, wondered why Gloria had called her. There had to be someone closer to Gloria Maxwell than Shirley McClintock!

"I'll have to go to school," Allison said, meaning it.

"Not tomorrow," Shirley told her. "Maybe later, but not tomorrow."

They sat stolidly before the fire, encouraging Allison to talk, answering Allison's questions, letting the warmth and the hot milk work until Allison began to have trouble staying awake. When the girl couldn't keep her eyes open, Shirley escorted her into the guest room, watched while she got into her pajamas and climbed into the tall bed, then sat on the side of the bed talking in a monotone about nothing of any consequence until Allison was soundly asleep.

She left the light on in the hall and the door slightly ajar.

"Poor kid's worn out," she told J.Q.. "She's probably been awake since her dad's body was discovered this morning. Two o'clock or so."

"What are you going to do with her tomorrow?"

"You're going to take her riding or hiking or out to count the cows or something, J.Q. I'm going into town to see the kid's mother. Allison is right. She may need a lawyer."

"Can't stay out of it, can you?"

"Isn't a case of can't. It's a case of won't. Remember that damned sixth arrow, J.Q.? When I found that arrow in that deer, I could have been the cause of that child's father getting killed."

At first the sheriff was not at all accommodating in the matter of Shirley McClintock having a personal visit with Gloria Maxwell, even though Shirley was at some pains to identify her needs as pertaining totally to Allison.

"I need to know about her school," Shirley said. "I need to know if she takes music lessons. I need to know if she has any pets. I need to know if she has any food allergies. For heaven's sake, Botts, you can't expect me to take this child on without knowing a few things about her."

"She could have gone to a short-term foster home," Botts Tempe said, digging in his heels. "She didn't have to go out to you."

"Oh, right, short-term foster care. Didn't I see in the paper last week where the county budget for foster care was used up in September? Didn't I see in that same paper some scandal about sexual abuse in some foster home here in town? Come on, Botts. I can always go after a court order if I have to. Judge Wilton knows me pretty well. His daddy knew my daddy."

Grumbling and glaring, he gave her a chit for the jailer. The jail, in the basement of the building, wasn't intended for long-term incarceration. Miscreants sentenced to weeks or months were housed in the neighboring county. Because it was a barebones, short-term lockup, there was no visiting room. Shirley was taken directly to Gloria's cell, an eight-by-ten concrete cube with a high window and a toilet concealed behind a curtain.

"Women's quarters," Gloria giggled hysterically. "The men's is the same except they don't have a curtain."

"Gloria, settle down."

"How can I settle down? They think I killed Charles. Why would I kill Charles? They say I did it to collect his insurance. I don't even know if he has insurance."

"Do you have a lawyer?"

"No. Why would I have a lawyer? I don't even know any lawyers." Her voice was rapid and panting. Her arms jerked from side to side.

"Have they questioned you, Gloria?"

"Over and over. And I tell them the same thing every time. I don't know who killed him." She broke into sobs, her hands waving before her face as though to erase some vision there.

Shirley shook her by her shoulders. "Gloria, listen to me. Don't talk to them any more. Tell them you want a lawyer, and you won't talk without a lawyer there. Do you understand me?"

"No. If I'm not guilty, why should I need a lawyer? That's what Sheriff Botts said. I heard him say that."

"To you?"

"No, to the deputy."

Sneaky bastard, thought Shirley.

"He said that to the deputy hoping you would overhear. That way you might decide to do without a lawyer, and they like that because they can trap you into saying things so they can pin it on you even if you didn't do it. Didn't they tell you a lawyer could be appointed for you?"

"Yes, but they sort of rattled it. Like the pledge of allegiance. Not like it meant anything."

Why are you out there defending Nazis and child pornographers? Shirley demanded silently of the absent ACLU. Why aren't you here in this cell with this stupid, stupid woman.

"Gloria, will you do what I say?"

Nod. A frightened, panicky nod. Shirley pursued the matter until the nods became firmer and more frequent and the rehearsed statement became intelligible. "I want a lawyer, and I do not wish to say anything more."

When that had been achieved, Shirley said, "Gloria, I need to talk about Allison."

Gloria did not think Allison had any favorite foods. Gloria did not know if Allison had any favorite books. Gloria could not remember if Allison had any special friends at school. Allison had never had a pet because Charles had been allergic to animal hair. Allison's doctor was whoever was available at the family health center. Allison's teacher was Mrs. Brand. No, Mrs. Brand was last year. Who was it this year?

Shirley took out the document she had prepared before leaving home that morning and asked Gloria to sign it. It asked Shirley to take custody of Allison while Gloria was unable to care for her.

"Why?" Gloria asked, stunned. "Why do I need to sign this?"

"Because Sheriff Botts is making noises about foster care for her. And because foster care sucks. Kids get abused all the time in foster care."

"But I'll be out in a day or two."

"If you get a lawyer, yes. But even a day or two of foster care could be pretty destructive, Gloria. I thought you'd like to make it clear you want your daughter to be safe. She will be safe out at the ranch. I don't want to fight the sheriff over her. That wouldn't do Allison any good at all. I don't want Botts Tempe trying to put Allison somewhere that wouldn't be good for her!"

Unwillingly, lips tightly compressed, Gloria signed the paper. "Only for a day or two," she repeated.

"Only for what it says right there," Shirley agreed. "Until you can take care of her again." She had no idea whether the thing was properly worded or not, but the intention was very plain. Allison Maxwell was to stay at the McClintock place until her mother could care for her. It would at least keep Botts Tempe at bay.

From the phone booth in the lobby of the justice building, Shirley called the office of Ehrlich and Grafton and left a message that Numa Ehrlich was to hasten to the aid of Gloria Maxwell in the county lockup, and that she, Shirley McClintock, would take care of payment for the matter if Gloria Maxwell was unable to do so.

"And tell Numa," she concluded, "to take somebody with him as a witness when he first talks to her and pay particular attention to how she looks. Her skin. Whether she's been . . . ah, scratched or scarred up any."

Shirley had brought Allison's key with her. She had to pick up some more suitable clothes for the child, and it wouldn't hurt to look around the Maxwell house, if she could get away with it.

There was a yellow crime tape across the front of the garage, but the front door wasn't sealed. Shirley had brought a small suitcase along, and she unlocked the door as though she owned the place, waving to a neighbor on the north who had her head out the window, staring. "Came to pick up some clothes for Allison," Shirley called, smiling. The neighbor nodded and pulled her head back into the house. One of those who would have borrowed stuff, no doubt, if the Maxwells had become acquainted.

The house was silent and smelled faintly of fried chicken. In the kitchen the Colonel Sanders Kentucky Fried cartons were still on the table along with a container of milk, two half-empty containers of slaw, and twisted foil containers that had held catsup. Shirley tilted and sniffed at the thick, sticky residue in the glass. Something sugary and alcoholic.

She looked in the cupboards and in the refrigerator to get an idea of what Allison liked to eat, but she found almost nothing. A rock-hard lemon. A container of coffee cream, soured. No cereals. No milk. No canned or frozen foods. What had they been eating?

At the front of the house, in what had been a small bedroom, she found Charles's office. He had a separate phone line there, a filing cabinet, a desk littered with bills, letters, and files. Shirley resisted the urge to straighten the desk, limiting herself to pulling out individual items and perusing them, then reinserting them into the pile. The bank wanted the last six mortgage payments. The Ford agency wanted the customized van returned and were getting increasingly nasty about it, as a sequence of three clipped-together letters made clear. A furniture store was making noises about repossession.

"*Tsuris,*" Shirley muttered to herself. That's what Martin used to call it. *Gehokteh tsuris.* All kinds of chopped-up trouble. Anybody in real-estate these days had to be crazy or paralyzed. Colorado was suffering from a deep depression, no matter what the rest of the country had going. When the

68

oil boom had collapsed, so had the hopes and dreams of a generation of westerners. No more real-estate boom. No more job boom. No more money boom. Now there was only an exhaust emissions boom from all the cars leaving the state. *Gehokteh tsuris* for everybody.

Gloria's closet was full with clothes hung on top of one another. Not expensive clothes, but lots of them, some still with the tags in them. Cheap clothes, to Shirley's eyes. Too short, too tight, too fancy. A shopper, Gloria was. A real hot shopper. The MasterCard people had corresponded with Charles as well. There was a letter in the office dated two months ago saying the card had been cancelled.

The drawer of the bedside table held Gloria's birth control pills, a bottle of prescription medication, and a wad of ten- and twenty-dollar bills—several hundred dollars—stuffed toward the back of the drawer, under wadded stockings. Shirley put the money back where she'd found it.

Allison's room was almost bare by comparison. The closet held dresses that looked unworn and too small. There were jeans and shirts in one bureau drawer, but the jeans were ragged, and Shirley guessed they had been outgrown a long time ago. Well, hell, she'd stop at the Wal-Mart on the way out of town and buy some. And some decent shirts. And some decent shoes. And socks. And a jacket. The kid had only a silly little plastic jacket, fake leather, like some motorcycle moll. Did they call them molls? Or were they something like "old ladies," as in "She's my old lady." The purple velour caftan was in the closet along with the silver sandals. Evidently identical outfits for mama and daughter had been part of Allison's birthday present. So where had Gloria got the money to pay for the outfits? Charles hadn't had any money.

The only toys were dolls and doll clothes and play jewelry and play makeup and play high heels. No blocks, no cars, no balls, no games. More stuff to get at the store. There was one stuffed bear who looked well loved. Shirley packed him and all the underwear and pajamas and socks she could find.

Some of Allison's books were dog-eared and sticky; Shirley packed them, leaving the clean ones behind.

At the telephone table in the hall, she stopped to read the notes Gloria had jotted down. "Alli, I'll be back before twelve." "Chas, Mike says call him about the church."

Had the Maxwells been churchgoers? There was no bible among the few books in the living room cases. No bible storybooks among Allison's things. No evidence they subscribed to some other, non-Christian religion.

Shirley went back to the office and pulled out a file drawer. Charles had put things away more or less alphabetically, and under the "L's" she found a folder for the Living Church of Jesus. Inside were appraisal forms and contracts, offers and counteroffers, all pertaining to the Winterburn place in the Palace Pines Country Club. When oilman Kramer Winterburn had died, Columbine Savings and Loan had ended up owning the house; not surprisingly considering the extent of the financial collapse after the oil bubble burst. Charles had been the agent for the sale of the property to the church, and the papers were signed by Mike Carmichael, loan officer of the S&L, which explained where the two of them had gotten acquainted. Though the appraisals were for almost a million, the church had paid only half that—in cash, fruit of Reverend Patterson's "radio ministry" no doubt, since his local congregation wasn't large enough to come up with that kind of money. The commission on the sale had come to almost thirty-five thousand, but that had been two years ago. Shirley leafed rapidly through the other folders. The sale of the Winterburn property was the most recent one she could find. What had the Maxwells been living on?

"Numa, I'll bet I'll have to pay your bill," she muttered to the air. Gloria would probably lose the house and the van. Had Charles had life insurance? Tempe thought he had. Well, well, well. It might be a good idea for Gloria to look into bankruptcy as well. Otherwise she might have nothing left.

Assuming she ever got out of jail.

Carrying the almost-empty suitcase, Shirley left the Maxwell house and drove to the shopping center where she shopped for children's clothes and shoes and games. When she got home, she took the tags off the new items, lost the tags at the bottom of the garbage pail, then put the clothes through the washer twice and the dryer once to take the stiff newness out of them. Once folded, not too neatly, she stacked them on the bed in the guest room, Allison's room, along with the clothes, the bear, and the dog-eared books from the Maxwell house.

Then she went hunting for man and girl. She found them in the barn, feeding compressed alfalfa range treats to a malingering cow and to Sean McManus, the biggest of the Galloway bulls.

"What's she in for?" Shirley asked, pointing at the cow.

"Warts," Allison answered. "She's got big old warts on her face, and J.Q. let me put stuff on them so they'll dry up and fall off. She likes me." Her eyes were sparkling and her cheeks were pink. Suddenly she came to herself, however, and sobered down. "Did you see my mom?"

This morning early it had been "mommy." Shirley accepted the change of title, probably the result of J.Q.'s influence. "I saw your mom. Your mom's all right. I got her a good lawyer. I went over to your house and picked up some stuff for you, and I went down cellar when I got home and found some more stuff my niece left here. That's my grandniece. She outgrew a lot of stuff last summer when she was here. It's probably a little big for you. She was thirteen."

J.Q. gave her an expressionless stare. He knew Shirley had no grandniece or any other kind. Shirley's only brother had been childless when he died in World War II. Martin had had nieces. They sometimes came to visit with their mother, but they were in their late twenties.

Shirley smiled blandly at him, wrinkling her nose in warning.

"What kind of stuff?" asked Allison doubtfully.

"Oh, just jeans and shirts and stuff to wear outside when you go camping. Stuff like that. It may be too grown-up. You can look and see. She left a bathrobe, too, and some moccasins. I'm sure you can use those. I put the stuff in your room."

Allison left them at a run.

"What's the story?" asked J.Q.

"The story is that Charles Maxwell was broke. I don't know what he's been living on for the last year or so, but he sure hasn't been paying any of his bills. He's behind on house payments, car payments, credit-card payments. Gloria hasn't the least idea what's going on. She thought she didn't need a lawyer. Of course, some of that was Tempe being sneaky. I got her a lawyer."

"Whom you'll pay for," he snorted.

Trust J.Q. to be grammatically correct under all circumstances. He had been grammatically correct back in the seventh grade, when they had been schoolmates and quiet sweethearts. He had been a pain in the ass then, just as he was now.

"What am I supposed to do? Leave her to the mercies of an overworked public defender system? Anyhow, there was a note on the phone table at their house saying someone from the church called. I snooped a little. Maxwell sold the Winterburn house to the Living Jesus bunch. Columbine Savings and Loan held the mortgage on it. The way it looks, they let it go for about the amount of the mortgage, which was about half the appraised value. Carmichael tried to make me a similar deal on the Finlay place. Somebody from the church could have been calling Charles about something to do with the property, I suppose."

"Which would mean?"

"Damn it, J.Q., I don't know. There's a connection, that's all I know. Those bones belonged to somebody. Patterson

72

came out here for a reason. I'd feel better able to theorize if I knew a few whos and whys."

"What are you going to do next?"

"I'm going to call that fat woman, the one who came out here to convert me, and I'm going to invite her to lunch. I'm going to tell her I'm thinking of being born again."

"You don't even know her name."

"I do, too. Her name is Mabel Brubacher, and she's a sister to the man who runs the bakery."

"How in hell did you find that out?"

"I looked up William Deitz in the phone book, called his number and the woman who answered told me who she was. I claimed the fat woman left something here that I wanted to return to her. I said, 'The fat lady that goes missionarying with William Deitz,' and the woman on the phone knew right away who I meant. Mabel Brubacher, she said. Miss."

They started back to the house. Halfway there, Allison met them. She had a new shirt on. An old shirt, Shirley reminded herself. A supposed hand-me-down shirt. "Hey, that fits pretty good."

"She must have been small for her age," said Allison, admiring the bright flannel as she struggled to button the cuffs. "It fits me perfectly, and it's hardly faded at all. And you brought my bear. Mommy wouldn't let me bring him when I came. She said . . ."

"Well, hey, people have to have their bears," Shirley interrupted, seeing the girl's mouth begin to crumple. "Mothers sometimes think stuffed toys are kind of babyish, but I've got a bear. He lives on my closet shelf, but every now and then I take him down and give him a hug." J.Q. had given her the bear when she was over fifty years old. He had told her at the time that people had to have their bears. Something from A. A. Milne about bears. Bears in the squares. Did kids these days even know A. A. Milne? Only Pooh, probably, from TV, but none of the verses. Pity. The verses were the best part.

Later that night, when Allison was asleep, Shirley showed J.Q. the document she'd had Gloria sign.

"Taking this pretty seriously, aren't you, Shirl?"

"Only seriously enough, J.Q. I called Numa Ehrlich to take care of her mother. I'm not playing around with that child."

"Just don't get used to her being here," he said warningly, his eyes soft. "Don't get hurt, Shirley."

"Oh, hell no, J.Q." she said, lying in her teeth. "No, I won't get used to her."

3

Sunday passed quietly, reading the funnies, having late breakfast, feeding the stock. Allison spent most of the day trying to get various animals to eat from her hand. By evening she had succeeded not only with the littlest Muscovy duck but with one of the goats as well, and she was feeling very pleased with herself when she came in at suppertime.

J.Q. had put her science book beside her plate. "Didn't you tell me you had a chapter to read?"

She wrinkled her nose at him. "I like ducks better than marlucipals. That's what we're reading about in school. Australian marlucipals."

"Marsupials," corrected Shirley. "And you need to know about them!"

J.Q. found this exchange a sufficient lead-in to a favorite and interminable story about possums. Allison, delighted at the reprieve, paid rapt attention interrupted only by a few questions designated to make the story even longer. Shirley, who had heard the possum story in exhaustive detail several times before, ate her chowder and cornbread in silence while considering her assault upon Mabel Brubacher. This became a colloquy between her better and worse selves that went on until bedtime.

Mabel arrived at noon on Monday in a cream-colored Ford station wagon with the back end full of boxed religious tracts. Shirley gave her no time to unlimber tract or bible before sitting down to lunch, which she had taken the trouble to lay very nicely in the dining room with place mats and matching napkins and Shirley's mother's flowered plates. Mabel cooed over the plates. Shirley's aunt Ethel used to do that, too, though Shirley had never found them particularly coo-worthy.

"What I want to do today, Mrs. Brubacher," Shirley said, awarding Mabel honorary marital status, "is just talk. Joining a church may be mostly a matter of religion, but it's also a matter of people."

"Oh, my, that's certainly true," Mabel said, digging into her casserole. The recipe was also Shirley's mother's: a combination of turkey, dressing, and sauce—moist, succulent, and aromatic. At that moment, J.Q. was at the kitchen table, feasting on a large portion of it.

Shirley went on pontifically. "When one adopts a religious way of life, one wants to be surrounded by sincere and dedicated people. Before we talk about the religious part, I want you to tell me about the people. Tell me about Reverend Patterson. Tell me about the people who work most closely with him."

"Well, Reverend Patterson is about the most wonderful man I've ever known. No, that's not true. He is the most wonderful man." Mabel wiped her chin and took a long drink of iced tea. Shirley had diagnosed her as an iced-tea drinker who would eschew wine as sinful and Coke as depraved. Mabel took up her fork once more. "He's kind and nice to people. He always has a nice word for you. He always says thank you for any little thing you do. His wife is the prettiest thing. Her name's Bonny. I know you've seen her. She drives that pretty little red car. Reverend Patterson bought it for her as an anniversary gift. She just loves that little red car."

Shirley smiled and said yes. On more than one occasion

she'd seen the red Porsche with its row of rally emblems on the door.

"Bonny's not what you'd think of as a minister's wife. She's very artistic."

"How's that? Does she paint or sculpt or something?"

"No, it's not that she does it. She's one of those people who can see art, you know?" Mabel fumbled for the word she wanted. "She's very discriminating. That's why we needed the house in Palace Pines for the Pattersons. The old parsonage was so ugly, it just hurt her to live there."

"Oh, did it really?" Shirley asked.

"It made her sick. Something about the insulation in it or something. She all the time had these headaches and couldn't even come to services sometimes."

"She's been better then, since they've moved?"

Mabel looked doubtful, as though the question had not previously arisen, then took a few swallows of iced tea to wash down the last bite of her first helping. Shirley supplied her with another large, sauce-oozing chunk and another bowl of salad.

"You were telling me about the people who worked most closely with the reverend."

Mabel thought a minute, chewed, swallowed, and said, "I guess the folks that work most closely with Reverend Patterson are probably the deacons. There's Deacon Deitz, he was with our group when we came out here to see you, and Deacon Zeb Ferris and Deacon Terhewling. I don't know what his first name is."

"All men?"

"Oh, yes, all the deacons are men. That isn't a proper job for a woman. I've got a pamphlet right with me that explains what jobs a woman should do. Bible quotes and everything explained very clear."

"You can give me that before you go," Shirley smiled.

"Then there's Deacon Ralph Buttner and Deacon John Brown." Mabel continued her inventory. "They tease him, you know, about having John Brown's body. Deacon Brown is a very wealthy man."

77

"That would be Brown's Equipment?"

"Um-hm. All that heavy road machinery stuff."

"How about women in the church. If they can't be deacons, what can they be?"

"They can work in the auxiliary. And they can be heads of the circles. Bible study circles and bakery sale circles and prayer visitation circles, all those."

"But the deacons are the main ones. How many of them are there?"

"Well, there was six. But Deacon Dabronski moved or something. Seems to me I heard someone say he moved back to his family home in the east or the south somewhere. I haven't seen him at services for months and months. He used to be the one Reverend Patterson depended on most."

Something moved in Shirley's mind, like a fish turning in muddy water. "Deacon Dabronski moved?"

"Well, he must have. I know he hasn't been around."

The fish glimmered and twisted. "How long has he been gone?"

"Golly, I don't think I've seen Deacon Dabronski all summer. I saw him at the church picnic up at Redstone Point the first Sunday in June, I remember that, because he helped me cut the pies and took pictures of us all. I know he was here the next weekend when they broke into that dreadful baby-killing clinic, because he got arrested. I don't think I saw him after that."

"Is your church involved in that anti-abortion stuff?"

"Not the whole church, no. But a lot of the members are."

"Are Dr. and Mrs. Fish members of your congregation?"

"You mean Elise Fish. No. She and her sister don't get along for some reason, so . . ."

"Her sister?"

"Bonny Patterson. Reverend Patterson's wife. She's Elise Fish's sister. And they don't get along real well, so the Fishes go to church somewhere else."

"I suppose that could be embarrassing. Having your own sister be the minister's wife."

78

"Well, it could! Especially if you . . . well, I don't think she's . . . she's what you'd expect a minister to marry, you know." Mabel was disturbed by whatever she was thinking. She bit her lips.

Shirley got off that subject. "So your church isn't directly involved, but some of your members . . . ah, picket the clinic with Elise."

"Um-hm. Some of them. Deacon Dabronski went down there every single Saturday with Deacon Deitz." Mabel wiped her mouth. "He was very dedicated."

"Did Deacon Dabronski have a family here?"

"No, no family, unless you count Reverend Patterson. Reverend Patterson used to say he was close as a brother. Right during services, Reverend would turn and say he wanted to thank Deacon Dabronski for all his help. Deacon Dabronski used to almost live at their house, I know that. I guess Bonny kind of objected to that, too. At least that's what I heard. Well, you can see that. She probably doesn't get to see enough of her husband as it is without some other person hanging around. Deacon Dabronski drove Reverend Patterson around and did business things for him."

"Business things?"

"Oh, you know, like picking up the cleaning or taking Bonny's dog to the vet, things like that."

Errands, Shirley thought, wondering when such duties had been promoted to the status of "business things."

"When he wasn't living with the reverend, where did he live?" she asked. The fish was still down there, swimming around.

Mabel furrowed her brow as she chewed. "I'm pretty sure he lived in the annex."

"The annex?"

"What used to be the old parsonage. We call it the church annex now. The janitor lives there, and the gardener—he takes care of the lawns and the greenhouse and the memorial park—and I think Deacon Deitz lives there, too. Andy Manning keeps house for them. Well, she cleans the church, too. She has a part-time helper. I know that, because I thought it might be a good job for me, but they'd already hired some-body."

Shirley took a small mouthful of salad and chewed it thoughtfully. "I may have seen Deacon Dabronski around. Tall man, wasn't he? About six feet? With dark hair?"

"Oh, yes, a real nice-looking man. Tell you the truth, I wondered why he wasn't married."

"Well, he wasn't too old to get married yet. What was he, about forty?"

"About that, maybe a little younger," Mabel said with a little sigh. Too young for Mabel, the sigh said. The sigh said a good bit more than that.

Shirley heard the yearning in the sigh and decided to make something of that. "I think it's real disturbing, his disap-pearing that way. Of course, you've told the sheriff."

Mabel's mouth dropped open. "Why, I haven't done any such thing."

Shirley shook her head sadly. "And you a good church-member! Why, it seems to me it's your Christian duty to report it to the Sheriff, Mabel. For heaven's sake. The man might be somewhere right now with a broken leg or a hurt back, unable to get help, just because nobody reported him missing."

"Reverend Patterson should . . ."

"Does Reverend Patterson do your Christian duty for you? My, my, that isn't the kind of church I'd want to belong to. One where everybody held back waiting for the preacher to do it all."

This seemed to strike a chord, but Mabel still wasn't com-fortable with the idea. "I heard he'd moved back home. I'd feel really strange going to the sheriff. You could tell him, though, if you think you should."

Shirley pursed her lips, appeared to consider the matter, finally shook her head. "No. It would only be hearsay if I told him. I never even met the man. The sheriff would just think I was meddling. You're the one who actually knows Deacon Dabronski is gone. Now, he may have moved back home, and maybe that's just what everybody assumed. He was your friend. He helped you cut the pies and took pictures of you. Maybe at this very minute, he's somewhere looking at your picture and praying that you, Mabel Brubacher, will come looking for him.''

''Do you really think so?''

Shirley smiled. ''How about coffee, Mabel? Are you ready for a piece of pecan pie?''

They had coffee and pecan pie. Mabel rather halfheartedly mentioned sitting down and going over some scripture, but Shirley demurred.

''I just couldn't concentrate on it now. I keep thinking of that poor man, maybe dying, and nobody knowing where he is.''

Mabel's plump face turned red. ''All right!'' she said. ''All right, I'll go into town and tell Sheriff Tempe. I will. I'm still not sure it's the right thing, but you could be right about his needing help and it being my duty to do something!''

''I just know it's the right thing for you to do.''

Mabel drove the station wagon out the driveway, slowing to a cautious five miles per hour as she edged past a gang of cows who were, as they often were at midday, sunning themselves on the gravel drive and not much interested in moving. Shirley gave her a minute's head start then got into the beatup ranch pickup that J.Q. used to move hay around and drove down the old mill road to its junction with County 64 and along the county road toward the interstate. She picked up Mabel's station wagon at the highway and followed it at a sedate forty-five to the first Columbine exit at the west end of town. The shopping center was also at the west end of town, just across from the Taco Bell and the McDonald's and the Kentucky Fried Chicken. Outside the shopping center the station wagon slowed and finally stopped on the gravel shoulder of the road. Shirley pulled into the nearby Pizza Hut and waited to see what Mabel was going to do next. After five minutes Mabel's car slowly pulled away from the shoulder and into the shopping center, past the Safeway and Hallmark Cards and the Busy Barbers: Unisex and the Ridge

County Savemor Liquors to the Justice Center. About ten minutes passed before Mabel got out of her car and went inside.

Shirley wondered if Mabel had been sitting in the car praying for guidance. She'd certainly taken long enough getting to the sheriff, if that's where she'd gone. When she hadn't emerged after twenty minutes, Shirley thought it fairly likely that Mabel had indeed gone to the sheriff's office, so she turned the pickup around and went home.

"Where've you been?" demanded J.Q. "I saw you light out of here. You're supposed to tell people where you're going."

"No time, J.Q. I needed to follow that woman and see she went to the sheriff. I think she knows the corpse, and I didn't want to go to Tempe myself. He's already peeved at me over Allison and my getting a lawyer for Gloria. I might need something from him later on, so no point in making him mad."

"And how come she knows who the dead man is?"

"Oh, she doesn't. She just knows somebody hasn't been around for a few months. Nobody's reported him missing, which is a little strange in itself, wouldn't you say? Particularly since he was closely associated with the good reverend, and the good reverend was right here on my patio going on and on about nobody knowing who those poor lonely bones belonged to."

"Well, how do you know it's him?"

"Well, hell, J.Q., I don't know it's him. I wouldn't swear to any such thing, but I've got my suspicions. Some little bird told me."

"A bird?" J.Q. thought he was being teased and was not amused.

"Did you ever learn that rhyme? 'Who killed Cock Robin? I, said the sparrow. With my bow and arrow, I killed Cock Robin.' "

"I thought the corpse was shot with a gun."

Shirley nodded. "The man in the scrub probably was, but he wasn't Cock Robin. Charles Maxwell, though, he was cocky, no question about it. And Charles Maxwell was shot with an arrow."

Sheriff Tempe called midafternoon wanting to know where Mrs. McClintock got off talking nonsense to Mabel Brubacher.

Shirley sighed. She should have known Mabel wouldn't keep her mouth shut once a possible connection to a dead body was suspected. "Is the body Dabronski?"

"She said you told her to come in here and report him missing."

"Is the body Dabronski?"

"I don't know if it's Dabronski," he shouted. "What I want to know is why you think so."

"I don't think so, Sheriff," she said in her most innocent voice. "For heaven's sake, the woman was here because I invited her for lunch. I'd been real rude to her group the other day, and I thought I owed it to her to give her a hearing. So she started talking about this man who used to be around all the time but wasn't around anymore, and he was the same height and the same age and the same hair color as the newspaper said the dead man was. Now I know what I should have told her was to keep it to herself, shouldn't I? I should have told her you'd be real upset if anybody gave you a clue as to who the bones belonged to. I should have told her Sheriff Botts Tempe didn't want that body identified, so she should just . . ."

"Shirley! That's a lot of . . ."

"Of course, I encouraged her to tell you about it, just as any good citizen would do," Shirley yelled.

"Everybody at the church says Dabronski moved back to North Carolina, where his family is."

"Maybe he did, Sheriff. Maybe he did. Maybe what you need to do is find somebody who knows for sure. Or call him up in North Carolina and see if he's all right."

"Suppose it is him. What about the perpetrator, Mrs. McClintock? You got any bright ideas about that?"

"Ms. McClintock. Ms. My first husband's name was

Fleschman, my second husband's name was Johnson. My father's name was McClintock. I'm not Mrs. McClintock, I'm Ms.''

"You got any ideas about the perpetrator? Or maybe perpetrators? Since you seem to think these two things are connected up?''

"You might ask the reverend when he saw his deacon last. I'm told they were very close.''

"Reverend Patterson? Now that makes me mad. That's my church, and you damn liberals are all the time accusing . . .''

Being called a liberal stopped her only for a second. "Hey, Botts, calm down. I'm not accusing anybody. I'm not suggesting anything. I merely repeat to you what Mabel Brubacher said to me, which was that Deacon Dabronski was very close to the reverend. At the very least the reverend can tell you when he saw Dabronski last. For heaven's sake, that'd help, wouldn't it?''

"I think you know something,'' accused the sheriff.

"Well, if you think I've got any guilty knowledge, Botts, you can arrest me and try to scare it out of me.'' She hung up, rather more strongly than necessary.

"Are you talking to the sheriff about getting my mom out?'' asked Allison. She had sneaked into the corner of the room like a mouse. Shirley hadn't known she was there.

"That's what you want me to do, isn't it?''

"Sure. Because she didn't do it.''

"That's right. So we'll get her out. It's just taking longer than I expected.''

"She didn't do it, but she said she wanted to.''

Shirley took a deep breath and held it. "When was that?''

"When we got home from going deer hunting. Mom said never again, she'd like to kill him dragging her and Arlette off in the woods that way, and they never did get their lunch.''

Shirley let the breath out. "That's a figure of speech. She didn't meant it.''

"Oh, I know that. She used to say it all the time. So did he. He used to say he'd like to kill her, too. When she bought

84

stuff. He'd say he didn't buy it, and he didn't believe the other women did it, and he ought to lock her up, and not having any money was no excuse. Stuff like that."

"What other women was he talking about?"

"I don't know. Some women my mom used to go shopping with. She'd leave me a note and tell me when she'd be home, and she'd go with somebody. She had to go with somebody, because when Daddy was gone, she didn't have a car."

"I imagine she got bored and lonely, Allison. Your daddy didn't really mean he'd kill her."

"I know. Sometimes he said he'd kill me if I didn't do stuff."

"Like what stuff?" asked Shirley, suddenly dry-mouthed, thinking of sexual abuse of children.

"Like forget to carry out the trash." Allison sat down and thumped the tile floor with her new—old—shoe. "Sometimes I forgot. Or I forgot to do my homework, and he'd say, Allison if you don't get that homework done, I'll kill you."

"Tomorrow," Shirley announced, disliking all this talk of killing, "I'm going to get you started at the school out here."

"Out here? There's no school out here."

"Oh, yes there is. One mile down that road is a private day school that teaches kids from all over out here. It's called the Wilma D. Crepmier School, after a friend of my grandfather's. It's a good, solid, old-fashioned, nonsectarian school that provides grades one through six. You'll get the Pledge of Allegiance and a strong emphasis on personal responsibility but no prayers unless you say them yourself."

Allison looked doubtful. "How many people go there?"

"About thirty. They have two classrooms and two teachers, and one reason it exists is the bad winter weather in this part of the world. Certain citizens don't want their children in school buses during blizzards, so they have banded together to support the Crepmier School. How does that strike you?"

"Very sensible," said Allison in a perfect imitation of J.Q.'s intonation. "Very sensible indeed."

The McClintock family had been longtime supporters of Creps, as the locals called the Crepmier School; so Ms. Minging, the head teacher, found no difficulty in including Allison in the upper level on a temporary basis. Allison spent two days finding her own level in reading, spelling, writing, and arithmetic workbooks, after which Ms. Minging sent a note home saying she was above grade level in the verbal skills, below grade level in math. J.Q. looked at Allison over the tops of his glasses and said he would be working with her at least one hour every evening until she was up to snuff.

"Mom says arithmetic is boy's stuff," said Allison dismissively.

"Nonsense," said J.Q. "If your mom is right about that, then she is also right about playing ball, living in the country, wearing jeans and shirts and boots, riding horseback, and a whole host of other things that are called 'boy's things.' You can't pick and choose among them, Allison. What you have to do is do your best at everything. That way the real you will emerge."

Allison looked slightly confused.

"You know about butterflies?" Shirley intervened. "Coming out of a cocoon?"

A nod, one of those Allison nods that admitted as little as possible.

"When you look at the caterpillar, you can't see the wings. There's simply no way to tell by looking at a caterpillar that it will ever have wings. There's no sign of them on the caterpillar's body. You can imagine all these people standing around looking at a caterpillar and saying, 'Hunh. That thing will never have wings. Wings are bird stuff.'

"Well, when you look at a fifth-grade kid, you can't see what they're going to be either. There could be a dancer or a doctor or a scientist or artist inside any boy or girl. There could be a good mechanic in there, or an exceptionally fine accountant. Nobody knows for sure. If you tell yourself math is for men and learning about tools is for men and only this or that is for women, you may be cutting off your wings before you've ever had a chance to grow them. Does that make sense?"

"You mean I could be *anything*? A pilot even? Something like that?"

Good lord, has nothing changed? Shirley wondered. After decades of all-out feminism, little girls still ask that question. "Anything you've got the talent for. But you'll never know what you've got talent for unless you try everything and give it your best shot."

After Allison had gone to her room, J.Q. said, "Pretty good lecture there, Shirl."

"It's what I told Sally," she murmured, the memory bringing sudden tears to her eyes. "It's what I told her the day that she . . ."

"Hush," he said, coming to put his arms around her. "Oh, hush, Shirl. Where's my tough old buzzard? Don't go back, dear love. That's time past. You've no time for that now. It looks like we've got our work cut out for us with time present."

On Thursday the *Ridge County News* carried a front-page story about the identification of the bones found on Strawberry Mountain as being those of Ira J. Dabronski, once deacon of the Living Church of Jesus and employee of that church as well as close associate of Reverend Orrin Patterson and his wife, Bonny. Mr. Dabronski had been thought by the Pattersons to have returned to North Carolina, his childhood home. Mr. Dabronski's remains had been identified through dental charts and through X-rays on file at the family health center in Columbine.

"I didn't know that was called Strawberry Mountain," J.Q. muttered, digging through his copies of forest service and geographical survey maps. "That *isn't* Strawberry Mountain," he said moments later. "That's the southeast slope of Starr Mountain. Strawberry is south of it by at least three miles."

"Botts Tempe released the information," said Shirley with a sly grin. "Botts Tempe knows it isn't Strawberry."

"Ah-ha. He wants to keep the curiosity seekers away from the site."

"That'd be my guess," she said.

In a seemingly unrelated item, the newspaper reported that bail had been denied to Gloria Maxwell, now under arraignment for the murder of her husband, Charles.

"That idiot," mumbled Shirley, referring to Botts Tempe, as she made her way to the kitchen door. "Allison," she said, "Finish up your breakfast. Time for school."

"Coming," said Allison. She appeared in the doorway, egg on her chin, hair on end, fully dressed in jeans, flannel shirt, and down-filled vest. "I thought of playing possum this morning," she confessed. "It was nice and warm in my bed."

"You'll be nice and warm out of your bed once you start moving around," Shirley said, wiping the girl's chin. "Where's your comb? Give it to me. You look like a Sebastopol goose, all ruffled up. There. Now you look almost like a person. I watched J.Q. pack your lunch before we were even up. He gave you cold fried chicken from last night and a peanut-butter-and-honey sandwich and cookies."

"And carrot sticks," yelled J.Q. from among his maps. "And an apple and a thermos of milk."

"I'll get fat," said Allison contentedly.

"Probably," said Shirley. "But I wouldn't worry about it yet."

"Ms. Minging wants my health card."

Shirley grimaced. She'd been trying to remember for two days to get that health card. "Where did you say?"

"In the kitchen, in that little desk where Mom keeps her recipes, in one of the bird holes."

"Pigeon holes," corrected J.Q. "Come on, kid. If we dally another two minutes, you'll be late." They went out the kitchen door, leaving Shirley to her second cup of coffee. She fumbled through the kitchen junk drawer for paper and a pencil and started a list with "health card" at the top. Actually the card was Allison's immunization record. State law did require children to be vaccinated against communicable diseases, though that had little enough to do with health. Ms. Minging had been unusually patient, for her.

Shirley added milk and cheese to the list. Allison couldn't seem to get enough milk. She said her mom hadn't always had enough money to buy milk, at which point Shirley had asked where her mom got the money to buy the purple caftans and the silver sandals and the fingernail set.

"She splurged," said Allison. "She took some of her own money for that, but she said daddy was supposed to buy groceries. If he didn't give her any money, we didn't get any."

Shirley clamped her teeth together in an angry line and put melon on the list. Allison was fond of melon, and Gloria Maxwell was a twit. What kind of a mother let her child go without milk! Add pork chops. Allison said she liked pork chops.

She couldn't keep her mind on groceries. It kept going back to that silly, silly woman in the cell who had been denied bail. Gloria should have been granted bail. She had been in there for almost a week! The fact that bail had been refused was bothersome. Though the judge was an old lady when it came to certain crimes, sex crimes mostly, he wasn't unreasonable. Not usually. He should have realized that Gloria was no danger to the world at large.

She called Numa Ehrlich and left a message for him to call her, then took her list out to the Wagoneer and left for town. J.Q. was going to drop Allison off at school, then go get his cast removed. Shirley had agreed to do the shopping, make the bank deposit, and stop at Columbine Feed and Supply for chicken feed and at the lumberyard for drive staples so they could finish insulating the new chicken house. She decided to stop at the bank first, then go to the Maxwell house for the health card, then to the grocery and lumberyard.

The exit from the highway that led into the west end of town was blocked. As she passed, Shirley saw trucks and cars backed up for a quarter of a mile, blocking the exit all the way to the cross road. Smoke hazed the intersection, blowing in acrid tatters across the highway. She took the second exit and came back from the other direction to stop at the bank, which was empty except for two tellers. Her business concluded, she stepped out of the bank and looked westward down Main Street. At the end of the street firemen, moving about in a haze of smoke, were summoning one car at a time through their tangled hoses. The building that had burned was a featureless cube next to a somewhat blackened garage.

One of the bank tellers emerged from behind her to peer curiously down the street.

"What burned?" Shirley wondered.

"Customer said it was the Benton warehouse. Where they have the sales, you know? The auctions of used furniture? Oh, damn. I never get to watch fires. I love fires, and I never get to see one. Everything always burns in the daytime when I'm working. See, they've already got it out." She seemed to take it as a personal affront, shaking her head at the firemen as though they had offended her. "You'd think some stuff would burn on weekends when I could watch."

"It's a real mess." Shirley gave the firebug a curious look. "Looks like the roof fell in. Suppose they'll have a fire sale?"

"I doubt there's enough left," the firebug responded with a scowl as she hurried back inside after a bank customer.

Back in her car, Shirley followed her curiosity to the fire, though there was little enough to see. The warehouse had had no windows. All the damage was inside, invisible. The roof, said a bystander, had fallen in, and the contents that hadn't been burned had been totally destroyed by water. The bystander was an astonishingly pretty blonde dressed in camel and cashmere, and when she turned to get into a familiar-looking Mercedes, Shirley realized who she was.

"You're Bonny Patterson, aren't you?" she asked.

The woman turned, startled, her initial surprise giving way to cool appraisal. "Yes, I am. But I don't believe we've met."

"No, we haven't met. I very recently met your husband, however. My name is Shirley McClintock. He came out to my place yesterday to . . . to explain about the missionary folks from your church.''

"Missionary folks?''

"Mabel Brubacher. William Deitz.''

"Oh, the housecallers.'' She laughed, a girlishly charming tinkle of laughter.

"That's what you call them? You know, I'd like to know a little more about that whole thing. Do you have time to come across the street and get a cup of coffee with me?''

Bonny Patterson looked first at the car then back at Shirley, as though judging between the two and deciding only with some difficulty that she could take time. Is she shy? Shirley wondered. Shyness would be quite a burden for a minister's wife. She didn't act shy, not really. Simply withheld. Self-contained.

"I can't stay very long,'' she said at last with that same tinkle of laughter. "I'm meeting someone in twenty minutes.''

"Just one cup.'' Shirley led the way across the street and into the Pizza Hut, where she bought two cups of coffee and set them down on a corner table as far as possible from the four other people in the room. Bonny Patterson slid into the opposite chair and lowered her head over her cup, her eyes focused on the coffee, which she stirred slowly, seemingly mesmerized by the swirling surface. Soft, ash-blond hair tumbled around a perfect face, lightly tanned, lovely as a porcelain and with about as much expression. She resembled Elise Fish in the way a painting resembles a poor copy. This was the masterpiece; Elise was merely an illustration.

"Do you ever participate in . . . in housecalling?'' Shirley asked curiously.

"No,'' she said. "No, Orrin says that isn't my job.'' She looked up, past Shirley, over Shirley's shoulder, her eyes sliding across Shirley's face to the other side, as though unwilling to make eye contact.

Some animals did that. If you looked them in the eye, they felt threatened. Shirley lowered her own gaze to her cup and said, "I was just very interested, not at the time the group came out, of course. At the time I was busy, but later on I called Mabel and asked her to come out and talk with me."

"Mabel is what Orrin calls a stalwart. Which is one way of putting it."

"What do you think of her?"

The face considered this without much interest. "She's . . . Mabel. A large, well-meaning woman of no particular . . . Well." She smiled, looking directly at Shirley for the first time. "You've caught me, Mrs. McClintock."

"Ms. But call me Shirley. How have I caught you?"

"The people in the congregation want to feel that they are our friends, so Orrin says. They want to be our warm, personal friends. They want to be part of our lives. At least, so Orrin tells me." She flashed a quick, almost hummingbird-like smile. "That's all nonsense, of course. Even Orrin can't manage to be friends with all of them. He's able to act it better than I do, that's all." She grinned fiercely, showing sharp white teeth. "I find some of them a little hard to take."

"I would, too," Shirley said sympathetically. "Having all those people competing for your attention."

Another smile, a slow one this time, full of unspoken amusement. "Oh, I confine my attentions mostly to domestic things. Have you seen our house?" Suddenly there was expression in her face, light in her eyes. "It's exactly the house I've always wanted."

"You like it," Shirley smiled, warming to her. People who loved beautiful things were, in Shirley's experience, worth getting to know.

Bonny laughed, "That house . . . it's a miracle. It's everything I've wanted my whole life. What I've dreamed of. The kind of place I used to long for when I was a child, with Elise." Her face changed. "My sister, that is. Elise Fish." She turned her face away, putting up a hand as though to shield it, her fingers playing with her ear, then with a dark mole on her neck behind the ear, then caressing her jawline and chin, a fluttering movement that stopped as quickly as it had begun.

"I know Elise," Shirley offered, wondering what lay between Bonny and Elise that made Bonny's manner change so greatly when her sister came to mind. "I can't say that I like her very much."

Bonny turned her face toward Shirley's, actually looked at her, her eyes glittering in an expression of covert amusement as she delighted in the fact that Elise was not much liked. "Elise always wanted to run everyone's life, you know. Elise was going to marry Orrin before I came home, but Orrin decided he wanted me. Elise said he'd never marry me, that he couldn't afford to. Elise can't bear the fact that he married me anyhow. She can't be content unless she's managing somebody—for their own good, of course." She laughed abruptly, her fingers at her ear once more, stroking her neck once more. "Poor Elise."

Shirley brought the subject back to something less emotional. "Well, if you have that beautiful Winterburn house, it probably makes up for a lot."

"Orrin says God intends it to make it up to me for . . ." Awareness slid across her face. Her eyes became shuttered. "Well. To make up for all the time he has to be away."

"I didn't know ministers could be *away*. I thought they had to stick to the congregation."

"Orrin goes to a lot of evangelical conferences. The church gets a guest preacher when he's gone. He just got back from a week in Atlanta, and it's about the tenth trip this year. He goes away all the time, for a few days or a week. Once this year it was almost three weeks, so he *should* make it up to me for that. Besides, the house isn't just for that. It's partly to make up for all the years we lived in those awful parsonages."

"I guess parsonages can be old and ugly," Shirley sympathized. "And I was in your house when Kramer Winterburn owned it, so I know what you mean. You're right. It's very lovely. I always think of that house as having wings. Those big decks, reaching out over the mountainside!"

"When I stand up there, it's like I'm a bird." Bonny laughed, like a child at a circus, full of delight.

93

"Are your families from around here? Yours and your husband's?" Shirley asked.

"I grew up here," she said. "I lived in Kansas City awhile. Orrin's family is from back east, but they moved to Denver when Orrin was in seminary here." She smiled again, a mere flick of expression, gone as quickly as it had come, and fumbled with the little purse in her lap. "Thanks for the coffee. It's been nice to talk with you, though I've been indiscreet. Orrin gets mad at me when I do that. But you're not a member of the church, so you won't tell on me, will you? Please don't tell on me. Mabel would be crushed. Elise would make all kinds of trouble. I really must go or I'll be late."

She stood up, as though uncertain where she was, then murmured a good-bye and went out and across the street without pausing or looking to either side of her, almost as though she felt nothing could hurt her, that women like herself needn't look both ways before crossing. Three cars slowed for her without honking and then dawdled past, the drivers staring after the striding figure.

Shirley, left behind, finished her coffee and wondered what Bonny's beautiful house had really been intended as reparation for. What disadvantage or habitual failing, real or imagined? What a pity Bonny had caught herself just as she had been about to say something revealing.

Mabel had been right about her. She was an untypical minister's wife. Beautiful, certainly. Tastefully and expensively dressed, with a hectic, slightly defiant manner, with tinkling laughter and strangely hooded eyes. "I've been indiscreet. Don't tell on me." Adult words; a childlike manner.

Shirley had once found a wounded owl. She had kept the huge bird until it healed, feeding it chunks of raw chicken from heavily gloved fingers. Though the owl took the food, seemingly with good appetite, it became no tamer with time. Once released, it had vanished on silent wings, plunging away into the dusk as though it could not bear the sight or sound or smell of her again, showing neither gratitude nor any memory of kindness.

Bonny Patterson reminded her of the owl. She had the same hooded eyes; she moved as though there were winged energies trembling just under her skin, ready to fly out and away, without looking back.

When Shirley was sixteen she would have given her soul to be like that. Over the years she had come to terms with herself as she was, with her ponderous bones and monumental height. Still, wild and fragile things moved her with a mysterious desire, a dreamlike longing to be. She shook her head at her own foolishness, stretched herself to her full height, and went to finish her errands.

At the Maxwell house she used Allison's key as before, stepping through into the quiet house, immediately aware of a different quality to the silence: an echoing, almost empty vacancy, which was explained the minute she went into the living room. Aside from a coffee table, two lamps, a scatter of magazines, and the assorted miscellany that might have come out of table drawers, the room was empty. The dining room was as vacant. China and glassware sat in a forlorn huddle on the carpet. The dining table, chairs- and buffet hutch, which had overfilled the room when she had been here last, were gone.

In the master bedroom nothing remained but the carpet and a jumble of folded clothes and odds and ends on the floor along one wall. Dust bunnies marked the place the bed had stood. Allison's room, on the other hand, still retained its slightly dilapidated furnishings: a single bed, a lamp table, a rocking chair, a slightly chipped chest of drawers. The drawers were pulled out, as though they had been searched.

The antique desk was still in the kitchen, though the appliances had been removed. No dishwasher, no stove, no refrigerator. Shirley checked under the sink to find the garbage disposal still in place. Evidently it had come with the house. In the laundry the washing machine remained but the drier was missing. In the front bedroom Charles had used as an office, no furniture had been taken, though the papers on the desk looked even more disordered than when she had seen them last.

The totality of the repossession indicated that the Maxwells had brought nothing with them to this house; they had furnished it completely, all at once, probably from one store on one contract. It might have been one of the "specials" heavily advertised by some dealers; one of those "no payments for six months" deals. When Charles had been unable to pay, everything had gone. Shirley went through the house again, checking the closets. A dress she remembered having straightened on its hanger was now twisted, hanging by a single sleeve. Someone had gone through the closets, though she could not see that anything was missing. The crew doing the repossession might have been curious, or light-fingered, of course. The money that had been in the drawer of Gloria's bedside table was not among the leftovers on the bedroom floor.

Back in the kitchen, Shirley fished Allison's health card out of the cluttered desk and went through the connecting door to the garage. The garage door, which opened onto the alley, was shut, and the van was gone, leaving not even a grease spot on the concrete to show it had ever been there. On one wall hung a few garden tools, a spare tire, Charles Maxwell's fancy PSE hunting bow, a target bow, a field quiver, and a target quiver. Shirley examined them with interest. Five hunting arrows in the field quiver. Six new target arrows in the other. All were fletched with magenta polymer vanes. Well, bright color made the arrows easier to find in the woods. As she turned to leave, she noticed several cardboard boxes stacked against the wall, crumpled newspapers hiding the contents. They were full of empty bottles, mostly sweet stuff: Southern Comfort, other liqueurs, port wine. When Shirley left through the side door, the neighbor to the north had her head out of the window again.

"I see the furniture company repossessed all their stuff," Shirley called, in as neutral a voice as she could manage.

"Furniture truck showed up Monday morning first thing," agreed the neighbor, nodding her kerchief-covered head.

Under the cloth the rows of curlers marched from forehead to neckline like soldiers on parade. "They broke a back window and went in. And the car people took the van at the same time. Had a sheriff's deputy with them. He stayed until after somebody fixed the window. I guess they have to do that, huh? Fix anything they break?"

"How long have the Maxwells lived there?" Shirley asked.

"Less than a year. They used to live over in Palace Pines, but I guess the real-estate market wasn't that good anymore, and he couldn't keep up the payments. My sister works for the credit bureau, and she told me they got repossessed there, too. My name's Mercer, by the way. Betty Mercer." She held out her hand, and Shirley took it.

"Shirley McClintock. Did you know the Maxwells at all?"

The woman shook her head, "Just to speak to her. He never spoke, not even if you spoke first. I got the impression he thought it was a real comedown, living here. He didn't want to get too friendly."

"How about the little girl?"

"Could have been a nice kid except for her mother's weird ideas. I raised three girls, and I never let them use makeup until they were juniors in high school. A little lipstick maybe, on special occasions, but nothing else. That was the rule. Makes me sick, seeing little girls all painted up around the eyes. Makes them look like little hookers."

Shirley nodded, agreeing with her. "You think Gloria killed her husband?"

"Naah," said the woman, shaking her head. "Her? She couldn't even pick up the paper off the front porch with those fingernails she always wore. I never saw her do anything that took any muscle. She was just, you know, like a pretty noodle."

Shirley nodded again. Gloria was, in many respects, like a pretty noodle. Attractive but limp.

When she got back to the house J.Q. had returned and was stalking up and down, trying out his ankle.

"How does it feel?" she asked.

"Like it belonged to somebody else," he grimaced. "Doctor says to take it easy for a few weeks. No fifty-mile hikes."

They went to the kitchen to make sandwiches while Shirley told him about the repossession. The phone rang and Shirley grabbed it.

"Numa Ehrlich," her caller identified himself. "You called?"

"Bail," she responded. "How come Gloria didn't get bail? Hell, child abusers get bail. Rapists get bail. How come Judge Benton . . ."

"Patience, Shirley," Numa's voice repeated. "In the first place, Gloria Maxwell would not consent to my representing her until late Tuesday afternoon."

"She what?"

"Shirley, she seems to be quite an odd person. If she's a dear friend of yours, please don't take offense. Given that the circumstances are disturbing, still one might expect a modicum of awareness. I saw her Saturday afternoon, not more than an hour or so after you called. I told her you'd retained me to represent her. She rejected me in favor of a court-appointed attorney. I called to tell you, but you weren't home, and then I became occupied with other things. Evidently when she met the court-appointed attorney, she rejected him in favor of me." Numa sniffed. Obviously, the sniff said, anyone sensible would have done just that. "Bail was refused yesterday, and I've been working on it since. I do have other cases, Shirley."

"Benton Furniture Warehouse," murmured J.Q. "He's Judge Benton's brother. And the Ford Agency is a brother-in-law."

"Numa," she said, "could the refusal of bail have anything to do with the fact that the Benton Furniture man wanted to repossess Gloria's furniture, and he's Judge Benton's brother?"

Numa sounded doubtful, but he also seemed to be taking notes. She could hear a pen scratching away. Shirley went on talking about poor Gloria and what she could do next, when and if she got out jail. When she hung up the phone she was scowling. "That rotten bastard."

"Your lawyer?"

"Judge Benton. I'll bet you're right. He probably got a call from his brother the furniture huckster—have you seen his ads on TV? Yech! Have you seen the furniture he advertises on TV? Cut velvet and tassels, for God's sake. Green and orange bolsters. It's enough to make a cat sick."

"Shirley."

"I can't understand why people buy . . ."

"Shirley."

"Yes, for heaven's sake, J.Q."

"Would you say that average TV fare appeals greatly to people of taste and discrimination?"

"Well, I watch it, J.Q."

"An hour a night, sometimes. You watch "NOVA." You watch "Masterpiece Theatre." What would you say is the discrimination power of persons watching sitcoms and mini-series for several hours every night? Oh, and game shows."

She thought about it. "Could take a toll, couldn't it?"

"I postulate a ten-percent loss of intelligence every year. That's only an estimate, of course. It could be greater. Then there's the inevitable blunting of discrimination that takes place. After all that, it should not surprise you that the furniture advertised by the Bentons of the world is chosen to fit that particular audience. We could make an axiom of it. Nothing advertised on TV is likely ever to win a MOMA award."

She glared at him. "What was I talking about before you started this lecture?"

"Judge Benton."

"Right. Well, I'll bet his huckster brother told him to keep Gloria in jail until he had a chance to empty her house, and he couldn't get anybody over the weekend, so Monday was his first chance. Benton probably gave him and his brother-in-law quick hearings and repossession judgements, too."

"Did I hear you say something about Gloria coming out here to the ranch?" J.Q. asked in a dangerously quiet voice.

"I did merely imagine your saying that to your lawyer, didn't I?"

"Where's she going to go?" Shirley asked him. "There isn't a stick of furniture in that house. She doesn't have a car. Her only sibling is in Albany, New York. I don't know if she has living parents. We'll ask Allison when she gets home from school. If Numa gets Gloria out of jail, she's got to go somewhere."

"You expect her to share the guest room with Allison?"

Shirley shook her head. "The bunkhouse. Allison needs a room of her own. Especially with Gloria as Gloria is."

"Nobody has lived in the bunkhouse for ten years. The plumbing doesn't work."

"We keep talking about fixing it up so we can hire somebody to feed the cows. So we can go to Disneyland."

"Shirley! I do not want to go to Disneyland! If television results in a ten-percent loss of intelligence per year . . ."

"I already have people coming tomorrow. Cleaning people, and a plumber and a painter. I told them it was an emergency."

J.Q. looked disgusted. Shirley pretended not to notice, meantime thinking sadly that it wasn't something she should have done without asking him. If J.Q. felt like it, he could pack up and leave. There was nothing holding him here, no marriage vows, no obligations. He stayed because he was fond of her, because they had known one another since they were little more than children, and because he liked the place. The prospect of having Gloria around might be the straw that broke the camel's back.

"I'm sorry, J.Q.," she said. "I should have asked you."

"It's all right," he said in an unconcerned tone. "Once you get the bunkhouse fixed up, and once Gloria gets sorted out and it's empty, you can hire somebody to do the stuff around here that I do. Then I can go traveling."

"Would you?" she asked him, holding his eyes with her own. "Would you do that, J.Q.? Without me?"

He went on slicing chicken and didn't answer her. She kept her hurt to herself. He would have done exactly the same thing himself if it had been up to him. He wouldn't have let that woman go home to that empty house either. No matter how limp she was.

Fixing up the bunkhouse turned out to be simpler than anticipated. Though the building was fairly spacious—two bedrooms, one bath, and a large living room/kitchen area—and though it hadn't been used since Shirley's father had died, the only problems were a leaking tub faucet, a stopped-up basin, filthy paint, and ten years worth of mouse droppings and spiderwebs. By four on Friday afternoon the walls were newly painted and the plumbing was fixed. By Saturday noon the carpet cleaner had been and gone, the curtains and bedspreads had been laundered, and there were clean towels in the bathroom. The place looked and smelled clean. A little Spartan, Shirley thought, but clean. Certainly better than the dusty vacancy of the Maxwell house.

Though Numa had managed to get an appearance before Judge Benton to argue the matter of bail on Friday, it was Saturday before bond could be arranged. Notwithstanding all Shirley's efforts to provide a safe harbor for Gloria Maxwell, when she and Numa got to the jail shortly after noon, Gloria obstinately refused to go along with their plans.

"I want to go home," she announced in a shrill whine with an incipient scream hovering at the back of it. "It's very nice of you to invite me, Shirley, but I want to go home."

Shirley looked helplessly at Numa, who shrugged. His tall, spare body always looked a bit stiff, and he had stiffened even more at Gloria's tone. His nose was pinched, too, and his bushy eyebrows were lifted. Shirley had always thought he looked like a handsome Lincoln. Or at least one without warts. At the moment he simply looked annoyed.

"And I want you to bring Allison home," shrilled Gloria.

Shirley took a deep breath. "She's looking forward to the school Halloween party next Tuesday, Gloria. They're having a costume thing and a softball game. She'd really like to go on out there."

"Softball! She doesn't play ball! Ballgames are for boys. Allison knows that. I want her back with me!"

Numa asked whether Gloria had considered how badly Allison might be treated by her schoolmates. He spoke feelingly of the unthinking cruelty of children, particularly children whose parents had read of the murder over their morning coffee and had asked their children if that wasn't the little Maxwell girl in their class. "You're suspected of murdering her father, Gloria. Her classmates are unlikely to be kind."

Gloria gulped and waved her hands. "She can stay home, with me."

Numa spoke of the truancy laws, of the requirement that all children attend school, how Allison herself would feel at missing weeks of her lessons. "I'd like to suggest that you leave her where she is for just a few days. Just until you can see how things go. Perhaps you'd like to ask her what she'd like to do."

Everything either of them said seemed to make Gloria more erratic and intense. Now she screamed, "It doesn't matter. She's mine. And I want her at my house. I need her there."

"I'll bring her in tomorrow," said Shirley, thinking of the empty house and wondering helplessly what was going on in Gloria's mind. How did Gloria expect to feed the child, or herself? "Or I can drive you out there to have Sunday dinner with us. You and she can have a visit, then I can bring you back to your house."

"I can drive myself. You'd better not pull anything," Gloria threatened. "I'm not going to put up with it if you pull anything."

"My dear woman, Ms. McClintock is trying to help you and your daughter," said Numa in a firm, fed-up voice that plunged half an octave and seemed to be addressing a crowd of at least five hundred. "If you don't want her help, simply say so. As I attempted to explain to you, it is she who is paying my bill. She also paid for your bail bond. If you don't want her help, you can arrange for your own bail and your own attorney, and we'll both leave you alone."

Gloria glared at them, like a frightened cat about to do something death defying from the top of a tall tree.

Shirley saw the panic, foresaw the leap into the abyss, and cried, "No, no, that's all right! Of course she wants our help, Numa, and of course she wants Allison back. We can talk about it at Gloria's own house if that's where she wants to go. Come on, Gloria, if you won't come to my place, I'll drive you home. You can talk to Allison on the phone, and tomorrow we'll have a whole long Sunday to decide what to do. Maybe you can call your sister and talk with her about it?"

Gloria did not reply, not to this or any other gambit. She glared out the car window in stony silence, chewing at her lips. It was enough, Shirley thought, to make one scream. What in heavens name was the woman thinking?

"You don't need to come in," Gloria declared as they drove up in front of the house. Her voice was as tight as a G-string, throbbing with barely controlled anxiety. "Thank you for the ride."

"You're welcome," Shirley said to her back as she ran up the sidewalk to the front door. Shirley turned off the motor and waited. She was not about to go anywhere just yet.

In three minutes the front door flew open and Gloria came shrieking down the sidewalk. "What have you done with it! What have you done with my things?"

Shirley got out of the car, took the screaming woman by the shoulders, and shook her gently while Gloria fought and spat and screamed. "Mr. Ehrlich told you," Shirley shouted over the bubbling hysteria confronting her. "He told you the furniture had been repossessed."

Gloria wrenched herself away. "But everything's gone!"

Shirley settled herself, took a deep breath, and brought her voice down out of the top of her head where it was threatening to roost. "That's what repossession means, Gloria. The furniture store came with a truck and took it because Charles hadn't paid for it." She spoke slowly, patiently, as when trying to train an uncooperative dog.

"The dishwasher's gone. I turned on the water and it ran all over the floor."

"They took the dishwasher away, Gloria. They took away the stove. They took away the refrigerator. Mr. Ehrlich told you all this. It happened last week. That's why I invited you to stay at my place."

"No," Gloria backed away. "No. I'm going to call my sister. I'm going to talk to her about this. Her husband is a lawyer. I'm going to . . . I'll let you know what I want to do. I don't want to go with you."

As though she were afraid of being kidnapped! Or perhaps afraid of being murdered. Who knew what was going on in her head? "Fine," Shirley agreed. "You have my phone number. Or it's in the phone book under McClintock Ranch. After you talk with your sister, you can let me know what you want to do."

She got back into the Wagoneer and drove away slowly, not speeding up until she reached the highway, even then driving rather more slowly than usual, trying to bring her twanging nerves under control. She had very much wanted to strike Gloria Maxwell. She had very much wanted to spank her. All this running back and forth. My God, what did the woman think repossession meant? Did she think it meant they'd posted some kind of notice on her door asking her if taking the furniture would be convenient? Did she realize the van was gone, too? Did she even have a phone working? And how about the electricity? Had that been turned off?

At the ranch Allison was waiting by the garage. "Did my mom get out? Where's my mom?"

"Honey, come on in here." Shirley put her arm around the girl and led her toward the house. "Your mom didn't want to come out here. She's all panicky and nervous."

Allison nodded sadly. "She needs a drink, Shirley. I'll bet they didn't let her have any at the jail."

Shirley was stopped. The best she could manage was, "Do you think so?"

"Mommy drinks when she gets all nervous. I saw all about

it on television. She only does it when Daddy isn't there, or when she gets lonesome, or when she's been shopping late.''

"She wanted you to come back to your house,'' Shirley said gently. "I asked her to let you stay here at least this weekend, because there's no furniture there, or even a refrigerator or stove. I think she'll change her mind if we give her a little time. Let's go in and call her. I think she'd like to hear your voice, don't you? And you can tell her what a nice place this is and invite her to come out and see.''

They tried the Maxwell number only to receive a recorded message that the number had been disconnected. After the third attempt the phone rang, and it was Gloria herself.

"My phone's been disconnected,'' she cried. "I called my sister, and she said she'd call me back, and when she didn't I called her, and she said her call wouldn't go through. But I can still call out. I called somebody to come help me because my car's gone.''

"Mr. Ehrlich told you, Gloria,'' Shirley repeated for what felt like the hundredth time. "He tried to explain to you all about repossession. He told you about the van being gone.''

"I wasn't listening. I didn't know that's what it meant. There's a notice here that says the bank has a judgment against me for the house. What does that mean?''

"It means they're taking the house back, Gloria. I think you have thirty days to pay up, or they repossess the house, too. Maybe it's sixty days. You can ask Mr. Ehrlich. He'll know. He will probably be able to get the judgment postponed.''

"But I don't have anywhere else to live! I don't have any money. I had some of my money in the bedside table, but it's gone. Whoever took the furniture took my money.''

"Gloria, I'll come help you pack your clothes and you can come out here.''

"I don't want to come out there,'' she yelled. "I don't want to. I want my own house. I want my own things.''

"Gloria, Gloria, stop crying. What's your sister's name? Brentwood? Okay, what's her phone number? Gloria, are your parents alive? How about your father? I'm sorry to hear

105

that. Gloria, Gloria, listen, why don't you ask your neighbor to give you a cup of tea. The one on the north side. She's a nice lady. I know you don't know her, but I talked to her, and she's a nice lady. Her name is Mercer. Betty Mercer, that's right. And you ask her if you can wait over there until I call you back, okay? Gloria, would you like to speak to Allison?''

Silence. Gloria had hung up.

''She's really upset,'' Shirley said to Allison, who had started shedding silent tears when she heard the shrill whine of her mother's voice. ''Really upset, Allison. She didn't realize all her furniture and everything would be gone. We have to give her a few minutes to get herself together.''

''Where's she going to sleep?'' Allison whispered. ''How will she cook? I always fix her dinner, and I'm not there.''

J.Q. put his arms around the child and hugged her. ''We'll get somebody to take her some food, and she'll sleep in your bed, honey. Unless we can get her to come out here and stay with us. Don't worry.''

Stay with *us*, indeed, after she'd made such a fuss! Shirley was dialing. ''Mrs. Mercer?''

''Yes?''

''This is Shirley McClintock. We met through your side window the other day, remember? The tall woman who was getting Allison's clothes?''

''I remember, yes.''

''Right. Well, Gloria Maxwell just got out on bail, and you know she doesn't have a stick of furniture, no stove, no car, and her phone's disconnected for incoming calls. I left her there about three-quarters of an hour ago, at her insistence. She was fairly hysterical. I thought if maybe you could invite her over for a cup of tea, it might calm her down. I suggested to her that she come over there.''

''Shirley—you don't mind if I call you Shirley, do you? I'm Betty. I saw her come out the side door of the house a few minutes ago. It looked like she was coming over here, but then she went back in the house.''

''Well, maybe she's still too upset. Listen, write down my

number, would you?'' Shirley stopped, trying to remember her own phone number, then recited it slowly. "That's right, nine-five-seven. Could you wait awhile to give her time to calm down, then go over and invite her? Then call me, and I'll try to figure out what to do next."

Betty Mercer agreed to go over after a while and invite Gloria to have tea with her. Meantime Shirley remembered the boxes of bottles in the garage and wondered whether Gloria had gone back into her empty house because she had wanted something stronger than tea.

Gloria's sister's phone in Albany was busy. Shirley tried again in fifteen minutes to find it still busy. She was about to try yet again when the phone rang. It was Gloria's neighbor, Betty Mercer, calling to report.

"She isn't there, Shirley. I waited almost half an hour and then went over there. The side door was open. I went all through the house, knocked and called. There's no basements in any of these houses out here. Her garage was locked, but unless she's hiding from me, she's not in the garage, and I looked everywhere else. Maybe she went for a walk."

Shirley did not believe it likely Gloria had gone for a walk, though considering the woman's illogical behavior, anything was possible. "Betty, if you see her, tell her I'll arrange to rent a car for her for a few days, and I'll lend her some money, but it will be Monday morning before I can do that. See if you can get her to call here so Allison can talk to her. Tell her Allison and I will come in to see her or get her or whatever she wants, if she'll just settle down."

Shirley suggested Allison go put on something clean, a dress, something her mother would approve of, just in case her mother called. Ten minutes later Betty Mercer called back to say Gloria Maxwell was not anywhere in the neighborhood; Betty had driven around a six-block area searching for her. "Could she possibly have called a friend to come pick her up? I did think I heard a car when she first went back in the house."

Gloria had mentioned calling a friend. "Who would your

107

Mom have called to come pick her up?'' Shirley wanted to know when she'd hung up. "The Carmichaels?"

"Is that Mike and Arlette?" asked Allison, struggling with buttons. When Shirley nodded, she said, "I don't think so. Mom didn't like Arlette that much. Mostly Mike was Daddy's friend and Arlette just sort of came along. Mom had some other friend she sometimes talked to on the phone, but I don't know her name."

Shirley bent forward to help with the buttons.

"A woman friend?" J.Q. asked. He had just come into the room to peer at both of them over his glasses.

"Yes. I think it was a woman friend."

"What makes you think so?"

"Oh, you know. Mom always sounded different when she talked to men. Kind of . . . silly. Like the girls at school when they talk to boys."

"But not you," J.Q. suggested. "You talk to boys in a normal tone of voice."

Evidently this was something they had discussed before. "I try," she said. "I do try."

"I came in to inquire about supper," said J.Q. "I find one of my ladies dressing to go out."

"I don't think we're going anywhere," sighed Shirley. "I goofed somehow. Gloria's gone off with somebody, J.Q. I wish I knew who."

"Maybe she's coming out here," sniffed Allison, eyes wet.

"That's possible," Shirley agreed. Barely possible, but Shirley wasn't counting on it. The best thing to do right now was to get hold of Gloria's sister in Albany and see what she knew about anything, but she was not going to do it in front of Allison. Since J.Q. was interested in supper, Shirley suggested Allison put on an apron to protect her frills and help get the pork chops ready to bake. When they had left the room, she dialed Gloria's sister, Mrs. Lawrence Brentwood, once more. This time the phone was answered by a firm, nononsense voice.

Mrs. Brentwood was al dente where Gloria was limp, assertive where Gloria was anxious, positive where Gloria was confused. When Shirley introduced herself as the woman who was keeping Allison, the assured voice said without a pause for further explanation, "As I told Gloria a little while ago, we cannot possibly have her and Allison here just now. Our youngest has just gone off to college, and Harold and I are leaving in two days for a long-awaited second honeymoon cruise." The voice did not make anything sentimental out of the words. The voice might just as well have referred to a long-awaited trip to the dentist.

"If your youngest is college-age, you're considerably older than Gloria, then?" Shirley said, slightly annoyed at the voice.

"I wouldn't say considerably," said the voice with an unmistakable chill. "I married young."

Shirley bit her tongue. "The problem here, Mrs. Brentwood, is not finding someone to take care of Allison. Allison's doing fine here with us. What I'm trying to do is get some understanding of Gloria. I'm trying to help her, but it's turning out to be rather difficult. She's a very hard person to help."

"Mother used to make that same comment," said Mrs. Brentwood. "Even though Gloria was only six when Mother died. Gloria simply comes apart under pressure. She always has. If there was to be a test at school, Gloria would have hysterics. If she had to recite, Gloria would have an anxiety attack. Trying to help Gloria deal with reality only made it worse. The only way to handle Gloria is to pretend that problems do not exist. She's all too willing to believe that problems do not exist. Considering her inclination to fall supine for any man who would help her pretend, Lawrence and I were extremely relieved when she married Charles. We thought Charles would provide a cushion against the world. Charles seemed a perfect husband for her, well-to-do, with excellent prospects. We didn't know Charles that well, of course, and as it turned out, we were mistaken."

"Can you tell me how? Anything you can tell me might help."

Mrs. Brentwood seemed not at all reluctant to slander her

brother-in-law. "Charles turned out to be a con man. I don't mean he does . . . what are they called, scams? I mean he does normal business kinds of things in the manner of a con man. Always lies a little. Much of what he told us about himself before he married Gloria turned out to be untrue. He always misrepresents a little, or simply doesn't explain to people what's involved. Always pares the law a little close. That's my husband's opinion." Mrs. Brentwood sniffed, letting it be known that a particular appreciation should be attached to any opinion of her husband's. "Charles always spends more than he makes, never puts anything aside for a rainy day. Charles has gone broke at least five or six times since they've been married. Every time it happens, Gloria falls apart; I send her money to come here; she brings Allison for a few weeks of tears and babying; then Charles gets back on his feet and she returns to him. I will say for Charles that he always gets back on his feet, somehow. We would have repeated the pattern this time, except that this time I said no. Lawrence and I are leaving in two days, and we're not going to postpone our plans because Charles has gone broke again." The voice had a certain money-in-the-bank hauteur to it that Shirley disliked.

"Did Gloria say that's what happened, that Charles went broke?"

"Well, more or less. I had someone here the first time she called, and I couldn't talk with her. I then tried to call her and couldn't get through. When she called back, she said all their furniture had been repossessed, and their car. It was all terribly *a capo*, the melody as before, so I cut her off rather quickly."

Shirley spoke through her teeth. "Mrs. Brentwood, your brother-in-law has been murdered. Your sister has been arrested for his murder and is now out on bail. She has no money and no possessions, and she couldn't leave the state if she wanted to."

Shirley imagined, with relish, the expression on the face of the self-possessed person on the other end of the line. That person was being rather quiet. When people have their furniture repossessed, damn it, other people ought to listen! Especially sisters. Not that Shirley had ever had one.

"Oh, good Lord," breathed Mrs. Brentwood in a voice that wavered between anger and embarrassment. "She didn't say a word about that."

Shirley felt that Gloria had probably mentioned first what was most important to her: the furniture. Probably her sister understood that even better than Shirley did.

Shirley relented enough to fill the silence. "At the moment I don't know where Gloria is. Allison is here with me, and she's fine. I'd like to leave my phone number with you so you can let me know if Gloria gets in touch with you again. Please, Mrs. Brentwood, do let me know. Allison is worried about her mother. If you or your husband want them, I can give references so you'll know I'm a substantial person who does not have any kinky interest in children. I know that goes through everyone's minds these days."

Silence. Then, "My husband, Lawrence, may want to call you when he gets home."

Lawrence did indeed. Lawrence called after supper, very officially wanting names of lawyers and business references in much the same tone and vocabulary his wife had used. When Shirley mentioned her former boss at the Washington Bureau, there was a momentary thaw in what had been a quite frigid conversation.

"I know Roger Fetting," Lawrence Brentwood said. "At least, we've met."

"Well, I'm sure Roger will attest to my rectitude. I didn't really intend my call to make problems for you, Mr. Brentwood. I was simply trying to get a line on Gloria's behavior, and your wife has given me that."

"I'll confer with Esther concerning the situation. At the moment she's considering dropping all our plans and coming out there. I don't know quite what we're going to do at this point." Mr. Brentwood's tone expressed annoyance at murder and peevishness that his sister-in-law might have been connected with any such thing.

Shirley frowned. "There's not much you can do to help at the moment."

The peevish tone returned. "I think Esther is thinking of Allison. If the worst happens, Allison would probably come live with us. That, or perhaps boarding school. Boarding school might be best. Esther thinks perhaps we should be there, getting things straightened out. Since we have very much looked forward to our own youngest leaving the nest, I can't honestly say I would anticipate refurbishing the nest for Gloria's child. Neither Gloria nor Charles have ever been what I would call stable, and there is a great deal to heredity."

Shirley shut her mouth on the flood of objections that threatened to bubble out. Allison was not unstable. There was a great deal in environment, too, and the damned fool Brentwoods should stay where they were.

She bit her tongue. They had a right to come. They had a right to consider taking Allison, if Gloria agreed, which she probably would. Despite the damage their patronizing attitude would do to the child.

The best Shirley could manage by way of comment was, "Let me know what your plans are."

Numa called the next morning. Since it was Shirley's habit to sleep in on Sunday, she spoke to him on the bedroom phone. "I don't suppose you have any idea where my client is, do you?"

Shirley had been trying to sleep, trying not to think of Gloria, trying not to think of anything but quiet and dimness and the soft warmth of the bed. Now she swore under her breath and reached for her robe. "If she isn't at home, I haven't any idea, Numa. I took her to her house yesterday. She saw everything was gone and panicked. According to her sister in Albany, Gloria has chronic panic attacks, so her behavior yesterday wasn't unusual for her. I called the woman next door, Betty Mercer, and she went looking for Gloria, but she'd gone by that time. The Mercer woman thinks maybe she heard a car. Gloria said something to me about having called somebody because she didn't have a car of her own. It looks like someone picked her up. I thought I'd go over there today, see if there's an address book lying around, and start calling her friends and acquaintances. What are you doing working today?"

"I'm not really working. I merely wanted to get a bit more information about Charles's activities the week he was killed. The matter of the sixth arrow is still perplexing. I have learned from Gloria that Charles Maxwell had no time from Sunday through Wednesday to retrieve the arrow. He left his home at ten on Monday morning to drive to Grand Junction, where he was meeting a putative client. That's approximately a seven-hour drive from Columbine. He stayed in Grand Junction until Wednesday morning at about nine-thirty. He returned home Wednesday afternoon, about five-thirty, just in time to bathe and go to his regular Wednesday evening brokers' meeting. On the previous Sunday, from the time they returned from their expedition with you until he left Monday morning, Gloria says he did not leave her side."

"What time did he get to Grand Junction?"

"You are interested in whether he had time to retrieve the arrow en route? No, he did not. He left at ten, his appointment with his client was at five-thirty in the bar at the motel, and he arrived at five-thirty. I talked to the putative client. Also, if you have a suspicious mind, as I do, you will be interested to know that he did drive his own van. He did not take a plane and then rent a car. I checked with the motel, and he was driving his own van with his name painted rather ostentatiously on the door."

"Who did he meet? Somebody who was going to bail him out?"

"Someone he hoped might mend his fortunes, I believe. However, the man I spoke with is unlikely to have the kind of resources Charles Maxwell would have needed to get out of the sizable hole he had dug himself into. I think the meeting was of two con artists, back to back, each seeking succor from the other."

Since Shirley had not told Numa of Mrs. Brentwood's

comments regarding Charles's con games, she found this perceptive of him. "Well, if he didn't have time on the way there, did he have time to pick up the arrow on the drive back?"

"It was pouring rain over the whole area, over most of the state, in fact. Gloria tells me his clothes were dry when he returned home, and he had not taken rain gear with him."

"Did you find out about life insurance?"

"Oh, by all means. Gloria had the name of the company in her purse, which the wardress had allowed her to retain in her cell. I called the insurors. Charles had borrowed against his policy so heavily that there's little, if anything, left. The prosecutor would have a difficult time showing she had any motive whatsoever for killing him. Tempe thinks she killed her husband for money, and that is the only motive he has alleged thus far. Even if we can show there was no money, Tempe may still claim that Gloria thought there was."

"Did you find out what time Charles left his meeting the night he was killed?"

"Gloria gave me the name of one of the brokers, and I phoned him. He had been at the meeting. He told me Charles left well before midnight after drinking rather too much and talking quite loudly about his supposed land deal on the Western Slope. When he left he was not in the best possible state to drive a car, according to my informant. My guess is that Charles went straight home, or as straight, at least, as his bibulous nature would allow him to do, arriving there at midnight or earlier. He could well have been lying in his garage for several hours before Gloria found him. I understand it's a quiet neighborhood. People were no doubt sound asleep."

"And she was probably sleeping very soundly because she herself was drunk," Shirley opined. "Not for sure, Numa. But she does drink, mostly sweet stuff. Southern Comfort and port and other stuff. I saw boxes of empty bottles when I looked into the garage to see if they'd taken the van. Also, Allison says her mother used to drink whenever her husband wasn't around."

"This meets my every desire," he said. "A female alcoholic as a client."

"I don't think she's an alcoholic," Shirley said. "Though I could be wrong. I think she just drinks because she's alone a lot, without a car, and it dulls the loneliness and the panic. If the situation changed, she might not drink."

"You will try to locate her tomorrow?"

"I will, Numa. Maybe even today. I think I saw an address book in her kitchen desk when I picked up Allison's health card. If Gloria didn't take it with her, it'll still be there. Maybe J.Q. and I'll take Allison to a movie this afternoon, then we can stop by and pick it up."

"Let me know."

She said she would and hung up, depressed.

Out in the kitchen smells of sausage and hot bread and coffee went some way to relieve the depression. Allison was perched on a stool, slathering cream cheese on hot split rolls.

"We were going to bring you breakfast!" Allison yelled. "Go back to bed."

"How about you bring it to me out on the patio?" Shirley asked. "It's real warm out there. The thermometer says over seventy."

"There's a chilly wind, Shirl," J.Q. said. "Comes up and nips at you right through the sunshine. We'll set the table in here if you don't want to be cosseted with breakfast in bed, but I don't think you want to have your *tochis* frozen either."

J.Q. had picked up a few of the words Shirley had learned from Martin. J.Q. liked *tochis*. He said it was so much more descriptive than butt, and he disliked ass as sounding crude. Of course, if you spoke Yiddish, *tochis* was probably crude, too. Martin had said his mother would never use the word. He'd had his mouth washed out with soap for using the word when he was a boy. It was strange how foreign words never sounded as dirty as domestic ones. The dirt wasn't in what they meant; the dirt was in how they made you feel.

Shirley sat down with a cup of coffee and the comic pages, pleased to be in the warm kitchen with Allison and J.Q. This was their second Sunday together. Almost a habit. One more

115

Sunday would make it a family tradition. She read *Cathy* with enjoyment, and then turned to *Calvin and Hobbes*, as usual admiring it as much for the drawing as the the humor. She missed *Bloom County*. She had always read it, except when they had Bill the Cat. Whenever she had seen Bill the Cat in the strip, she hadn't bothered reading it. Bill the Cat was a road-kill, and road-kills weren't funny. Basket cases weren't funny. Like little deer running around with arrows through them. *Doonesbury* hadn't been all that funny lately either. She skipped all the soap-opera strips. None of them were amusing.

On Sundays they got the Denver papers, both of them, mostly for the comics and because it gave them two papers to read or at least to glance through. At one time the two papers had differed editorially, but they had both adopted a follow-the-mob mediocrity in recent years, telling their readers that Reagan had to have done it right because everyone felt so good, and any minute Bush would start making them feel good. Cocaine could make everyone feel good, too, but the papers didn't see fit to mention that a Reagan high and a cocaine high had many things in common. Such as the day of reckoning, when all the borrowed joy would have to be repaid in blood. She glanced at the editorial page and munched on hot rolls and bratwurst.

Dog began to bark out near the inside cattleguard, the one leading into the area near the house. J.Q. got up to see what was being barked at. "Sheriff's car," he said.

Shirley moved her glasses down from her forehead and got up to go to the door. It was Botts Tempe himself, getting out the car, pulling at his trousers, wriggling his butt to get his holster to settle. He came stalking up as she opened the door.

"Morning, Botts," she said. "Come for coffee?"

He flushed, took off his hat, and came in when she opened the screen door for him. He looked around the room, saw Allison on her stomach on the floor with the comics, and beckoned Shirley to come outside. With a glance at J.Q., she followed him.

"Shut the door," he murmured.

"What the hell, Botts?"

"I didn't want to say anything in front of the girl," he said. "Columbine police got a call from Mrs. Maxwell's neighbor this morning. Neighborhood dog was sniffing at the bottom of the garage door, whining. She knew Mrs. Maxwell was missing, so she called. The chief knew the sheriff's office was on her case and called us. We went out there and broke in."

Shirley didn't ask. She already knew. Inside, she felt she had known since yesterday.

"She was dead," said the sheriff. "Pushed right up against the garage door on the inside, completely out of sight. She'd been shot through the chest."

"With an arrow?"

He shook his head. "With a gun."

4

TELLING ALLISON WAS the worst part. Shirley got J.Q. aside while they figured out how to do it. J.Q. wanted to wait until a little later in the day, until Allison had a chance to digest her breakfast.

"She's all eyes," said J.Q. "No flesh on her."

"She's wiry," agreed Shirley.

"Her mom hadn't been feeding her well," J.Q. insisted. "The kid's too thin."

It might have been pure funk, but Shirley agreed to wait. They finished breakfast. They went out to the barn and fed the bull range cake and spent an hour halter-breaking a couple of calves. While they diddled about, Shirley tried various combinations of words, trying to find some miraculous phrase that would make it less painful to hear that a mother had been murdered. She couldn't come up with one. On the way back from the barn they sat down on the old bench overlooking the duck pond, and they told her then, both of them, fumbling, doing it badly.

Allison's face went very white. Her lips trembled for a time that seemed to go on forever; then she cried. She didn't scream, she just cried, sat there white-faced with the tears streaming down her cheeks, begging to know why. Why, why, and there wasn't anything they could tell her. There was no why. Shirley held her, rocked her, tried to comfort her. She wanted to know if they'd hurt her mother or just killed her. Shirley, stopped utterly by this, gave J.Q. a beseeching look.

J.Q. understood what the child meant. "They just killed her, very suddenly," he said. "She didn't feel any pain or anything, it just happened all at once."

Which started the tears again.

"Where'm I going to live?" she asked at last. "Not with Aunt Esther! Please, not with Aunt Esther."

"Why not with Aunt Esther, baby?" asked J.Q. "Isn't she very nice?"

"She's awful. She's always telling Mommy not to panic, not to be nervous, not to be scared. But then she says things like, 'Of course this will distress you, Gloria.' And then she tells some awful story about somebody getting beat up or killed or dying of diseases or going bank . . . that word when people lose all their money."

"Bankrupt," supplied J.Q.

"Or going bankrupted and having to go to the poor farm."

"The poor farm?" he asked with a quirked eyebrow.

"That's what she says. And she says how lucky Mommy is to have a sister who can look after her, because those poor people didn't have anybody. She says how we ought to be grateful, Mommy and me. How we ought to show our gratitude. Like Aunt Esther has a maid who lives there, and she says if we were properly grateful, we'd do the maid's work, and she could let the maid go and get back some of the money she spends on us. Like for tickets and things. And after a while Mommy says she can't take it anymore, and we come home."

J.Q. nodded thoughtfully. "I suppose your aunt says the same kinds of things to you."

"Only I don't listen. It doesn't do any good to listen to her," she said with an unchildish wisdom. "No good at all, but Aunt Esther keeps trying. She always wants to hurt Mommy's feelings and make her feel . . . inadequate.''

So much for heredity, thought Shirley.

"You won't let her have me, will you? If you do, she'll fire the maid and make me clean the house for her forever.''

"I'll do my best,'' said Shirley grimly, trying to remember the exact wording of the document she had had Gloria Maxwell sign.

"Mommy and I were getting along all right. It didn't matter whether Daddy was ever there or not. Aunt Esther used to yell at Mommy all the time about Daddy not being home, but it didn't matter. We were doing all right. Mommy said so. I took care of her. And I just want to know why,'' and she was off into tears again.

They did not leave her for a moment during the rest of the day. J.Q. said he felt like a tick on a dog, the way he stuck to the child. That night Shirley got up three or four times to check on her, twice encountering J.Q. in the hall on the same errand.

"She's sleeping as though she hadn't slept for days,'' Shirley murmured. "Sunk in sleep, drowning in it. Should she be sleeping like that?''

"It's almost as though . . .''

"As though what, J.Q.?''

"As though she'd laid down some burden.''

The only similar thing Shirley could remember was a young employee of hers who had lost a profoundly disabled sister after months of ceaseless care. She had told Shirley she had slept for two days after her sister died. "Maybe she did lose a burden, J.Q. Maybe that's exactly what's happened.''

On Monday morning Shirley called Ms. Minging to say Allison wouldn't be at Creps that day, maybe not for a few days, then phoned Botts Tempe and Numa Ehrlich and made appointments to see them both. By ten J.Q. had Allison out in the barn, treating a calf for an imaginary condition that required dipping range cake into a mysterious potion and then feeding as much as possible of it to the calf. "A stomach tonic,'' J.Q. called it. "To cure a failing appetite.''

Allison was grieving, but her feelings seemed to be almost remote from what she was doing as she methodically dipped the green chunks of compressed alfalfa into J.Q.'s mystery medicine and fed it to the eager calf. The child's face was very white and still with tear stains down both cheeks and an occasional tremble of chin and mouth. Shirley went outside where she could cry a little in private and wondered whether Allison's behavior was normal. Maybe it would be better if she screamed for a few days. Maybe she should get hold of a child psychologist.

All such considerations would have to wait. Shirley had to go into town and meet some people.

Botts was first on the list, and when she was in the office with him she decided to be at least partially honest.

"I'm crazy about the little girl, Botts," she said. "I don't know when I've been so impressed by a child. I lost my own little daughter when she was just a little older than Allison. I'd very much like to offer Allison a home. I'm seeing my lawyer later this morning about that."

Botts grunted. "Mrs. Maxwell's sister's coming out, you know. Woman named Brentwood. She's next of kin."

"I talked to her a couple of days ago. Do you know when she's coming?"

"I told her there was no hurry unless she knew something helpful, which she says she doesn't. I told her the kid was fine with you, and I wasn't going to release the bodies any-time soon anyhow. Told her she could give me a week or so if she wanted, see what turned up."

Shirley took a deep, thankful breath. "Allison doesn't want to go live with her aunt. Of course, it may end up that she has to, but we're going to at least offer to have her stay with us. In any case, I'm telling you this to explain my interest in the case. I feel like she's my own . . . well, not daughter. I'm too old for that. Say granddaughter. Allison needs to know why her mother was killed. It's not like an accident where you can simply say it just happened, nobody's fault, nobody meant to do it. It's obvious someone did mean to do it, and Allison needs to know why. Well, you and I do, too, but in Allison's case, it's an emotional need rather than a professional one.

"Funny thing is, she understood it happening to her daddy. Frankly I don't think she was very close to him, and maybe she had some perception of him as the kind of man who might get killed. It didn't . . . oh, it didn't surprise her much. You know what I'm saying?"

Botts Tempe, who had seen a number of deaths that surprised no one at all, said that he did.

"Allison was close to her mother, though. And her mother simply wasn't the kind of woman to . . . to . . ."

"To get people that mad at her?" suggested Botts. "I'm not sure about that. Talk to the people downstairs at the jail. They were ready to throttle her, her screaming and yelling all the time."

"She was scared. She was subject to panic attacks, Botts. Her sister told me that. I didn't used to believe in panic attacks either, but I had to read up on them once, and they're real enough. I mean, they're not just tantrums. She was locked up for no good reason; she was scared; and she had these attacks."

"I had a good reason for locking her up."

"Botts, I know you think you did, but she did not kill her husband, which I have tried to tell you over and over. She couldn't have. She didn't have the damned arrow it was done with."

"She could have gone up there anytime from Sunday to Wednesday and got it! Kid was in school! He was gone! Anytime, Ms. McClintock."

"Call me Shirley, Botts. Let's not yell at each other. Let's cooperate. Just listen to me. She didn't have a car. They only had the van, and Charles drove that."

"I don't know that."

"Well, Numa Ehrlich does. He talked to the people at the motel in Grand Junction where Charles was, and he had the van. So, she didn't have a car. Then, even if she had had a car, she was absolutely hopeless in the woods. She wore heels, Botts. Everywhere she went. The day we went hunting, she had on high-heeled boots. I don't mean cowboy boots, I mean dress boots. I went through her closet when I picked up Allison's stuff, and she didn't have one pair of flats. Even her bedroom slippers had two-inch heels. Then, on top of that, she didn't have a scratch on her. Look at my forehead, my neck. It was two weeks ago, but I've still got scratches, and there are some on my arms, too. You've got scratches, Botts. J.Q. has scratches from when we found the shoe and the wallet. Anybody who's been in that scrub has scratches. Ask the jailer or wardress or whatever you've got down there if Gloria had a scratch on her. Numa has a witness who saw her. She didn't have a flaw in her pretty skin."

Botts sat back and simmered. "You've got no right going through people's closets."

"So arrest me. Charge me with doing an illicit closet inventory. I was curious, Botts. For heaven's sake!"

"I suppose you've got other stuff to tell me."

"Yes. I do. You ever done any archery? Target shooting? Bowhunting? Anything like that?"

Botts shook his head, glaring at her.

"Well, there was a time it took a strong man or a very strong woman to hunt with a bow. It took a lot of upper body strength to pull a bow strong enough to shoot an arrow through a foot or two of meat or into a distant target. I was good at it, for a woman, because I'm big. I guess that's why I took it up in the first place. When I was a teenager, being a girl over six feet tall meant there were a lot of cute girlsy things I couldn't do. So, I concentrated on things I could do that weren't considered unfeminine, and archery was one of them. It took strength then. These days anybody can do it. They use cable strung around cams at the ends of the bow limbs, and the ends of the cable are attached to the bowstring. It gives an enormous mechanical advantage. You don't need to be strong anymore. But, even so, you have to know *how*. You can't just pick up a bow and shoot an arrow straight the first time you try, even with the bow sights and the overdraw platforms all the bows have these days."

"Overdraw platforms?"

123

"That's an extension on the bow, above the handgrip, that extends back toward the shooter. The arrow rests on it. That way you can use a shorter arrow and get flatter trajectory and higher velocity on the shot. Charles Maxwell's hunting bow had an overdraw platform. He used arrows two inches shorter than he'd have had to otherwise. I don't know why the hell he was worried about arrow velocity. The time I went with him was the first time he'd been bowhunting, and his hitting that deer was pure luck. Stupid little doe came up close and just stood there. With those short arrows he had a flat trajectory, and he just lucked out, that's all. Gloria Maxwell could not have shot him that way. Good lord, with those fingernails of hers she couldn't even pick up the paper, according to her neighbor!"

Botts scratched his nose and frowned. "We been figuring Charles was shot with the bow hanging there in the garage. I should've brought it in as evidence the first time, but I didn't. I figured it wasn't like a gun, where you can prove which gun shoots a particular bullet."

"You're exactly right, and that's something I wanted to tell you if you hadn't already thought of it. It's easy to figure out why whoever did it used Charles's arrow. There aren't that many places selling good hunting arrows. If you found an arrow in a body, you could probably find out who ordered it, even if it didn't have a name on it."

"They're not all alike?"

"Far from it. There's a dozen different lengths, to start with, for people with varying arm lengths, using various bows, and depending on whether they use an overdraw platform or not. Then there's different nocks. Different heads. Then there's about ten colors of vanes in about six or seven lengths, anywhere from about two inches long to five or six inches long, and on top of that there's different vane arrangements. You put all those variations together and call PSE or some other shooting equipment company and say, 'Who ordered arrows like this?' and you probably wouldn't get more than one name. Or at least no more than one in a given geographic area. A good arrow is almost as specific as a fingerprint, and I'll bet that's why whoever shot Maxwell used Charles's arrow.''

Botts had become interested despite himself. "But you don't think whoever it was used Charles's bow?''

"Well, not necessarily. All I'm saying is, it *could* have been another bow.''

"What you're really saying is find somebody who's done some archery.''

"I'm suggesting the person who shot Charles probably had done some bowshooting, that's all. One other thing. We both know the *Chronicle* prints every word you say, Botts. It would be nice if you could say something about Gloria no longer being suspected of her husband's death. That would mean a lot to Allison.''

He grunted, not agreeing but not refusing either. "I don't suppose you can help me out with motive on either one of them, can you.''

"My hunch is it has something to do with Dabronski's death. I think it does, but I can't prove it. I also know that Charles had a reputation as a con man, maybe not a real, criminal type, but still somebody who cut things pretty fine. I also know he'd gone broke before, more than once, and that he sold your church the house over there in Palace Pines that the reverend occupies. And I am not accusing anybody of anything. It may be a coincidence, or it could be somebody associated with your church. From what I understand, it's got a lot of members, so it's not like I'm pointing a finger at anybody in particular.''

"I don't suppose everybody in the church is necessarily pure as snow,'' grunted Botts with an uneasy shift of weight in his overloaded chair. "There's about eight hundred of them, and there's a few members I know of who're not exactly what you'd call vessel virgins. Anything else?''

Shirley had a mental picture of vessel virgins that threatened her train of thought. "Ah, let's see. Yes. I'll try to find out from Allison the names of any people her mother or father knew. There's an address book in the desk in the kitchen. . . .''

125

"I've got it. Picked it up yesterday."

". . . and Mrs. Brentwood may have some names for you. And in return for all this help I'm giving you, I'd like to know what you know, Botts."

He stared at her for a long moment, turning a pencil in his fingers, evidently deciding that it would do no harm to talk to her. When he decided to talk, it was almost as though he stripped off armor. His face lightened. His very body seemed to lose ten or twenty pounds. "Well I'll tell you, Shirley. I don't know much, and that's a fact. I got two coroner's reports that tell me two people got shot through their hearts, one with an arrow, one with a bullet. I got another one that tells me some bones have been lying out on the mountain for six months."

"You're comparing the bullet that killed Gloria with the one that killed Dabronski, aren't you?"

"Useless. The bullet that killed Dabronski was all scratched up on his rib, so we can't make a match."

"What else?"

"I got you and your fancy lawyer telling me the woman didn't kill her husband, and I guess you were right. I got some odds and ends my men picked up and some odds and ends you and your friend John Quentin picked up."

"Anything in that wallet?"

"Just what you saw."

"What was the folded-up paper?"

"Just that. A piece of plain white heavy paper, almost like cardboard, with a few letters left in one corner. Unfolded the whole thing was about twelve by twenty, and the letters were small eye, el, el, space, capital dee."

"Somebody's name. Bill Dawson. Will Dorset."

"I had thought of that," he said heavily. "But we haven't come up with anybody yet. . . ."

"Bill Deitz!" she said. "Deacon Deitz. He knew Dabronski."

"I know," said Botts. "I may be just a country sheriff, Shirley, but I'm not stupid. I even studied law enforcement. I sent a deputy to talk to Deitz a week ago. He says he's never

126

seen the thing and doesn't know what it is. He could be lying, but I've got no reason to think so. Furthermore, I talked to all the deacons at the church, asked them if they had any idea what the paper was or if they had any information that could help me, and they didn't.''

She had the grace to blush. "Sorry."

"The only other thing about the paper was that there's a smear of color along one edge; blue, the lab says. Maybe purple.''

"What? Ink?"

"Well yes, ink. Only not letters. Just a stain."

"Not exactly helpful."

"Not exactly." He looked at his watch. "It's after my lunch-time. You want to stop at the hamburger place then go over to the Maxwell house with me and look it over, tell me if anything's different?''

She checked her watch. Almost one. "I can't right now, Botts. I've got an appointment."

"I'd like you to look around over there. You still got the little girl's key?''

She nodded, slightly shamefaced.

"Use it first time you have a chance. Give me a call."

She left to keep her appointment with Numa, which did not start out to be particularly enjoyable.

Numa perused the document she gave him and frowned. "Shirley, this is an extremely dangerous document."

"I wasn't sure about the wording," she admitted.

"Wording! The wording's the least of it. The fact that it exists is damaging to you. Gloria Maxwell signed this and then you arranged her bail. She signed this and you got me to represent her. There isn't a judge in this county who wouldn't consider that coercive. She wanted out of jail, and the only way you would help her was if she signed her daughter over to you?''

"That wasn't it at all. . . ." she cried, stung.

"There isn't a court that would hold this as having any legal value. Any attorney would dig into your past and find you lost a child. Next thing you know, you'd find yourself

127

being examined by a panel of psychiatrists to see if you are sane or whether perhaps you killed Gloria Maxwell yourself!''

Shirley kept her temper with some difficulty. "Allison doesn't want to go to her aunt!''

"Then let's work on that. For the time being, forget this piece of paper. Forget it exists. There aren't any copies elsewhere, are there? Very well. Simply forget it. Now, I know you had no nefarious motives, but something must have moved you to take this child in. What were your motives? Assuming you can remember.''

"In the first place, Gloria called me and asked me to take Allison. I knew the alternative would be a foster home, at least temporarily. There's been all that scandal in the paper about kids being abused in foster homes. . . .''

"Ah,'' he said. "Well. That puts a better complexion on it. Perhaps we can do something with that. You were responding to the mother's own request. You were trying to save the child from possible abuse and loneliness. It is noteworthy that the mother did not call her sister, she called you.''

"The sister's in Albany!''

"Still, it's noteworthy. It's only a four-hour flight from Albany, probably five or six hours if one has to make connections. Counting time to pack and reach the airport, the sister could have been here in Columbine anywhere from eight to twelve hours after receiving Gloria's call. The child could have been cared for that long by someone else, but the mother rejected this option. That fact is helpful. You had met the child before?''

Shirley thought of the meeting; the huddled, pale little form in the back of the van; the purple velour and silver sandals; the eye shadow; the little birthday girl, leaning against the door in her geisha finery, wanting to play softball. "Yes," she said. "I'd met her. I had seen her last on her birthday, as a matter of fact. Her eleventh. While her daddy was in Grand Junction, putting together his big land deal.''

128

"When Mrs. Brentwood arrives—you did say she was coming? Well, when she arrives, we'll have a talk."

"She doesn't want Allison and her husband doesn't either. Without actually saying 'We don't want Allison,' they made it perfectly clear that they didn't. Mr. Brentwood believes she is too much like her mother. He talked about heredity. And from what Allison says, her aunt evidently bullied Gloria and Allison whenever they were there. Nonetheless, I get the impression they are the kind who would be dog-in-the-manger about the whole thing. If I seem to want Allison, they'll fight me, Numa. Out of some territorial pride if nothing else. She's *theirs*, and they don't strike me as the kind of people who let others take things that are *theirs*, even if they don't particularly want whatever it is. I do want Allison. Not selfishly, really. Or not completely, at any rate. No one else really does want her, and the kid needs someone who does."

"Self-interest," mused Numa.

"I don't understand?"

"Self-interest. We should try to make it clear to the Brentwoods, assuming your estimation of their characters is correct, how very much in their best interest it would be to leave Allison where she is. And you, my dear, would be well advised not to show eagerness to have the child. It might not be a bad idea to talk to Allison about that as well. If she is as bright as you say she is, perhaps she can help. If I'm ever asked, by the way, I could never have suggested any such thing."

Shirley was eager to get back to Allison, but she took time to stop at the Maxwell house on her way out of town. She walked slowly through the rooms, noting differences where she could. The desk in the kitchen had been rifled. Botts had done that maybe, or a deputy? The drawers in Allison's room were dumped on the floor. Also Botts? She wandered out to the garage, noted that the boxes and the quivers were gone but the boxes of liquor bottles were still there. Dust had settled over everything. Entering the kitchen she wiped dirt and grease from her feet and looked around again. Nothing spoke to her. She went into the front office and flipped through the files. More or less as they had been, except that she couldn't find the file on the Living Church of Jesus. On further consideration the drawer looked much less full than it had when she had first seen it, but Botts might have taken folders from it.

When she got back into the car something tugged at her, teasingly, annoyingly. Something she'd seen? Smelled? Felt? It bothered her so much that she stopped at the Pizza Hut to have a slice of pizza and a cup of coffee and think about it. The front corner tables were occupied, so she carried her cup around the long counter to a single table, partly hidden behind a display rack that someone had half unpacked. Only then did she notice who was sitting at the corner table where she and Bonny had sat a few days before. It was Bonny Patterson once again, with Arlette Carmichael, the two of them bent across the table like conspirators, whispering to one another. Only their intense involvement with one another could have let Shirley get to her seat without their seeing her.

Bonny said something stern, her face very serious. Arlette put her hand in front of her mouth and giggled. Bonny ran her hand along her jaw, fingering the mole there, just as she had done when she had been with Shirley. Arlette leaned forward and whispered something that made Bonny flush and slap at her, only half in play. Shirley was reminded of an unruly dog, leaping around its trainer. Arlette was the dog, ears flapping, and Bonny was trying to teach her to heel.

Strange. She wouldn't have thought Arlette was quite Bonny's type. Though it would be hard to say what Bonny's type really was. Shirley watched, head bent over her coffee, while the two of them bent toward one another again. When they rose Arlette's expression was contrite, and she seemed to be apologizing for something as they left the place together. Bonny's little red car was out in front, and the two of them got in and went zooming out of the parking lot and onto the ramp that led to the highway. It was late in the afternoon for a shopping expedition. By the time the two of them got to Denver, if that's where they were going, it would be almost dark.

Seeing Bonny and Arlette had put whatever it was out of Shirley's mind. She remembered she thought she'd seen something at the Maxwell house, but she could not think what it had been.

At home Allison wanted to talk about where she was going to live; she was beginning to feel threatened by the imminent arrival of the Brentwoods.

"My lawyer thinks we need to plan," Shirley told her. "If I tell your aunt and uncle I want you to stay here, what do you think they'll do?"

"They'll make me go with them," said Allison, her mouth turning down into a disconsolate arc. "They sure will."

"Allison, why do you think they'd do that?"

"Because you want me," the girl said promptly, without bothering to think it over. "If you didn't want me, they wouldn't either. They always want what other people want. My cousins are the same way. Whenever I visited there the only thing they ever seemed to want was what I was playing with, and they were lots older than me, too. Like I was nine and they were seventeen and eighteen."

"So, what if your aunt and uncle thought I didn't much want you?"

Allison peeked at her from beneath lowered lids. "You do, don't you? J.Q. said you did. He said you had a little girl who died, and you like little girls."

"Well, not all little girls, no. I find many little girls quite boring. Many little girls seem to have nothing in their heads at all but rock music, clothes, and boys. I do happen to like you a lot. What I'm suggesting is that we don't let Aunt Esther and Uncle . . . Uncle who? What do you call him?"

"Uncle Lawrence."

"Uncle Larry."

"Uncle *Lawrence*," Allison corrected. "Laurence Linton Brentwood the Third. I have to call him sir. Cousin Melanie and Cousin Cheryl don't call him sir, but they don't like it when I don't."

"What I'm suggesting is," Shirley struggled on, "that we

131

don't let your aunt and uncle *know* how much I want you. If they think I don't, maybe they won't be so eager.''

"Something else they don't like," said Allison, as though she had not heard what Shirley said, "is braces. Melanie had braces, and Uncle Lawrence said it cost a fortune. He was always fussing about it.''

"Orthodontia," smiled Shirley, getting the idea. "What else did Uncle Lawrence hate?''

Allison was able to be quite descriptive about a number of things Uncle Lawrence disliked, or at least disliked paying for, such as music lessons and dancing lessons and clothes. When Allison and Shirley had finished talking, Shirley filled J.Q. in on the possible strategy.

"You know what Allison needs," J.Q. remarked, "is a horse. Didn't her mother want you to start her on a horse? And lessons, of course. Got to teach her to ride right, not just kind of sit there like we do.''

"A dressage horse," Shirley said. "I'm sure I recall Gloria telling me to get the child a dressage horse. Oh, God, J.Q. where're we going to get one in a hurry? The Brentwood's aren't coming today, but they might show up tomorrow!''

"Shirley, you're sitting here in the middle of horse country all up and down the valley, all your neighbors trading horses back and forth among themselves like they were baseball cards, and you wonder where you're going to get a *horse*?''

"It needs to be a *good* horse.''

"Well, yes, when the Brentwoods think of paying for it, it should be. When you get it, though, it could be a cheap horse. Even a borrowed horse. It really could.''

"J.Q., we could lay it on too heavy.''

"Well, fit the laying on to the layee. You won't know until they get here. You send Allison on out here. We'll go find a horse. I'll find a riding instructor, too. You get a stall cleaned out. We can't let a *good* horse run around loose like Zeke and SBH and the Idiot Mare.''

Shirley had time, after cleaning out a stall for an as-yet

theoretical horse, to call Ms. Minging and explain—more or less—the situation.

"She's a sweet child," said Ms. Minging in her usual I-am-right-about-this-don't-contradict-me voice. "A very nice nature, which astonished me quite frankly. When you told me about the family I expected her to be whiny and spoiled."

"I think she was the mother in that relationship," Shirley surprised herself by saying. "I think we'll find she did most of the meal preparation, when there was any. I think we'll find she took care of her own clothes, did her own washing, probably her own ironing. And maybe some of her mother's, too."

"That might explain it." Ms. Minging sounded sad. There were few familial permutations that Ms. Minging hadn't seen over and over. It no longer surprised her to find alcoholism or drug dependency or hypochondria in parents or extreme nurturing behavior in sons or daughters one would think too young to nurture anyone.

"Mr. Brentwood feels Allison would not be a good addition to his family, her heredity being what it is," Shirley nudged.

"Oh, really!" said Ms. Minging, beginning to sound angry.

Shirley had scarcely hung up the phone when it rang again; Mrs. Brentwood, saying that she and Mr. Brentwood had postponed their cruise, though they had lost a large portion of their deposit in so doing. She gave the distinct impression they considered this to be Gloria's fault or perhaps Allison's. They would be flying out, she said, on Wednesday to "take care of things."

Shirley said she would look forward to meeting them, then cut the conversation short, inasmuch as J.Q. and Allison were at that moment coming into the driveway in the truck; the headlights reflected off the barn enough to show they were towing a horse trailer.

"It's borrowed," J.Q. announced when she came striding out onto the front porch to meet them. "Please admire Allison."

133

Allison wore boots, riding breeches, a proper tweed hacking jacket over her white turtleneck, and a hard hat, each item looking like a perfect fit.

"Where? How?"

"Same place we got the horse. Cavendish place. Martha Cavendish has all the outgrown riding clothes her four daughters wore dating back to the time they were five. Among 'em we found a set that fits. She says when Allison outgrows these, there's another set waiting. She was happy to lend the clothes and Beauregard."

Beauregard was an eighteen-year-old bomb-proof sweetheart of a gelding on whose shining back a number of valley children had learned to ride.

"Why didn't I think of Beauregard?"

"Because you're in a tizzy. When are the people coming, do you know?"

"Wednesday. I don't know what time."

"Well, Martha's going to show up here at four on Wednesday afternoon for Allison's first lesson. Also, she has put a very high price tag on Beauregard, just in case she's asked."

Beauregard was a blessing in horsehide. After a quick supper out of leftovers Allison brushed Beauregard and forgot to grieve. There was so much to do; feeding Beauregard, learning to saddle Beauregard, learning to clean out his hooves. Beauregard, who had been through all this several times before, was condescension itself, nobility made manifest. He was accustomed to the adoration of little girls.

"Never could figure out what it is with little girls and horses," Shirley commented to J.Q. as she watched Allison struggling with brush and blanket. "I wasn't horsey when I was a kid."

"You had horses around you from the time you were born. Horse was just a tool to you, like a fence-stretcher."

"That's not true!" she said, stung. "I liked some horses a lot."

"You liked the ones who did what they were supposed to and didn't break your bones in the process and were thrifty and sensible."

134

"True."

"Same qualities you liked in a fence-stretcher."

"J.Q.! You make me out to be some kind of chilly monster who doesn't like horses. I like horses. I just don't know what gets into little girls that they go all gooshy over them. Horses don't have much sense. Dogs are smarter. Pigs are smarter."

"What it's all about is power," said J.Q. "Little girl on a good horse is the equal of any man. Look at the '88 Olympics. There's an example for you. Five riders came in even, four men and one woman. Officials made 'em trade horses, ride each other's horses. Four men said it was stupid, ridiculous, made no sense. One girl among 'em said fine, she didn't mind. And she settled down, rode all five, and beat all four men, because she was depending on the horse. Men, they're so egocentric, they thought they were doing it. She was the only one knew it was the horse all the way. She just got up there, told the horse she was depending on him, and went. Horses like that."

"True," said Shirley.

"Trouble with you is, you've always been big. Big woman like you doesn't understand how a little woman feels sometimes. Sort of at the mercy of the world."

"Your wife tell you that, J.Q.?"

"Among other things, yes. So did a daughter or two."

Shirley, who had once longed to be short and curvaceous, found this a revelation that kept her quiet and thoughtful for the better part of the day. Allison wasn't a big girl. Allison might have some of those same feelings, and Shirley should watch out for that!

When Beauregard was settled with Allison sitting on his stall partition adoring him, and J.Q. was settled with his paper and postprandial coffee in the living room, Shirley called Botts Tempe, hoping he might still be in his office. He wasn't, but in about ten minutes he called her back from home.

"Drawers in the girl's room had been rifled through and dumped, Botts."

"Could have been my men. I'll ask them."

"The file on the Living Church is missing from Maxwell's office. I think some other files may be missing, too."

"That wasn't my men, because I don't have any files."

"There's something else teasing at me about the place, but I don't know what it is. Maybe it'll come to me overnight. If it does, I'll call you back. I'm not sure it's anything important."

"Anything'd be a help. Now, Shirley, one of my deputies down here belongs to this Ridge County Bowhunters Club. He's given me the names of the members, all ten of them, and nobody on it rings a bell. Nobody matches to any of the names in Gloria Maxwell's book or any name in any of Maxwell's files, except Maxwell himself, of course. He was a new member. And you're not on the list."

"I know I'm not, Botts. I'm not a joiner. I hate clubs like that. A few people who like to do the same thing get together and do everything but the thing they like. Poultry fanciers don't do poultry; they do meetings, minutes, and fund-raising. Bowshooters don't do bowshooting; they do meetings, minutes, fund-raising. It's silly. And I'm not really a bowhunter either. I used to take a deer every now and then, because I like venison, and I told myself it was cheaper than gamefarm prices around fourteen dollars a pound. I took them here on the place with my target bow, and the last one must have been five years ago." She ticked her front teeth with a fingernail, making a beetlelike click. "Botts, read me the ten names."

He read them off.

"Fish?" she cried. "I'll be damned. Dr. Fish?"

"Doesn't say M.D.," Botts said. "Just Bertram Fish. I guess that'd be Elise Fish's husband, right?"

"He's also Bonny Patterson's brother-in-law."

"I didn't know that! Is he in this thing somewhere?"

"Lord knows, Botts. I don't. I can't see how. You must know who he is. Since his wife is the woman all the time picketing over at the women's clinic, there's a connection there with Dabronski but none with the Maxwells that I know of. Lord."

136

"Could be just coincidence."

"Well, you'll know that after you talk to him, won't you? Find out how long he's been a member and when he took up bowshooting and so forth."

"But if it is coincidence with him, there must be more than ten people in Ridge County that know something about archery. How do I find out who the others are?"

Shirley pushed her glasses up on her forehead, furrowed her brow, twiddled a lock of hair, pulled her glasses back down, and scowled at the wall. "You could ask the bow manufacturers for all the customers in and around Columbine," she said. "They could do that easily, because their lists are sure to be divided by postal code. But it probably won't help."

"Why do you say it might not help?"

"Because anybody could go into Denver to one of the big sporting-goods stores and buy a bow, maybe pay cash, and the customer might or might not end up on their mailing list. You could try Gart Brothers. Their mailing lists will be divided by postal code, too. Nothing on the list will tell whether the customer bought a bow or a canoe or a pair of skis. Besides . . ."

"Besides?" Botts prompted.

"A lot of people move here from the east, from California, away from any old where. They move here, they move away. You could have a shooter from anywhere with his own bow, and you'd have no way to know. And the shooter could have used Charles's bow. I don't think we're going to get at him through the bow, Botts. Unless it is Fish, and I can't figure out why it would be."

Botts Tempe sighed. "Tell you the truth, Shirley, I can't either."

"Knowing if a suspect has done some shooting will help at the other end of it, though. Once you have a suspect, knowing if he's a shooter may help you narrow it down," she said hopefully.

"If we get a suspect," he said in a depressed tone. "Which

right at this time nothing much makes me think is going to happen. I'll go talk to the doctor. See what he has to say.''

Shirley attempted to be encouraging, but she, too, saw a dead end looming. Though she could imagine why someone might have wanted to kill Charles, she could not imagine why anyone would have killed Gloria. And she could not imagine why Dr. Bertram Fish would have wanted to kill either of them.

''Botts, if you're willing to go a little way with me, maybe we could narrow this thing down. I've got a short list of people I think might be involved. Only thing is, you've got to promise not to get mad if I tell you who's on it.''

He grunted at her.

''Promise?''

''I can't guarantee anything. You tell me and we'll see.''

''Okay. Reverend Patterson.''

''*McClintock!*''

''I said you couldn't get mad, Botts. Do you want the rest of the list or not?''

''Give it to me,'' he growled.

''Mike and Arlette Carmichael. William Deitz. Dr. and Mrs. Fish. Henry Rizer . . .''

''Who the hell is Henry Rizer?''

''Some guy who goes missionarying with Deitz. Also, Mabel Brubacher.''

''You're kidding. Mabel?''

''I want to know if any of those people has ever shot a bow. That's all.''

''You're out of your mind. Mabel Brubacher?''

''I'd really appreciate it, Botts.'' Then she hung up, wondering if he was right. She might be out of her mind.

When Allison came in from the barn she surprised Shirley by saying she wanted to go to school the next day.

''Fine by me,'' Shirley said. ''It's Halloween. I've got stuff you can wear. You can be a pirate if you want. Or maybe a bullfighter.''

''Shirley . . .''

"Yes. What's on your mind?"

"If I go, is it . . . is it disrespectful?"

"You mean of your mom?"

"Yes." The color left her cheeks, and she turned up a white face in which the eyes were enormous, like one of the forlorn waif pictures popular during the seventies. "I want to go be a pirate, but I don't want to be disrespectful. Aunt Esther and Uncle Lawrence are always talking about being disrespectful. I don't care whether I am disrespectful with them or not. But I don't want to be with Mommy. Because . . ."

"Because she's gone now, and there's no way to say you're sorry later on, right?"

Allison nodded, tears spilling. "When somebody dies, you have to do it right, don't you? No matter what you feel like. Because it's the only time you have!"

Shirley perched, drew the child onto her lap, hugged her, and rested her chin on the girl's head. "You know, Allison, there aren't any rules anymore about what's respectful when somebody dies. When I was a girl, there were lots of rules. I remember my grandmother when my grandfather died. She put on black, and she didn't take it off for a year. That was being respectful. When the year was over, she put on white collar and cuffs. Then, when another year was over, she bought a lilac dress. I remember her telling me how tired she was of black."

"Should I have a black dress?" Almost eagerness there. Need for some ritual to comply with. Something correct to do.

"No. That's what I'm saying. We don't have rules like that anymore. I think these days people are supposed to do what they feel like. If you feel like crying, you cry. If you feel like going to a movie, you go. If you feel like sitting quietly in a corner, you do that. You try to remember the dead person kindly, too. I think that's important."

"I loved Mommy," she said. Shirley heard doubt in the words. Self-doubt.

Shirley gritted her teeth, bit her tongue, prayed for the

right words. "I know you did, Allison. Because of the way you acted. You took care of her. You couldn't have done that unless you loved her."

Long silence. "I couldn't, could I?"

Shirley felt the small body in her arms relax, as though a some tightly wound coil had been released. "No, you couldn't, honey. You did everything you were supposed to. You did even more than anyone could have expected. You were respectful, and you were kind." And I'm not going to let those bastards have you, she finished silently. She rocked the child, and the child let herself be rocked.

A shadow brought her eyes up to see J.Q. standing in the door. Like an Indian he was sometimes. Sneaking around.

"What's up?" she asked.

He brought his hand from behind him, holding a good-sized pumpkin.

"I thought Allison might like to make a jack-o'-lantern," he said. "There's just time before bed, and Ms. Minging says most of the kids are bringing one to school tomorrow."

Shirley did not bother to ask what he and Ms. Minging had been talking about. Up to no good, the two of them.

"Cocoa," she said. "I'll fix it while you do that."

When J.Q. had taken Allison to school on Tuesday morning, when the stock had been fed and the necessary chores done, Shirley saddled Zeke and rode out toward the northwest corner of the ranch. The northwest corner was forested mountainside, sloping up onto a high promontory facing southeast with a flat rock outcropping at the edge. It was an excellent sitting and thinking place, and Shirley much felt the need of sitting and thinking. Even as late in the year as it was, there was fresh green grass under the south edge of the pines, and Zeke munched away contentedly while she settled herself on the rock ledge with her thermos of coffee and her half-dozen oatmeal cookies. The cookies were in lieu of breakfast. Eating always helped her think.

She started her consideration with the dead man, Dabronski. No matter how you looked at what had happened, Dabronski either had on him, or was believed to have on him, something that someone else wanted. She believed this, first-because her house had been searched, and second-because someone had retrieved the arrow from the place Dabronski's body had been found. There would have been no reason to go there unless someone was looking for something. Why the arrow had been retrieved, she wasn't sure, though it could have been simply because it had a name and address on it.

However, she did know the "something" was small enough to put in a sugar cannister or behind a sack of coffee beans. Call the thing "X." Call the somebody who wanted the thing "Mr. Jones." Of course, it could be Mrs. Jones. So call the person simply Jones, he or she, and keep in mind it could be more than one person.

Jones shot Dabronski in order to get X. It was unlikely that two people would fight their way into a scrub thicket to engage in a shoot-out. Not impossible, just unlikely. There-fore, Dabronski was probably shot somewhere else and took refuge in the scrub. The place the body was found was down-hill from a road and a picnic area, and that was possibly, most likely, the site of the shooting.

Had Jones followed Dabronski when he ran away? If Jones had done so, Jones hadn't caught up with Dabronski. Why? Because Jones couldn't? Couldn't follow or couldn't find Da-bronski, either one. Perhaps Jones knew nothing about track-ing. Or perhaps it had happened at night, or late evening, and Jones couldn't see to track. According to the pathologist who had looked at the bones, they had been out in the weather for four to six months. Dabronski had died in the spring. There had been a lot of rain this past spring. If the shooting took place at night, by the time morning came rain might have washed away the trail. Whatever the reason, Jones had not been able to track Dabronski. Jones did not know where he was, whether he was alive or dead. However, Jones be-lieved Dabronski had the "X" thing that he, or she—Jones—wanted.

All right so far, Shirley thought as she took a bite of soft, raisiny cookie and followed it with a swallow of coffee.

After the shooting all remained status quo. Dabronski died in the brush. Nobody knew where he was. Nobody reported him missing. That was odd, because Dabronski had been much in evidence up until then. According to Mabel, he had been involved with the abortion protesters and had been arrested during the clinic break-in. He had been working for the Living Church. He had been running here and there for the good reverend. In general making a highly visible nuisance of himself. Then, bammo, gone and nobody saw fit to ask why. The reverend assumed he'd gone back to his childhood home. Everyone else assumed the same thing. Why?

Shirley took a small notebook from the breast pocket of her shirt, fished out a pencil stub, and wrote the numeral one, followed by, ''Why did nobody report Dabronski missing?'' She laid the pencil and notebook down on the rock beside her, shifted to a more comfortable position, and took another bite of cookie.

Now, next step. Dabronski is found. Accidentally. Nobody knows who he is at that point except the person or persons who shot him. Jones knows or is pretty sure who the body is, because Jones shot him. So when Jones sees that Shirley McClintock discovered the body, Jones figures maybe Shirley McClintock may have found X; so Jones searches Shirley McClintock's house.

Shirley is upset by being searched. So Shirley and J.Q. go back up on the mountain to see what they can find, and they do find a shoe and a wallet, which they turn over to the sheriff. *And* they see the arrow is gone. Sometime between Monday of that week, when the paper carried the story about the bones, and Wednesday of that week, when Shirley and J.Q. found the wallet, somebody had removed the arrow.

Shirley wrote a two, followed by, ''Who could have found the site and removed the arrow between Monday and Wednesday?''

Presumably Jones had done so and had retrieved the arrow with Charles Maxwell's name on it. There was only one Charles Maxwell in Columbine. Jones decided to . . . to what? Kill Maxwell? Why? No reason at this point. Does he think maybe Maxwell found X? The newspaper didn't say Shirley McClintock was alone when she found the bones. It said she was with a bowhunting party. So . . . so Jones decides to search Maxwell's place.

How would Jones go about that? Gloria Maxwell was at home during most of every day. She had no car, because her husband had taken it to Grand Junction. Jones might prefer not to deal with someone being in the house. Jones would wait until it was dark. Jones would wait until the lights were off in the house and the occupants asleep. Probably Jones didn't know Charles had returned. So Jones goes to search the house, is interrupted, and shoots Charles.

Shirley made a face. The only way it made sense was if Jones grabbed Maxwell's bow. You wouldn't be carrying a bow around while searching a house. Also, Jones brought the arrow with him. Because—because he wanted to see if it matched others in the house? Because if he ran into one of the Maxwells he could claim to be returning the arrow? Possibly. So Jones had the arrow in hand but no bow. A person might carry a gun or a knife while searching a house but not a bow. Besides, Jones had already used a gun at least once, on Dabronski. A person who had once used a gun went on using a gun, not a bow.

Shirley wrote down a three, followed by, "Why not a gun?"

Suppose Charles comes into the driveway, heaves open the garage door, and finds Jones searching the garage. Charles is fairly drunk, he starts after Jones, Jones grabs the bow and shoots Charles. After killing Charles, Jones panics and runs off. He couldn't search the house with a dead body lying there, with a car in the driveway, with lights on, possibly having already wakened someone. So Jones runs. Later Jones comes back and searches the house, this time finding Gloria there; so Jones has to kill her, too.

Wait. Charles was killed on Wednesday night. Gloria was arrested on Friday night. Shirley had gone through the house on Saturday. At that time the file on the Living Church had been there, Allison's bureau drawers were intact, the closets showed no sign of having been searched. If Jones had been scared off when Charles had been killed, surely the killer would have come back as soon as possible.

Perhaps the first opportunity had been after Gloria was in jail. Gloria had been in jail for over a week. The house could easily have been searched during that time. Had it been?

Wait a minute. The house had not been searched on Saturday when Shirley was there. If it was not searched between then and Monday morning . . .

On Monday morning all the furniture was removed. If the searcher had tried after that, chances are nothing had been found. Suppose Jones found the furniture had been moved to the Benton warehouse. Then the Benton warehouse burned.

Shirley wrote her next question. "Ask Botts about arson on the warehouse fire."

By now Jones has searched the Maxwell house at least twice. The first time he was interrupted. The second time the furniture was gone. So maybe Jones burned the warehouse where the furniture was stored, just in case X was hidden in the furniture. Could Jones believe that Gloria might have X with her in jail? Or put away somewhere, in a bank deposit box maybe? Suppose Jones thought Gloria knew where X was. Jones would wait for Gloria to come home, demand to know where X was, then, when she said she didn't know—or if she did know—kill her.

Why? Because even Gloria would make the connection between someone's threatening her and someone's having killed Charles. Jones couldn't threaten her and remain safe unless he was an unknown who could disappear. Therefore . . . therefore Jones was known to Gloria.

Why didn't Jones wear a mask? A stocking, a ski mask? He could have threatened her, knocked her down, and run-off. Why did he have to kill her? Question six.

This would all be so much easier if one knew what X was.

Start over. Dabronski had been carrying a wallet with four

144

thousand dollars in it, all in hundreds. Dabronski worked for the church, running errands. His title of "deacon" was probably more or less honorary, in lieu of a decent wage. Where had he obtained four thousand dollars? This was question number seven.

What came to mind, of course, was some kind of payoff. Jones being blackmailed by Dabronski. Dabronski saying, "Meet me at such and such a place and bring me four thousand dollars and I'll give you X."

Four thousand wasn't a lot. Minor-league stuff. Either it was a minor-league blackmail or it was supposed to be one payment, one of many. Maybe Jones had no patience with being blackmailed. Maybe he or she had expected to receive X, didn't get it, and shot Dabronski thinking he was carrying X.

Why would they think Dabronski had X? Because he said so? Because he proved it? With what?

There had been nothing on the body, nothing in the wallet but the folded piece of heavy paper, the money, and the tickets. Which could be pawn tickets or claim tickets.

Question number eight. What were the tickets for?

Shirley sat for a considerable time while the sun reached noon and started down the sky again. At last she got up from the ledge and read the list over to herself:

1. Why did nobody report Dabronski missing?
2. Who went off into the scrub between Mon. and Wed. ?
3. Why didn't Jones use a gun on Charles?
4. What about arson in the warehouse fire?
5. Where did Dabronski get $4000?
6. Why did the killer have to kill Gloria?
7. Where did Dabronski get X?
8. What were the tickets for?

Botts probably knew the answer to some of these. Question number one would be where she personally would start looking.

* * *

"Nobody reported him missing because everybody thought he'd left," Botts said when she called him later that morning. "He got arrested for that clinic break-in. Right. That was the second Saturday in June. He spent Sunday in jail along with four or five others."

"Elise Fish?"

"Dr. Fish bailed her out right away. Monday the judge released the rest of them on their own recognizance and set the hearing for ten days later. Tuesday morning Dabronski's clothes were gone, his car was gone. He'd talked a lot about going back home; everybody assumed he didn't want to face a possible jail sentence and just went."

"Reverend Patterson didn't know anything about it?"

"He was out of town. He left Sunday afternoon for an evangelical meeting in St. Louis, and he didn't get back until late Monday night. His wife Bonny met him at the airport about midnight, and he told me it took them hours to get home in a pouring rain. Tuesday morning they slept in. When Patterson went into the church office at almost noon Andy Manning, the woman who cleans the church and annex, called and told him Dabronski had cleaned out his room and gone."

"There was four thousand in his wallet. Where'd he get it, do you suppose?"

"Nobody knows. According to Deacon Deitz—he lives in the same building where Dabronski lived—Dabronski had no savings and was always griping about money. Of course, he could have had savings without Deitz knowing. He could even have inherited money without Deitz knowing."

Shirley sighed, ran down her list mentally, and tried again. "Do you know what those tickets were in Dabronski's wallet?"

"One was his dry cleaning. There's another one, looks like it could be from a shoe repair place or something, but we haven't located it yet."

"Was the Benton warehouse fire arson?"

"How the hell did you know? The investigators have been real quiet about that."

"My theory is Charles Maxwell came home and surprised somebody searching his garage. After killing him the killer ran, but he came back the following week to continue the search. The furniture was gone, and he had no way of knowing which furniture in the warehouse was the Maxwell furniture, so he burned the whole warehouse."

"My God," said Botts. "How in the hell did you come up with that?"

"It's only a theory."

"What was he looking for?"

"I wish I knew."

"You must have some idea."

"Botts, I have no idea. Something small. That's all I know."

"And you think that's why the woman got killed, too? This guy came back?"

"Maybe he came back and demanded she tell him where the thing was. Or is. Though I can't figure out why he needed to kill her unless he was someone Gloria knew. I don't think either she or Charles knew anything about it. I was the only one who went into that scrub. I was the *only* one who could have found anything. Or me and J.Q., when we went back. Or you, Botts, and your men. Killing the Maxwells seems like panic to me. Thrashing around."

"That's partly the newspaper's fault. Saying you were with a party of bowhunters when it was just you."

"Well, yes. You can correct it though."

"It doesn't matter now, does it? We're a little late."

"Not too late for Allison. Panicky people do dumb things. I wouldn't want anyone thinking Allison knew something she didn't. Give something to the newspaper, Botts. Tell them Allison has no information of help."

Shortly after noon Shirley drove north out of Columbine toward the Palace Pines exit that would take her to the landscaped hundred acres occupied by the Living Church. Long ago the land had been donated by a local philanthropist to a congregational group calling itself the Little Church of the

Hills. A few decades later the Little Church had merged with one of like belief and moved into Littleton, one of Denver's southwest-stretching suburbs. The land and church buildings had been bought by Reverend Patterson's group and had since undergone a considerable transformation. The small church had become a chapel with a new, larger church attached. The old parsonage, with its wings and gables and surrounding porches, had become a church annex. A long, low education building stretched like a wide-flung arm along the flank of a hill, and whatever acreage was not taken up by blacktopped parking lots was filled by lawn, groves of trees, a "memorial park," and excellent views of the entire front range of the Rockies from Long's Peak in the north to Pike's Peak in the south.

Shirley ran the Wagoneer next to the annex porch. She had in mind a little conversation with Deacon Deitz, if she could find him in. However, her plans changed abruptly when the door was answered by a girl of seventeen or so who looked up at her, frowned, then smiled, and said, "Hi! Remember me? I'm the one you rescued at the clinic. Diane Underhill, remember?"

Shirley nodded. "I didn't expect to see you here."

"I work here. Part time. Helping Mrs. Manning. She's the housekeeper and cook. I'm the gofer. Come on in."

Shirley followed her into the hall, then left into the living room. It was furnished with pleasantly battered pieces, old but sturdy, and was cluttered though not dirty. It looked rather like the McClintock house had before Shirley had it redone. What her decorator friend had called "bunkhouse baroque."

"How many people live here?" Shirley asked, turning around to get the full effect.

"Oh, not as many as you might think, even though it's a big old house. There's six bedrooms," Diane said. "Would you like some coffee? Mrs. Manning just made some, so it's fresh."

"I'd love some. Yes. Can I come with you?"

"Sure, come on back to the kitchen. That's where we spend most of our time, anyhow. If you wanted to see her or me. Maybe you wanted to see somebody else. I didn't even ask!''

"No, that's all right. I wanted to see you. Or Mrs. Manning. Or anybody who lives here. I want to ask about Deacon Dabronski.''

Diane's face wrinkled into a mask of distaste. "Oh, him."

"You didn't like him."

"Nobody liked him. Except the Rev. The only reason the Rev liked him is he sucked up to him. He was a real slimeball. Talked this junk about sexual purity, you know, and then was always finding some excuse to push up against you.''

"Mabel Brubacher said he was a nice man.''

"Oh, well, Mabel. He could push up against her all he wanted, and she wouldn't even feel it. She's got about a foot of padding all the way around." Diane pushed open a swinging door, and they went through into the kitchen where a stocky, bright-faced, black-haired woman sat at the table peeling potatoes. Diane said, "Andy, this is . . . hey, I guess I don't even know who you are. I heard you introduce yourself at the clinic, but I don't remember.''

"Shirley McClintock.'' She offered her had to the seated woman, who wiped her own hand on her apron and took Shirley's with a firm grip and a winning, white-toothed smile.

"Andy Manning. Andrea, really, but I've been Andy since I was about two. Have a seat. Diane, get her some coffee or something else if she wants.''

"She already said coffee, Andy. I'm getting it. She wants to ask about Dumb-Bronski.''

"Deacon Dabronski,'' the cook corrected. "I know you didn't like him, but show respect for the dead." She leaned forward as Shirley seated herself and whispered, "I didn't like him much either, to tell the truth.''

"I'm making some inquiries because I'm currently caring for the Maxwell daughter,'' Shirley said. "You may have read about her mother and father being murdered?''

Expressions of horror, with much shaking of heads, from both Diane and Andy Manning.

"The sheriff and I are convinced that the killings are connected with Dabronski's killing. I'm trying to find out more about him.''

Andy Manning tossed a peeled potato into a water-filled pan and began moving her knife steadily around another. ''He wasn't a very nice man,'' she said. ''I agree with Diane. He tended to be sneaky with women.''

''How do you mean, sneaky?''

''Well, there's men that are men, you know? They flirt with you. They tell you you're pretty. They tell you they wouldn't mind a little, you know. Or there's the kind who cry on your shoulder and tell you they have needs.'' She cast a sideways look at the girl and snorted. ''Diane knows. Oh, yes, she does. Well, that kind of man is all right. Maybe a little pushy from time to time, but all right. You know where you stand with that kind of man. You either do or you don't, but you know where he's coming from is he wants to get into your panties. But Ira? Ira was all the time talking about taking vows of celibacy. All the time talking about—what was it, Diane?''

''Giving his sex life to Jesus,'' Diane grimaced. ''I don't know why he thought Jesus would want it.''

''Diane! Shame on you. Anyhow, he was all the time going on and on about things like that, then you'd find his hand on your bottom when you weren't expecting it. Like I said, sneaky.''

''He went to prostitutes,'' said Diane.

''Diane!''

''Well he did, Andy! For heaven's sake, I wouldn't make it up! Me and Jimmy Bryant and Sally Wilson and her boyfriend were all in Denver at a movie last spring, and afterward Jimmy said let's drive down East Colfax and see the working girls, and we got some pizza and Cokes and drove up and down looking at the prossies, and it was just like in ''Miami Vice.'' And who do you think I saw going with one of the girls but good old pure Deacon Dabronski.''

''You couldn't be sure she was a prostitute,'' said Andy.

''With four-inch heels and a skirt up to her ass and a little short sequin blouse that showed everything but her nipples?

150

Oh, sure, Andy. She was a Sunday school teacher out for the evening.'' Diane made an oh-yeah face and put a cup of coffee together with saucer, spoon, and paper napkin in front of Shirley. ''Cream's in the pitcher, sugar's in the bowl,'' she said. ''Unless you want skinny sugar. I'll have to go over to the church kitchen to get that. We're out.''

''Real sugar's fine,'' said Shirley. ''Dabronski lived here?''

''Back bedroom on the north,'' said Andy. ''He lived here, and Deacon Deitz, and the gardener, and the church maintenance man, and now this new man the Rev has driving for him. Deacon Dabronski used to do a lot of the driving.''

''Who's in his room now? Dabronski's?''

''Nobody. You want to see it?'' Diane asked, looking eager. ''Are you going to solve the crime?''

''I'd love to,'' said Shirley. ''I wish somebody would. Maybe knowing more about Dabronski will help. What else can you tell me about him? Hobbies? What did he read? Where did he go on his time off? Other than East Colfax Avenue in Denver.''

''He used to read spy stuff and dirty books,'' said Andy. ''That's the only kind of books I ever saw in his room. The spy stuff was on his table, and the dirty books he hid under his shirts in the dresser. Real kinky stuff, you know? Women tied up and everything. He used to watch TV, I guess. He always had the TV guide open on top of it with all the spy shows marked. You know, like James Bond.''

''He went to those *Say Yes to Life* meetings,'' said Diane. ''They had meetings every week, and he went to them all. He picketed on Saturdays. I don't think he had any hobbies at all.''

''He wasn't a bowshooter, was he?''

''A what?''

''An archer. He didn't shoot with a bow and arrow?''

Both Diane and Andy shook their heads with expressions of doubt. ''I don't think he did anything like that,'' said Andy. ''No sports.''

''I hear he used to talk about going back where his family lived.''

151

Andy tossed another potato into the pot. "He used to get teed off at the Rev every now and then. He didn't get paid much, Ira didn't, and he used to say he couldn't use Sunday thank-yous to pay his bills. Not that he had many bills. He lived here for nothing, food included. But he'd get teed off and say he was going back to North Carolina. It was North Carolina, wasn't it, Diane?"

"I think so. I didn't pay that much attention."

"He used to talk about it enough that I wasn't really surprised when I went up there and found all his clothes gone."

"What made you look?"

"Well, I make the beds and clean the upstairs bathroom every morning. Diane helps the days she's here. Not weekends, of course. We don't work then. Monday we wash half the sheets, Tuesday we wash the other half, so we strip some beds on Monday and some on Tuesday morning. But when I went up there, his bed was still made up, his coat was gone—he always put that over the back of the chair. So I checked the closet and then the dresser and everything was gone."

"He used to have a suitcase under his bed, and that was gone. His car was gone," said Andy. "Don't forget that."

"He had a car?"

"He had an old blue one. Four-door. Chevy, I think. There's a garage next to the house here, and him and Deitz got to use the two parking spaces in it."

"You don't live here?" Shirley asked.

"Lord no," said Andy. "I've got a home and family and church of my own, thank God. I come in every morning about eight. Mondays, Tuesdays, and Fridays Diane comes in. We clean up and do the wash or whatever and fix lunch for the men—they have to get their own breakfasts. Then I fix something for their supper and leave it in the oven and the refrigerator, and we're out of here around three, sometimes earlier."

"Except Fridays when we clean the church," said Diane. "And sometimes we have to go out to Palace Pines and help out there."

"There's a crew that comes in Friday afternoon to do the church," Andy agreed, "and I see they do it right. And Bonny Patterson has her own cleaning people on Fridays." She made a little face, not quite distaste. "Mrs. Patterson does not do any of her own cooking or cleaning. Mrs. Patterson has a very sensitive nature." She wrinkled her nose again and said, "Sometimes if they're entertaining at some other time of the week, she'll have us come out and help clean or prepare the meal."

"I trust you get paid by the hour."

Andy smiled grimly. "After the first month I worked here, I think Bonny understood that." She turned to glare at Diane. "Which younger people should take heed of."

"Can I see his room?" Shirley asked, draining her coffee cup. She rose and followed Diane into the hall while Andy went on peeling potatoes. There were enough potatoes already peeled to make mashed potatoes for an army, and Shirley wondered idly which of the tenants had so huge an appetite.

They walked up the stairs onto the landing, which had a door at either side with a corridor directly ahead. As they moved down the corridor Shirley saw bathroom doors standing open to the right, opposite a shorter hall leading to the left with a door on either side of it. Past the bathrooms, at the end of the long hall, were two more doors. Diane opened the one on the right and walked into a room at the rear corner of the building overlooking a parking lot at one side of the church. The room was of generous size, furnished in the same worn but respectable manner as the ground floor. The bed, wide and comfortable-looking, was across from a six-drawer bureau topped with a television set and a mirror. A work table and several straight chairs plus an easy chair did not crowd the room, and there was a huge closet in addition.

"He didn't need all this closet space," said Diane. "He didn't have that many clothes."

"Do you do laundry for the men, too?"

"No, they do their own. We do towels and sheets, stuff like that. That reminds me." She flushed, "When I stripped this bed the day after he disappeared I found his camera stuck down between the bed and the wall. And he had a new jacket, still in the box, over behind that chair next to the door. I didn't want to tell you in front of Andy, because I forgot to tell her about it, and she'd be mad at me.''

"What did you do with the jacket and the camera?"

"Put them in the hall closet downstairs.''

"But there wouldn't be any of Dabronski's laundry lying around, because they do their own?''

"That's right. I guess it's kind of like a boardinghouse. Andy fixes two meals a day, five days a week, but if they want snacks or stuff, they have to get it themselves. On Friday Andy leaves lots of cold stuff for the weekends, and they can either eat that or eat out. Most of them keep food in their rooms. Andy's always on them about cockroaches and mice. She buys them plastic baggies to keep stuff in.''

"She does the grocery shopping?"

"For the meals she fixes. They buy their own breakfast stuff, because everybody wants something different.''

"She orders the food, and the church pays for it?''

"She draws money from the church to pay for it. She has a food budget. She says that's how the church makes out so cheap. They figure the cost of meals in the guys' salaries, only the cost they figure is like what it would cost in a restaurant, not what it costs Andy to do it.''

"Speaking of salaries, what did Andy mean about your taking heed.''

Diane blushed. "She says I ought to get paid for every hour I work. Sometimes . . . sometimes Bonny gives me stuff instead.''

"Stuff.''

"Like dresses. Bonny has nice clothes, but she gets bored with them after a while. We're about the same size. She gave me some of her clothes she said she was tired of. She says I remind her of her little sister back in Kansas City. Andy snorts, you know how she does, when I tell her things like that. Andy says Bonny Patterson is very strange and should never have married a minister. Andy says if Bonny Patterson

154

ever had a little sister in Kansas City or anywhere else, she'll eat her food processor. She says Bonny Patterson has one sister, and her name is Elise Fish, and she lives right here in Columbine, which is enough to make Elise want to move. Don't ask me what Andy means, I don't know. Andy knows a lot about people here in town; she's lived here all her life.

"I like Bonny, though. She gave me a VCR once. It'll be great when I get it fixed."

"She gave you a faulty VCR instead of paying you?"

"Well, there's not much wrong with it, and she said it was more friendly. I give her stuff, too. I gave her a little angel to hang in her car. I've got one downstairs in the kitchen. I make them myself out of cornhusks."

"I agree with Andy," said Shirley in a dry voice. "I think you ought to get paid in money for every hour you work, and you should also try to keep your personal life and your work separate. Otherwise, you will end up being exploited, and that will be your fault, not anyone else's."

The girl flushed and was silent. Shirley opened drawers, peered under the bed, ran her hands across the shelf in the closet.

"I'd like to see the camera. I'll tell the sheriff about that and the jacket." Shirley went back out into the hall and peeked into one of the bathrooms. "Do the men leave personal stuff in the bathroom?"

"There isn't enough room. I mean, it's really two rooms, one with just a toilet and lavatory, one with a toilet and lavatory, tub and shower, and there's a huge linen closet, but there's no medicine cabinets."

"So his shaving stuff was gone, too."

Diane nodded. "He kept it in his top drawer."

Shirley went back downstairs, the girl following her. Halfway down Shirley stopped so suddenly that the girl bumped into her.

"Diane, Deitz lives here?"

"Yes."

"Then he knows you. You're no stranger to him."

"I guess."

155

"But he was hassling you in front of the clinic the other day."

"Oh, yeah. He loves to do that. Dabronski used to do that, too. Both of them are real . . . Andy says they're being holier-than-thou. Every time I go into that clinic one of them seems to be hovering around like some old crow."

"Why don't you go to some other clinic?"

"You sound just like . . . Anyhow, why should I! I don't have a car to go driving fifty miles into Denver or someplace. I've got a right to go where I want. They know me here in Columbine. I even have a friend who works at the clinic."

Shirley shut her mouth on the personal questions she wanted to ask. Instead, she stared down the long hall. "Which is Deitz's room?"

Diane pointed to the side. "He's down the other hall, toward the front."

"Which were the empty rooms? When Dabronski was alive."

"The one across from Dabronski's and the front one."

There were four bedrooms to the south of the corridor, two to the north, six altogether. Two opened at either side of the landing, two off the side corridor, one on each side at the end of the main corridor. Dabronski's room had been isolated from any occupied room. "So if he packed up late one night, nobody would have heard him?"

Diane thought about this, then nodded in verification. "The bathrooms are between his room and the empty front room," she said. "The room across the hall was empty, too. So the closest room with anybody in it would be the gardener's room, Mr. MacIntyre. He's opposite Deacon Deitz down the side hall, and he's deaf anyhow."

"And the maintenance man?"

"Mr. Thomas has the one on the south front."

"Who knows about this house? Which rooms the men have?"

Diane looked puzzled. "Anybody. They have company in their rooms if they want. Sometimes the Rev comes to visit them. Before they got their new house, the Rev and Bonny

156

used to live here, so they know the house. I do. Andy does. Before I worked here, there was another girl. Lots of people know about this house. Why?''

''No special reason,'' said Shirley. ''I just wondered.''

Diane got the camera and jacket out of the hall closet and laid them on the table and then went into the kitchen. The jacket was new; the pockets were empty. The camera was set for the tenth exposure. Shirley quietly wound the film, removed it, and slipped it into her pocket; then she followed Diane into the kitchen where she admired the cornhusk angel hanging over the sink and offered to buy one for Allison. She paid for the angel in advance, thanked Andy Manning for the excellent coffee, and let them both get back to their potatoes.

Botts Tempe did not yet know where Deacon Dabronski's car was but he was looking, he said, when Shirley called at four o'clock.

''There's a canyon about half-a-mile downhill from the Redstone picnic grounds,'' Shirley said. ''Have you looked there?''

Long silence.

''Why would I have looked there?''

''Because that may be where it is.''

''Any special reason, Ms. McClintock?''

''Call me Shirley, Botts. When you call me Ms. McClintock it sounds like you're mad at me.''

''Any special reason you expect this car to be in that particular canyon, Shirley?''

''Uphill from where we found the bones is the Redstone picnic grounds. If he drove there, and he probably did, somebody made off with his car. Also, somebody made off with his clothes, from his room at the church annex.''

''We knew his clothes were gone. He may have taken them himself.''

''I don't think so. He wouldn't have left his new jacket, still in the box, and he wouldn't have left his camera. There was exposed film in the camera, so I took it to be developed. I figured you'd want it developed anyhow.''

A simmering silence at the other end of the line. ''I asked Andy Manning if she'd stored any of his stuff for him, and she told me she hadn't.''

''Well, she hadn't. Her helper, Diane, was the one who put the stuff away. Did you try for fingerprints?''

''By the time we looked at the room it'd been cleaned, probably about a dozen times. We got a few of Dabronski's. We got the women who clean the place. We got some other people from the church, but no strangers we couldn't iden- tify.''

Shirley thanked him and hung up. She didn't have the heart to suggest it probably hadn't been a stranger who had killed Deacon Dabronski. He had probably known his killer as well as Gloria Maxwell had.

5

THAT EVENING SHIRLEY called her old friend John Fogg and made a date to meet him for coffee the following morning. During the night she rose in the late and early hours to check on Allison, who was restless though not actually wakeful. When morning came Allison had had far more sleep than Shirley herself.

The Wednesday newspaper used up most of its second page covering an interview with Botts Tempe, in which he said, in effect, that evidence connected the killings of Ira Dabronski and the Maxwells, that the investigation had been inconclusive thus far, but the recent discovery of Mr. Dabronski's car offered further possibilities for inquiry. In response to a question from the reporter (planted), Botts said the Maxwell child had been unable to supply any useful information: she had no idea why or by whom her parents had been killed. The paper arrived only moments before a phone call from Botts Tempe himself.

"Dabronski's car was there, Shirley."

"I saw the morning paper, Botts. Thanks for telling the

reporter Allison didn't know anything. I'm not sure it was necessary, but it does relieve my mind some.''

"While your mind is relieved, would you mind stopping by and making a statement as to how you knew about the car?''

"I'll probably be coming into town, Botts, but I didn't really know about the car.''

"You told me to look there.''

"That doesn't mean I knew it was there. I just thought it might be.''

"Would you mind running through that for me. I'm feeling a little slow this morning.'' Botts was not angry, only slightly grumpy, but his annoyance came through.

"Before J.Q. and I went up into the scrub looking for clues, I figured our route on a USGS topographical map of the area. You know, trying to find a way to get up there on horseback. I just happpened to notice that canyon along the road. It's almost straight down, with a wooded bottom. A good place to drop a car.''

"Sure, Shirley, but what made you think somebody had dropped a car!'' It wasn't a question, really. More of a complaint.

"Well, if Dabronski went up there with the killer, then his car would have been someplace else. But if he drove there himself and was shot, then the killer had to get rid of Dabronski's car to keep someone from finding the deserted car and searching for the owner.''

"Why there? Why didn't the killer drive to the city, to a parking lot, to the airport?''

"Because it was night and it was raining cats and dogs,'' she said. "Because the killer undoubtedly got there in his own car, and he couldn't drive two cars at once. If it were me, I wouldn't go any farther than I had to to ditch the other guy's car so I wouldn't have any farther than necessary to walk back to mine. Especially in the rain.''

"And how do you know it was raining?''

"For chrissake, Botts, you told me it was raining. You said the reverend didn't get home until late after he came in on a plane from St. Louis because it was raining like crazy. And that was the same night Dabronski disappeared.''

"Oh," said Botts. "Right."

"Of course, I'm guessing that it was nighttime, but Dabronski was in jail up until noon that day, so he had to set up his meeting after that. Besides, if a guy is up to something nefarious, he wouldn't meet anybody in broad daylight, would he? He'd probably wait until dusk at least. Wouldn't you?''

Another silence; then, with great dignity, "I haven't had your obviously wide experience with the nefarious, Ms. Mc-Clintock, so it might not have occurred to me.''

"Oh, sure it would, Botts," she said. "If you gave it enough time." She snorted, only slightly.

"Was that an insult?" he asked in a labored effort at humor.

"Me, insult a lawman? Come on.''

"Have you got any other suggestions?''

"Not at the moment. I wish I did. All I've got are questions.''

"Like what?''

"Like why did the killer use a gun and then switch to bow and arrow and then back to a gun again? Oh, and whether Dr. Fish was involved? Was he?''

Botts grunted, a negative, displeased sound. "He took out a membership in the Bowshooters Club for a birthday present for his son, Bertram Junior. The kid is eighteen years old, living at home while he's going to school in Denver learning to be an athletic coach. Evidently they have to know about all the sports, not just football and basketball, so he does archery and golf and tennis and every other kind of athletics in his spare time. However, the doctor claims golf is his game, and he personally has never tried to shoot with a bow in his entire life. I can't think of any reason he could be lying.''

"That's disappointing," she mumbled. "Damn. Did you find out about any of those other people on my list? Including Fish's wife?''

"Yes, I did. I happen to know where Orrin Patterson went

161

to school and where he had churches before this one. I know where his mother lives. I called all those places and asked if the reverend ever was involved in archery, and the answer I got everyplace I asked was no, he wasn't. I did pretty much the same thing with the other folks on your list, plus I checked their names against the mailing list of those manufacturers you gave me. Same thing with the sporting-goods stores in Denver. I can tell you that Mabel Brubacher bought a bowling ball, and Arlette Carmichael bought her husband a fishing rod, but none of the people on your list have ever done any bowshooting. So I guess our murderer is somebody else."

"One of them is."

"What do you mean, one of them is?"

"We could have two, Botts. One with a gun and one bowshooter. The more I think about it the more likely I think it is we might have more than one. You still want me to come in?"

There was another long silence before he said, "Just to sign a statement, yes. Or if you get any other bright ideas. Or when you get those pictures developed you took out of Dabronski's camera. And, by the way, that sister of Gloria Maxwell's called to say she'll be here this afternoon. Her and her husband."

"Yeah, I know," said Shirley. "Oh, Lord," she howled after hanging up the phone.

"Trouble?" asked J.Q. from the kitchen door.

"Allison's aunt and uncle. They will be here this afternoon. I was hoping they'd put it off. Or forget about it."

"They're a day late."

"How?"

"Last night was Halloween. Don't witches usually arrive on Halloween?" he smirked.

"True, but not funny, J.Q. Did Allison have fun at school yesterday? You know, I was so full of the stuff the Manning woman and Diane told me I didn't even ask."

"I don't think she's quite up to having fun yet, but she

162

enjoyed being with other kids. Enjoyed taking part. Her team won the ball game, by the way.''

"Where is she now?''

"Petting Beauregard.''

"First riding lesson this afternoon?''

"Four o'clock.''

"Let's not say anything about Aunt Esther and Uncle Lawrence until she gets home from school.''

"Coward.''

"No. Just let her have as good a day as she can. I've got something to do this morning, and there's no point in my worrying about her worrying all day. Let her look forward to her riding lesson.''

John Fogg had balked only slightly at meeting Shirley this morning at ten, though he'd questioned the appropriateness of the place Shirley had picked for their meeting.

"The Bee! Nobody goes to the Bee. Little old ladies go to the Bee.''

"That's why I want to meet you there, John. Tête-à-tête. You and me. Playing kneesies under the table.''

"Come off it, McClintock. What are you after?''

"John, please, just refresh your memory about the deal your nice little S&L made with the church over the Winterburn property and then come meet me at ten at the Bee. Oh, and John!''

"Yes,'' he growled.

"Don't ask anybody at the bank to get the records for you. Get them yourself. And don't tell anybody at the bank who you're going to have coffee with either.''

When Shirley got to the Bee she sat alone for fifteen minutes, wondering if John was going to show up. Considering how bad the coffee was, maybe she should have chosen somewhere else; but she hadn't wanted anyone to see them. The Bee was an Antique Shoppe and Tearoom(e) run by two white-haired women who, so far as Shirley could tell, were the same two who had managed it when Shirley's mother had brought her here for lunch fifty years ago. The neat Victorian house on the well-kept side street had been a much-enjoyed

163

treat when Shirley was ten. It had been filled with all sorts of wonders and delights.

Now, as she looked around herself, Shirley wondered if the wonders and delights of yesteryear had been similar to the current collection of Korean and Taiwanese junk, kitsch, and cliché. Bill had called this kind of thing *junque*, giving it the Mexican pronunciation. Hoon-kay. Cute kittens made of glass, porcelain, paint, clay, straw, wood, plastic, wax, cast metal, wire, and other less-identifiable materials. Cute rabbits: ditto. Cute birdies: ditto. Cute babies: ditto. Mottos and tea-towels and dainty wee pot holders with nylon lace around the edges. Grab a hot pot with one of those and third-degree yourself with melted plastic, but daintily.

Sighing, Shirley turned her attention back to her coffee as John Fogg slipped through the front door, looking furtively around to be sure he was unobserved by anyone who mattered. John had filled out a little with the years, but he was still tall and erect and had those lovely squinty eyes and lots of hair. White now, of course, but it became him. She grinned and beckoned.

"I'm the first man who has been in this place in thirty years," he breathed into her ear. "Except maybe the plumber."

"You probably are, John, but the coffee won't actually kill you, and I needed to talk to you."

"What's this stuff about the Winterburn house. We sold it. Got out from under, thank God." He perched on the too-small chair and regarded the plate of putative blueberry muffins with disfavor. "We took a loss, but not a huge one."

Shirley poured him some coffee. "What can you tell me about the deal, John?"

"What can I? Or what should I?" He took a bite of a muffin and made a face.

Shirley nodded companionably. "You should tell me nothing; we both agree to that. You know I have a reason for asking; I know you're going to tell me. Let's not waltz. I'm too tall for you."

John Fogg giggled. Shirley used to tease him about his

giggle years ago, telling him it made him sound like an eight-year-old. She was delighted that he still did it. He caught himself and grinned.

"Okay, old friend. When Winterburn died we got caught holding almost five hundred thousand on his house. Normally it would have been worth over twice that. Recently, in that location, however, we're lucky if we can even get an offer. So when the church, which seems to be stable and has a good financial report and looks like a reasonably safe bet, offers to pay not much less than the amount of the mortgage, interest only for five years, and then balloon . . . ."

"Whoa," she said. "Slow down, John. When the church offers to do what?"

"Pay interest only on half a million for five years and pay the entire balance at the end of five years. . . ."

"John, hold your hat. Charles Maxwell was the agent, right?"

"Right."

"I saw with these, my very own eyes, in Charles Maxwell's office, signed papers and receipts indicating that Mr. Maxwell and Mr. Carmichael of your bank received in cash almost half a million dollars from the Church of the Living Jesus. Two years ago, John. They got it in cash then."

John set his cup down with a careful, almost finicky gesture, wiped his mouth with a tiny napkin, crumpled it in his hand. "Cash? Shirley, you must be . . ."

"No. I'm not mistaken, Johnnyboy. Honest to God, this is Shirley McClintock talking. I read the thing. I had no business to, but I did it anyhow. So far as that church is concerned, they paid cash. Just under five hundred thou."

"What the hell!"

"How much interest, John? What interest rate did you think they were paying?"

"Carmichael sold me on eight percent. Not too bad a deal, considering. He said a low price and low interest rate would clinch the sale. Quite frankly we're trying to cut our losses where real estate is concerned. Have you any idea how many savings and loans have folded over the past year?"

Shirley thought hard. "Two years ago, what would have been the going rate on that amount tied up for five years, Johnnyboy? Ten? Eleven?"

"Two years ago? They might have got eleven, or a little higher. For five years they might even have got twelve."

"So, that'd be what? Three points difference? Fifteen thousand a year, more or less, times five years. Seventy-five thousand? Neat. At twelve percent it would be an even hundred thou. Carmichael tells you you're getting interest only at eight; the papers you have at the bank say you're getting interest only at eight. Meantime he and Maxwell tie up the money at eleven or twelve, and they pay themselves the difference. You get your interest payments on time, so you don't worry."

"But if the church paid cash, it would have expected to receive clear title."

She gave him the look he had hated when they were children. "Answer that one for yourself, Johnny. Does Carmichael have authority to release deeds of trust? Oh-ho, yes he does! What a very nice little fiddle the man has going. I wonder if this is the only one. He tells the buyer he can reduce the price if they buy for cash; he tells you to reduce the price and the interest to clinch the sale. You're trying to cut your losses and get out from under. Neat. I wonder how many more interest-only deals you may have going. He could be earning some nice change on the side."

John stared at the table, glowering. "He's in deep, Shirley. Damn it, I knew that."

"Carmichael?"

"He made some investments, real estate mostly. He's having a hell of a time holding on to them. Damn. I feel like a fool."

She laid her hand over his. "John, hey . . ."

Then, as he rose abruptly, she caught his arm and whispered, "Johnny, be careful who you ask to get the files for you. Don't forget he may have some little girl clerk down there working with him."

One of the two elderly ladies came to the table, asking

166

worriedly if everything was all right; hadn't the gentleman liked his muffin?

"That's no gentleman," Shirley said solemnly. "That's a banker. He loved his muffin, but he just remembered he left his steam iron on at home."

Esther Brentwood called Shirley shortly after noon to say she and Mr. Brentwood would like to drive out that afternoon. Shirley suggested four-thirty. When they arrived, Allison was receiving a riding lesson in the small front pasture and pretending not to see her aunt and uncle's car. She was so intent upon what she was doing—riding briskly in a circle at the end of a lunge line—that she may not, in fact, have seen them arrive. Beauregard, who was capable of making any rider look experienced, was doing his best for Allison. No one would have known it was her first lesson.

The car stopped. The occupants seemed to be taking inventory of their surroundings, including the small figure atop the horse. After a time Lawrence Brentwood got out of the driver's side and stood up, turning slowly to continue his assessment. He wore country tweeds and an open leather topcoat. His manner conveyed that everything he wore was handmade and that each garment was the most appropriate garment anyone could have worn in similar circumstances. Men might differ from his paradigm, his manner said, but only at their peril. Expensive teeth gripped an exclusive pipe above a massive, well-massaged chin. Ruddy cheeks joined an unlined brow, and the overall impression of implacable self-confidence was only augmented by the half-bald head fringed neatly in well-barbered gray. I am a successful man who has much deserved success, the face said, the body said, the clothes said.

He saw Shirley standing in the doorway and smiled. I am a good man, even a jovial man, the smile said. I am known to be kind to those who take the trouble to please me.

She might almost have believed it, but his eyes gave it away. They punctured the mask like the sharp tips of two nails driven through from some colder place.

167

Shirley went out to greet them. Lawrence opened the car door for his wife. Esther fingered pearls, a discreet single strand, though her restless fingers had brought the less modest diamond clasp forward to rest upon her cashmere bosom. Her skin was taut, as though from countless tiny tucks. She gleamed like enamel, like a mannequin in everything but the darting eyes that moved across Shirley's face without alighting; moving on, hovering, darting like hungry bats, finding nothing worthy of resting upon.

Shirley took a deep breath and welcomed them. They smiled slightly and came into the house as though they had just bought it. Shirley had put on her newest jeans, her good boots, had brought out the Scottish shortbread, and had made tea. Further than that, as she had said to J.Q., she had been unwilling to go. Now she found herself longing for her own former cashmeres and tweeds and one, or perhaps two, well-trained Great Danes.

"You folks come on in," she said in a carefully countrified voice. Shirley had decided, after considerable thought, to be unsophisticated and let them play at upsmanship. Her strategy was that the Brentwoods should feel superior to her, but not uncomfortably out of their class. They should consider Shirley McClintock to be inferior but acceptable. *My dear, we met this ranch woman when we were out west. Such a genuine type. Rather rough-hewn, but quite acceptable really. Considering poor Allison's limitations, we felt she would be more comfortable remaining there, among her own kind.*

Being *acceptable* meant bringing out the Limoge cups and saucers and the sterling tea service, which she had spent an hour polishing. Both had been part of her Washington life, her life with Martin and Bill, the life of constant entertaining and being entertained, of luncheons for a dozen and teas for forty and weekly sit-down dinners for twenty or more. Here at the ranch, silver and china came out of their cupboards only on exceptional occasions, usually for people she didn't like, since those she did like would not be at all impressed.

168

"Join me in a cup of tea," she invited the Brentwoods, "unless you'd rather have a drink."

Both her guests consented to tea, he in a haughty murmur, she in a patronizing mew. While she poured—from a low chair intended to minimize her height—Shirley extended sympathy on the death of a sister and brother-in-law. Lawrence Brentwood stirred his tea moodily and did not respond, his abacus eyes toting up the worth of the house, the land, the livestock, and Shirley herself. Esther fished in her eelskin purse for a pristine linen handkerchief which she touched delicately to the corner of each eye. Despite her claim that she had married young she was at least fifteen years older than Gloria had been, almost old enough to have been Gloria's mother rather than her sister.

"Did I see Allison out there riding a horse?" Esther asked in an almost offended tone, as though wishing to be assured some fancied impropriety was not, in fact, occurring.

Shirley nodded soberly. "One of Gloria's last wishes was that Allison continue to be provided for in the manner she and Charles had planned. Of course, Gloria didn't know it was a last wish, which makes it even more sacred, don't you think?" Shirley crossed her fingers, remembering that the childhood penalty for telling lies was having one's mouth washed out with soap. She hadn't actually told any lies yet. Gloria had undoubtedly wanted Allison to be raised as she planned. Any mother would.

"Gloria was not at all interested in horses!" Esther said, setting down her cup with a tiny slosh of its contents. "Not at all."

Shirley nodded in agreement. "That's quite true. I think Charles was more the sportsman. As a matter of fact, I got to know your sister through Charles's interest in sports."

Lawrence Brentwood frowned as he left his teacup and went to the window. "Looks like a rather good horse she's riding."

"Oh, Beauregard certainly is a good horse. I'll say this for Charles, he always wanted to go first class." Shirley topped up Lawrence's teacup and tried not to sound smug.

"That horse belongs to Charles?" Pained astonishment, annoyance, pique. Esther Brentwood's nostrils lifted visibly, as though she had smelled something questionable.

"No, it was a present for Allison." Which was certainly true, though no transfer of moneys had as yet taken place. "Of course, it isn't all paid for yet. Charles's death rather interrupted things."

There was little or no causal relationship between any two statements she had made thus far, but the Brentwoods were not to know that. Mr. and Mrs. Brentwood exchanged a singularly meaningful stare, which Shirley noted with interest while pretending not to notice at all.

"She will be able to go on with her riding, won't she? It would break Allison's heart to give up her riding on top of everything else. Allison was sure she'd be able to get really good instructors if she lived with you. She said your daughters, her cousins, ride. I think it's so fortunate that you're well provided for, since poor Charles may have left very little. And, after all, it can't be that expensive to ship a horse across country. Heavens, people do it all the time." Shirley sipped at her tea and wondered if she were overdoing it.

"I'm sure," breathed Esther. "I'm sure they do."

Shirley patted her lips and settled herself, hands folded in lap, legs crossed at the ankles, wishing again that she'd put on a skirt. Nothing to do but plow forward, full speed, getting in one's licks where one might. "Esther, I know Ms. Minging wants to talk to you about possible boarding schools for Allison. Ms. Minging is Allison's teacher at the local private school. I told her you had mentioned boarding school, Lawrence, and since she knows a great many people in the best private schools back east, she wants to make recommendations to you about Allison's future education."

Another moment's strained silence.

"Such a surprising girl," Shirley said, pouring herself another half cup. "Having known her parents, I find her quite surprising. So very gifted in so many respects."

"Gifted?" inquired Lawrence, coming back to sit down, his face suddenly stiff and suspicious. "I hadn't known."

"Very intriguing child," said Shirley. "Quite advanced in language skills."

J.Q. came to the living room door from the kitchen, hat in hand, and cleared his throat to attract Shirley's attention. She introduced him—as ranch foreman, which is what he called himself when he needed a label—and he said, "I just wanted to mention that Allison has a visit to the orthodontist scheduled tomorrow. If Allison's folks have other plans for her, the appointment should be cancelled."

"Orthodontist," said Lawrence in a flat tone. "What's the matter with her teeth?"

"Crooked," Shirley sighed. "Just a little. In my day they'd have let it go, but we all know how important a perfect smile is these days. And I guess the surgical removal of supernumerary teeth has become almost routine."

"Mrs. McClintock . . ." muttered Lawrence Brentwood.

"Ms.," said Shirley, beaming cheerily at him. "Ms. McClintock. My maiden name. I've been married, but out here at the ranch I use my maiden name because my family has lived here for three generations. However, I've been forward enough to use your first names, so please, call me Shirley."

"Shirley. May I ask who is going to pay for the horse, the riding lessons, the dentist, the private school? Since Charles may have left, as you say, very little?"

J.Q., who felt that the question could not have come at a better time, grunted, gestured at Shirley, and said, "She was planning to, the more fool her." He used this rudeness as an exit line, playing the rustic to the hilt.

Shirley managed a self-deprecating little frown. "J.Q. has been with the family a long time and sometimes is a bit familiar. It is true I felt I was committed to paying for Allison's care. Gloria had no idea how long she would be in jail, and then when she got out, she had no place to live and no money. She asked me to take care of Allison, and I agreed to do so. We talked about Allison's education and her health needs. The fact that Gloria subsequently died doesn't relieve me of that responsibility. However, I *must* stress that all that

171

occurred before I knew that Gloria had a sister who would want Allison. At the time, I simply didn't know."

"Why would Gloria have come to you in that way?" snapped Esther. "Why would she have asked you to take her daughter?"

Shirley shrugged. "Why, Esther, I imagine she was thinking of you. I imagine she knew that you and Lawrence had plans for the upcoming years and that adopting a new daughter would cause a major upheaval in your lives for many years whereas it would require almost no adjustments at all in mine."

"No adjustment at all?" Lawrence said with what was almost a sneer. "I find that hard to believe."

She shook her head at him, giving him her most innocent look. "Well, I know that sounds silly, Lawrence, but it would not, not really. I have no plans to travel, and Allison is quite content with the school here. It's a very fine one, despite its small size, and because of my family's involvement with it over the years, it doesn't cost as much for Allison to attend as it might cost someone else. Ms. Minging is able to obtain scholarships for many of her students who wish to continue in private schools, and she has assured me that will be no problem when Allison finishes there. Also, I know that maintaining a horse involves considerable outlay for stabling and feed if one is a city dweller; it's no problem on a ranch. For example, I am able to trade hay for riding lessons. Both the teacher and I benefit, but there is no cash outlay."

"I see."

"Gloria knew some of this, of course, but I can't say what precisely moved her to ask me to take care of Allison. Gloria was so upset at the time that I scarcely liked to press her for explanations. I simply agreed to do as she asked." Shirley batted her eyes at them, conveying sincerity. "But, as I say, that was before I knew about *you*. In any case, I've grown quite fond enough of Allison that no matter where she goes, I've promised her I will go on being her honorary grandmother who will visit her frequently, wherever she is."

"Could we, ah, talk with her teacher?" asked Lawrence,

his hand on his wife's arm, squeezing it. It was a signal that Esther evidently understood, for she was suddenly very quiet, lips drawn together in an unaccommodating piggybank slit.

"Oh, most assuredly." Shirley rose to get paper and pen from the mantle. "Yes. Here's Ms. Minging's number and address. Allison's riding teacher is Martha Cavendish, you can introduce yourselves when you go out, and Mrs. Cavendish also provided the horse. She'll want to recommend some instructors in your part of the country, I'm sure. Martha's well-known nationally in the equestrian world. I believe she has coached Olympic riders from time to time. Do you want to talk to Allison's dentist? Her doctor? Now it *will* be necessary for you to get in touch with the attorney, Numa Ehrlich, because he was representing Gloria at the time of her death, and there were some legal fees that had accumulated at that time. Her death cancelled the bond I'd paid for her release, except for a small fee, so there'll be only minor expense for you there. Then you'll want to arrange for the funerals."

"Funerals? Plural?" Lawrence barked.

"Well, Charles's body hadn't been released when Gloria was arrested, and Gloria's hasn't been released yet either. I had been going to take care of Charles's burial for Gloria, but as next of kin, you'll undoubtedly prefer to make arrangements yourselves. I'm acquainted with most of the local ministers or priests if you want a religious ceremony."

"We're Anglicans," said Esther. "Charles and Gloria were nothing until recently when they took up with that church . . . that . . . what was the name of it?" she asked her husband.

"Living Church," said Lawrence, shaking his head in remote distaste.

"Gloria wrote that she was thinking of becoming a member because she had become friendly with someone from the church," Esther continued, ignoring her husband's warning glance. "Though as usual she was obscure, hinting at having secrets. Gloria never outgrew the childish pleasure of having secrets. Quite frankly I thought she'd taken up with some

173

man. The choir director, perhaps. Or a young custodian. That would have been Gloria's style.''

"Esther!'' her husband said firmly. "Your sister merely said she had a friend in the church and that she was thinking of joining it. There's nothing improper in that.''

Esther threw him a rebellious glance and said maliciously, "What she actually said on the phone was that she and Charles had found their connection with the church very *profitable*. Then she giggled, as though it were a joke. With Gloria everything was either a panic or a joke.''

Shirley rose to bring the visit to an end, meantime biting her tongue to keep from following up on what Esther was saying. It was the wrong time to get into that. There was another, more important agenda at the moment: Allison, and Shirley intended to stick with it. She gritted her teeth and accepted Esther's fulsome thanks. Lawrence gave none. She walked them as far as the drive then went back into the house where she could watch them from the window without being seen.

They strolled to the pasture fence and beckoned to Allison. The girl dismounted as though she had been doing it for years. She walked over to them, standing very straight as she offered a small, chilly-looking hand. There was something ritualistic and elaborate in her stance, in the expression on her face. Shirley realized Allison was being polite—stiffly, bone-crackingly polite. No hug, Shirley noted. No hug at all. They talked only for a moment. The instant they turned away Allison went back to her horse.

"What did you think, J.Q.?'' she asked the air.

He replied from the kitchen, where he'd been listening. "Not exactly my kind of people. I expected to hear at least one or two exclamations of 'That poor child,' or 'Poor motherless baby.' A few such remarks are almost de rigueur for the occasion, I should have thought. Can't say I like them much.''

"Neither does Allison.''

"What do you think?'' he asked, bringing in a tray to remove all evidence of consorting with the enemy.

"I think Mr. Brentwood will start adding up the expenses of raising Allison properly, which he can well afford to do if he wants to. Then he will consider that he needn't spend that kind of money, that he can treat Allison as a poor relation. He'll almost talk himself into that. Then he'll recollect I said I was coming to visit Allison frequently. He will recall that I have friends who know him, friends to whom I might mention the fact that Lawrence Brentwood is a weaseling turd, and his wife is a witch, and he'll decide he wouldn't like that."

"And her? The Mrs.?" J.Q. was grinning at her as she got into the flow of it.

"She won't be swayed by powerful friends or being considered coprophilic. She will simply go on being viciously annoyed that her baby sister, whom she resented from the hour of her birth, whom she bullied and mistreated and probably detested, preferred someone else as Allison's guardian. Which may not even be true. Poor Gloria wasn't all that levelheaded. She may have grabbed me because I was closest, or because I'd require the least explanation. I have a feeling she hated explaining anything to big sis. Funny, if Esther was fifteen or so when Gloria was born, you'd think she'd have had very little contact with her."

"You're forgetting their mother died when Gloria was what? You told me. Six?"

"Oh, that's right. She told me that on the phone."

"And that means Esther was the substitute mother, and as a kid in her teens she might well have resented it. If mama died when Gloria was that young, twenty-year-old Esther was left with a child to raise. Which would help explain why Esther is glad to get her own daughters out of the nest and is irritated at the idea of raising Allison. She's already raised one child that wasn't her own. She doesn't want to do it again."

"She seems to have gone out of her way to make Gloria unhappy about it."

"Whatever Gloria's reasons were, when she needed some-

175

one to take Allison, she called you, Shirl. Keep that in mind. So? What do you think?''

Shirley shrugged. ''I think it's a toss-up whether greed or territoriality wins.''

Ms. Minging called later that evening to report on her own conversation with the Brentwoods. ''They called me from their hotel, Shirley. I explained to them how bright she is and what special schooling she should have. There's one very fine and famous school near their home. The Houghton Academy. Perfect for Allison. Twelve-month boarding school. Summers in Europe. And it only costs about twenty thousand a year. Plus fees and air tickets for the summer trips, of course.''

Shirley gulped. ''How did they respond?''

''Mrs. Brentwood said she'd tried to get her daughters Melanie and Cheryl into Houghton, but they'd have had to have been registered when they were born in order to have been accepted. Mrs. Brentwood was a little snippy about it.''

''Ah.''

''I told them I am an alumna, and that there will be no difficulty admitting Allison as I have already spoken to the administration.''

''Oh, Lord, Mingy, you didn't.''

''I did. And furthermore, it was true. I did have to twist the arms of a few old friends, but I told them it probably wouldn't come to anything anyway, that we all hoped Allison could continue here with me.''

''I didn't know that about you,'' said Shirley in wonder. ''I didn't know you were a proper easterner from one of those awesome schools. I thought you were a maverick, like me.''

''Shirley,'' said Ms. Minging severely, ''there are no mavericks like you. I am afraid you are truly unique.''

''Was that Ms. Minging?'' Allison asked after Shirley had hung up.

Shirley avowed it was and that Ms. Minging had been doing her best for Allison.

''I did my best for me, too,'' the girl sighed. ''When Aunt

176

Esther asked me if I liked it here, I said it was all right but I was sure the riding instructors in the east would be superior. I said it in the same tone of voice she always uses when she talks about me and Mommy.''

"Who suggested that gambit?"

Allison threw a quick look at J.Q., who was, an usual, immured in the *Wall Street Journal* and paying no attention to either of them. "I forget. Do you think it will work?" she asked.

Shirley shook her head doubtfully. "It will work with your uncle, I think. Provided we didn't overdo it. I'm not sure what might work with your aunt. Did she say they'd be coming out to see you again any time soon?"

"She said they'd be in town for a few days, that's all."

"Well, cross your fingers and hope. Don't you have homework?"

Allison pursed her lips thoughtfully. "I have to wait for J.Q. to finish the paper so he can help me with fifteen problems in math."

"No," said J.Q. "You have to do all the math yourself, after which I'll help you with whatever you couldn't do. I'm not going to waste my valuable time doing parts you can do. I've heard both Ms. Minging and Shirley going on and on, telling people how bright you are, so you can't get away with playing dumb around here."

Allison's lower lip came out, but she sat down among her books at the kitchen table without further protest.

Shirley and J.Q. perched in the living room. Shirley tried to read and ended up staring at the carpet. After rattling his paper for twenty minutes J.Q. discarded it for his memo pad and began mumbling to himself.

"I asked you," he repeated, "whether there's anything you need from town?"

Shirley jerked to attention. "Oh. Yeah. We need milk. Since Allison's been here we keep running out. Buy two gallons. And you can pick up the film I found in Dabronski's camera. I told Botts I'd taken it to be developed, and he'll

177

want to see the pictures—after I do." She dug into her hip pocket and brought out the claim ticket.

He turned it over curiously, looking at both sides. "This looks like one of the tickets you found in Dabronski's wallet. You did put that one back in the wallet, didn't you?"

"I did," she said. "This is the one I got yesterday."

"It looks the same. Isn't it the same?"

She went to the drawer of her desk to find the facsimiles she had drawn on a sheet of typing paper. One of them did very much resemble the ticket she had just given J.Q. Same size, shape, arrangement of numbers. "I never thought of it being a claim ticket for photographs," she said wonderingly. "Evidently Botts didn't either. He said one of the others was a laundry claim slip."

J.Q. turned it over curiously. "We always take film to the Fotomat. This isn't a Fotomat claim. It doesn't even have a name and address on it, only the number."

"I *know* that, J. Q. If it had had the name and address on it, Botts would have known what it was and so would I."

"How did you come to take it there?"

"It was entirely fortuitous. I was coming back from that church annex where Dabronski lived, what used to be the parsonage out at Patterson's church, and I stopped at that little drugstore on the corner of Fifth and Creek streets because they had a sign in the window saying they develop film. When you come into town from the north, it's the first place you come to where they do develop film, which is undoubtedly why Dabronski left his film there as well. To get to the Fotomat I'd have had to go all the way to the west end of town and double back."

"If Dabronski left his film at the same place, whatever film he left will still be there." J.Q. actually sounded excited.

"Probably pictures of the church picnic," Shirley said with dampening calm, trying to keep her own excitement and chagrin from showing. Here she'd had a marvelous clue in her own two hands and J.Q. had had to point it out to her.

"I'll pick up the ones you left there, and we'll see," he

said, refusing to be dampened. "Next time I go to town. Tomorrow or the next day."

"I'm finished," called Allison. "Except for three things I need help on."

"Only three things," marveled Shirley.

"Problems one through five, five through ten, and ten through fifteen. That's three things," muttered J.Q. as he hoisted himself from the chair and went to offer succor.

Thursday morning brought a twenty-minute blizzard, then the skies cleared and the snow melted, leaving the ground damp and smelling like spring. Shirley took it as an omen and sang tunelessly, to everyone's dismay but her own, as she fixed breakfast while J.Q. packed Allison's lunch.

Just before noon Lawrence Brentwood called to say he had made arrangements for Charles and Gloria to be cremated locally, whenever the bodies were released. Shirley made sympathetic noises and held her breath.

"If that church they were associated with wishes to hold a memorial service, that's up to them," he said heavily. "Esther and I do not need to arrange that. We have called the attorney and arranged for him to send us a bill for whatever necessary services he performed. As to Allison's future, we have not made any decisions at this time. I presume it would not be inconvenient for Allison to stay with you for the time being."

Fighting down the alleluia that threatened to burst forth, Shirley said, "Well . . ." drawing it out in a long, dubious monosyllable. "I suppose not."

"We will be better able to make a decision when Charles and Gloria's affairs are settled," he said pompously. "When insurance has been paid, things like that."

"Um," said Shirley, struggling to sound anything but joyous. "Will you be going back to Albany?"

"Temporarily," he said. "Just temporarily."

Shirley hung up the phone and did a war dance.

J.Q., having his lunch in the kitchen, asked, "They're going home?"

"Temporarily," she quoted. "Just temporarily."

"What will you bet that's the last you see of them?"

"I'll have to talk to Numa," she bubbled. "Find out what they said to him. He'll do something sneaky, I'm sure. Get us some kind of interim paper that will lead inexorably into some kind of permanent paper. Oh, golly, J.Q. It'll be so nice to have a kid around. This particular kid around."

"Let's drive over to Creps and tell her. She'll be having lunch right now, and she's been worried."

"Sure. Sure we can. Mingy won't mind. She'll be tickled as we are. She probably cast the deciding straw, all that business about the Houghton Academy." Shirley waited impatiently for J.Q. to wrap up his sandwich; then the two of them took off in the truck, whooping like a couple of juveniles while the wheels threw gravel in all directions. Creps was only a couple of miles from the gate: a mile north on the Old Mill Road and a mile northeast on the county road, just past a private road leading off to the southwest into the old Crepmier Farm. They slowed down to approach the school decorously, searching eagerly for Allison's birdlike form among the scattered groups of young people in the half-cleared playground and along the rail fence that separated the grounds from the forest on the north.

"Where do you suppose she is?" Shirley asked as she got out and shut the truck door.

"Inside with Ms. Minging probably. Or in the little girls' room. Or hiding out along the creek, having a cry." He gestured toward the copse of cottonwoods along the creek, bare of leaves but still offering the concealment of multiple trunks and willow brush.

J.Q. went into the school, and Shirley followed, savoring the smell of it—sweeping compound and chalk and floor wax and young sweat. The smell hadn't changed at all in fifty years. Ms. Minging was in the classroom to the right, the upper-level room corresponding to grades four through six. She looked up as they came in. "Well," she said drily, "to what do I owe the honor?"

"We came to give Allison some good news," Shirley

smiled. "At least, I hope she'll think it's good news. Her aunt and uncle are leaving her with us, at least for the time being."

Ms. Minging actually grinned. "I had a hunch they might. Didn't you see her outside?"

Shirley shook her head. "We didn't find her."

Ms. Minging rose to her full five-feet-two-inches and preceded them into the hallway and thence onto the tiny portico. The Crepmier school contained only two classrooms, plus boys' and girls' toilets, a sizable office with a couch and easy chairs—which served both as infirmary and conference room—and a cavernous basement used in bad weather as lunchroom and gym. After peering around outside Ms. Minging went back to the girls' toilet, then opened the basement door and peered into the darkness. "Where did she get to?" she asked anyone within hearing. She went out to the porch once more.

"Harlan?" she called. "Betsy? Dorothea? Have you seen Allison?"

Three figures appeared in stages of dishevelment, each saying politely some variation of "No, ma'am. I don't know where she is, ma'am. I think she's down by the creek, Ms. Minging."

Ms. Minging, her two visitors trailing behind, set out for the creek, which cut diagonally across the school ground from a shallow culvert under the Crepmier drive on the southeast to a brushy gully in the northwest, a total distance of some two hundred yards. Past the fence the gully wound its way through a narrow woodland to another and deeper culvert that cut under the county road.

"There," said J.Q., pointing. "There" was a stump near the road, chair-high, with a blue lunch box open beside it.

"Allison's?" asked Shirley, who had paid no attention to what Allison's lunch box looked like.

"Allison's," affirmed J.Q., picking it up and rummaging through the contents. "She'd started her sandwich, that's all. She hadn't touched anything else."

Ms. Minging was already plodding back to the school,

181

gathering children as she went. "Please, children, I want you to think. Allison seems to have wandered off. Have any of you seen her? Have any of you heard her?"

"She was crying about her mother," said someone. "She wanted to be by herself, she said."

"There was a car," said someone else. "I heard a car."

J.Q. was coming back from the road. "The ground's moist along the shoulder. There's recent tracks there, tracks and what may be an oil stain. As though there'd been a car parked for a while. Would she have gotten into a car with anyone?"

"The Brentwoods," said Shirley through gritted teeth. "If they'd parked there. If they'd called to her. All that phone business. Was that just to mislead us? He called me while his wife picked Allison up and left with her?"

"Could have happened," he said. "But would they do that?"

"He could," she said with absolute conviction. "Oh, yes. He might figure once they got her to New York nobody would bother coming after her."

"She might have gone for a walk," offered Ms. Minging, not believing it.

"I've got to call Numa," Shirley cried. "I have the number of the hotel where the Brentwoods were staying. It's at the house. Let's get back there. Mingy, keep an eye out for her. Call me if she shows up." She was already running toward the truck, J.Q. huffing along beside her, limping on the recently healed ankle. He pulled the truck in a tight circle and sped back the way they had come.

The short distance seemed endless. The four or five minutes seemed hours. As they approached the drive Shirley saw that the red flag on the mailbox was raised. There was no reason for it to be raised unless she or J.Q. had put mail in the box. "J.Q., slow down. Did you put a letter in the box?"

"No. Not this morning."

"Slow down! The flag on the mailbox is up. It's way too early for the mail. Besides, Henry wouldn't put the flag up."

"Kids," he suggested, stopping with her window six inches from the mailbox.

She pulled the box open, reached in, and retrieved a small brown envelope. "What the hell?"

He started off again as she tore at the tightly gummed flap.

"Oh, God, J.Q. Oh, Lord. It's a ransom note. Oh, shit."

He skidded the truck to a stop and took the paper from her shaking hand. The words had been written on a plain sheet of typing paper, black block letters made with a marking pen.

"If you want to see the girl alive again, you'll see I get what belongs to me. Wait for a phone call."

"Not the Brentwoods?" he asked, unable for the moment to believe what he was seeing.

"Not unless they're in it with Gloria's murderer!" Shirley wept, tears streaming down her face. "No, J.Q. Whoever has Allison has already killed three people. Damn it. I don't know why. And I don't know who. And I don't even know if Allison's still alive. This is all crazy!"

By the time they reached the house Shirley had herself under control, control enough at least to shout at J.Q. as he started to dial the phone, "No, don't call anyone."

"The sheriff, Shirley? Botts?"

"No. Damn it, J.Q. He talks to somebody. Somebody at that church."

"It was you who told him to put that business in the paper about Allison not knowing anything."

"That wasn't what caused this. God, J.Q., by this time everybody in Ridge County knows the investigation is stalled, that nobody knows anything, that nobody's found anything. Not until yesterday. *Yesterday* I found the film in that camera. When did I tell Botts about Dabronski's camera, huh? Yesterday afternoon? The women out at the annex didn't see me take the film. Nobody else knew except Botts and you and me. You and I haven't mentioned it to anyone. Who has he mentioned it to? Can you get into town and pick up those pictures without being seen? You're kind of inconspicuous. You don't go around making a spectacle of yourself, arguing with people. . . ."

"The pictures won't be ready yet, Shirley. You only took them in yesterday. . . ."

"*Not* the ones in the camera, J.Q. The ones Dabronski left there last spring before he was killed! The ones Botts has the claim ticket to."

"Botts has it. Not us."

"I wrote down the number when I drew the facsimile of the thing." She rummaged in the desk, drawing out the paper with an exclamation. "Here. Right here. Give the woman this number. Tell her the dog chewed up the ticket, but you wrote down the number. Tell her anything. Get those pictures, J.Q."

"You think that's what the person who took Allison wants?"

"What else *is* there? Yesterday I tell Botts about film in Dabronski's camera, today somebody kidnaps Allison! What else? Maybe it's what was in his camera. Maybe it's what he left there before. I need to know who Botts talked to. Who he's seen. I can't ask him."

"Maybe I can."

"Later. Pictures first. I can't go, I have to wait for the phone call. Go get them, J.Q., please. Now!"

He left. She heard the truck speeding away, sliding on the gravel. She sat, fuming, made a pot of coffee, stalked to and fro while it dripped, poured a cup, and promptly forgot it was there. She had the terrible feeling she used to have in Washington sometimes, the feeling she had the answer to something but couldn't come up with it. "What do you think, Shirley?" Roger had often asked her, and she'd sat there with her mouth open, not knowing what she thought because of something looming in her head, throwing an enormous shadow, balking any easy opinions with a monstrous and implacable barrier. And then later, waking in the morning perhaps, or suddenly over a postprandial glass of brandy, or for no reason at all, in the shower, it would come to her, and she'd know what she thought, what she actually thought, which was sometimes much more significant than Roger had been asking for, so that his mouth would drop open in turn when she told him.

"All that?" he'd whisper. "From three reports, a novel, and some TV shows?"

"It's all there," she'd say. "Not just those things, but everything. Newspapers. Magazines. They've all been waltzing around the subject. . . ." Just as now, everything she'd done for weeks had been waltzing around the subject, the killing subject: Who shot Dabronski? Who killed Charles Maxwell and Gloria? Who took Allison and why?

Jostle her brain as she would, the information wouldn't come loose. Was Carmichael's money fiddle part of it? Maybe. Could he have killed Maxwell? A falling out among thieves? She didn't know. Would he have killed Gloria? The puzzle needed a final piece, something she hadn't thought of. She couldn't get on the phone, not this phone at least.

There was a remote phone in the office. Sometimes when she was working outside she took it out with her. There was a separate phone line coming into the bunkhouse. She'd been paying for it for years, just to keep it, because getting lines out here in the country was impossible sometimes. She didn't even know if it still worked, though it had damned well better. Leaving the kitchen door open so she could hear the house phone if it rang, she took the remote phone out, ran across the gravel drive to the bunkhouse, and plugged the phone into the bunkhouse phone jack. She returned with the remote receiver in hand, already at ear, taking it down to dial—who?

Bess Willison, the manager at the women's clinic, her mind said, making connections she hadn't even been aware of.

She got the number from information, punched it in, heard it ringing. The woman who answered wasn't Bess but someone else, someone suspicious and unwilling to give information.

"When will she be in?" Shirley demanded. "I've got to talk to her. It's an emergency."

"Lunch," the phone said. "Half an hour."

"Have her call me the minute she comes in, please. This may be a matter of life and death," she said, wracking her brain, trying to remember the bunkhouse number, finally giving up and telling her own. "Please. It's terribly important."

Then, who? Andy Manning? The phone wasn't listed under Manning. How had she called before? By calling Deitz, of course. This time the phone was answered on the second ring.

"Ms. McClintock, she's out shopping," said the spritely female voice. "This is Diane. Can I help you?"

"Diane, what did you tell me your last name is?" Shirley asked, playing a wild hunch out of extreme left field.

"Underhill," said Diane. "Diane Martha Elaine Underhill, isn't that some mouthful. Why?"

Too good, her mind said. Too good to be true. "Diane, if I paid for your time, would you come out here to the ranch and talk with me about something important? I can have a friend of mine pick you up."

"Gee, Ms. McClintock, Andy's expecting me to be here when she gets back. There's a party out at Palace Pines tonight, and we're supposed to go help cook."

"Diane, this is a matter of life and death. You may be able to help save a child's life. Can you . . . can you leave Andy a note saying you've had a family emergency? Please . . . please don't say anything in the note about coming to see me."

It took further urging, but eventually the girl agreed, saying she would bring Ms. McClintock's angel since Ms. McClintock had already paid for it and everything.

Shirley didn't know the name of the drugstore where J.Q. was going. She looked up drugstores in the Columbine yellow pages, almost missed it, punched it three times before she got it right. "A Mr. John Quentin will be coming in to pick up some film. An emergency, please have him call home at once. He's a tall man with salt-and-pepper hair and a mustache. Thank you."

She strode once more, to and fro, back and forth, so deeply drowned in supposition that she started half out of her skin when the phone rang. It was J.Q. telling her he had one set of pictures from last spring. The ones she'd dropped off yesterday for twenty-four-hour service would be in anytime.

"J.Q., don't wait for them. Please go out to Reverend Patterson's church, to the old parsonage building, and pick up a girl named Diane Underhill and bring her back out here with you. Please, J.Q., don't ask questions. I'm not even sure I know why."

Then she was off the phone once more, off it long enough for it to ring. "Bess Willison, Shirley. You called?"

"Bess, I can't tie this line up just now. Let me call you back on the other phone." She hung up her own phone, punched again from the remote. "Bess? Forgive me if I don't make much sense, but the answer to this question is terribly important. Please, describe to me the records that you keep on your abortion patients."

"Describe?"

"Paper? What color? What size? How many sheets?"

"Ah, well. At the time of the procedure there'd be four sheets, regular eight-and-a-half by eleven. Four colors: pink, blue, yellow, and green. Counseling notes on one. Lab tests on one. Physician's notes on one. Recovery notes on one. Different colors so we can see at a glance that they're all there. Then there's an informed consent sheet."

"What color?"

"The consent sheet? White."

"Heavy, like cardboard?"

"Just ordinary paper, Shirley."

"Nothing that's heavy, like cardboard?"

"Only the folder they're kept in."

She could feel blood rushing to her face then away, like a tide. "A file folder! With the patient's name typed on it?"

"That's right. The patient's name plus two color tabs to file by. Alphabetically within color categories."

"What colors would you use for . . . for someone named Delia Unger."

"Blue is U, purple is D," said Kate.

There had been a blue smear on the paper Shirley had found. "One final thing: Were any records missing after the break-in last June?"

"No," Kate replied. "We have a master list of current patients, a card index, which is kept in a safe in the back office, so we were able to check against a list of records we should have had. When we started putting things away we thought a lot were missing, but they were only thrown around and mixed up. I was surprised to find them all, quite frankly. Elsewhere in the country when these invasions have taken place records have been destroyed or stolen and then used for harrassment."

"Even though all the records were there, were any of the file folders missing?"

"Several. Missing or just trampled and torn. We did have to make out a few new folders. Mind telling me what this is all about, Shirley?"

"Later," she said. "As soon as I'm sure. I promise. Oh, Bess? The counseling notes? Would they say who the father was?"

Bess spoke for two minutes, without pause, after which Shirley hung up and sat staring at the phone, willing it to ring again.

It did not ring again. Shirley poured out the cold coffee and replaced it with a hot cupful, leaving the hot one to cool on the kitchen counter as she moved from kitchen to dining room to living room to office then back again.

The sound of a car in the drive brought her onto the porch. J.Q. And Diane, looking agitated and worried. Shirley went out to take the girl by the hand. "Please, Diane, come in. Did J.Q. tell you what's happened?"

"He wouldn't tell me anything. I thought there for a while I was being kidnapped. . . ."

Shirley barked laughter, unamused, and started toward her office, only to be stopped by J.Q., who asked, "Have you heard from them?"

"Not a word," she replied.

"Anything new?"

"I'm working on it, J.Q. I really am."

She followed Diane into the office and shut the door behind them, sitting knee-to-knee with the girl and reaching for her hand. Maximum contact: she had no time to spend building a relationship. "Look, Diane, somebody's taken Allison, Gloria Maxwell's little girl who was staying here with me. She's eleven years old, a nice little girl. Somebody's taken her and sent me a ransom note. I've got to figure out who's got her, and in order to do that, I have to figure out some other things as well. Now listen . . .

"Near where we found Ira Dabronski's bones, we found a wallet. It had a folded-up piece of paper on it, a heavy piece, almost like cardboard. I had no idea what it was until today, when I finally figured out it was a patient record folder, probably from the women's clinic. The letters we could make out on it seem to be your name. Underhill, D. for Diane."

The girl flushed red. "That bastard," she said.

"Dabronski got it when they broke in there in June, didn't he?"

Diane shifted uncomfortably, obviously trying to decide how much or how little to tell. "That Monday afternoon, after he got out of jail, he came back to the annex and said he knew all about me . . . me and somebody. Thank God Andy was out shopping! He said he'd taken my records from the clinic to prove what a bad girl I'd been. He said if I gave him money he'd forget about it. Where the hell did he think I could get any money? I don't make much, and it takes every dime I make just to live on. Mom's on social security; she doesn't have anything. I told him to go to hell; if he said anything to anybody, he'd lose his job. He yelled at me. He begged me for money. He was real strange, like hysterical, you know? Like if he didn't get money, he'd die.''

"How did he know who the man was, Diane?''

"He said he read it in the record.''

"It isn't in the record. I asked the clinic manager. She says they never put information in the record that might be harmful to the patient if the record is ever subpoenaed. They don't put the father's name in the notes. They just abbreviate. MCP. Man causing pregnancy.''

"That bastard.''

"How did he know?''

The girl flushed again, tears in her eyes. "He must have seen us.''

"You and the reverend.'' That's who it had to be. It couldn't be anyone else.

Now she was weeping angrily. "Andy told me I was nuts to have believed him. The Rev. She said just because he was holy in the pulpit didn't mean he was holy anyplace else.''

"When she was nudging you, teasing you the day I was there, that's who she was talking about? The reverend was the man who had 'needs.' ''

"He told me Bonny . . . she didn't like it. You know.''

"Diane, that's the oldest line in the world. All men learn that line while they're still in junior high, I swear to God they do. How could Dabronski have seen you?''

"We were in the back of the Rev's Mercedes,'' she confessed, shamefaced. "I guess he looked out his window and saw me get out of the car or something.''

"In the church parking lot?''

A nod. "One night, late. I thought it was too dark, but he must have seen me.''

"And you got pregnant.''

"Yes. Only it wasn't necessarily him.'' She flushed. "I had a regular boyfriend then. Not the one I have now. But I wasn't in love with the Rev or anything. I feel so stupid! He, just talked and talked and told me how much it would mean to him, how much it would help him by relieving his ten-

190

sions! He's a good-looking man. He's sexy, too. But I wasn't in love with him. I didn't tell the Rev it might not be his when I told him I needed the money for an abortion. I knew my boyfriend didn't have the money, and the Rev did. And then, afterward, I got on the pill, so *that* won't happen again. I feel so dumb.''

"I see." And she did see, dimly. Too dimly. "Did the . . . the Rev say anything to you when he gave you the money about not telling anyone, anything like that?''

"He said if the church found out, he'd be out of a job, and if he was out, I was out. I told him I wasn't going to tell. If my mom found out, I'd be out of the house! She's dead set against fooling around with married men. That's how she lost Dad, and she's got no patience with it.'' She sighed, paddled through her purse looking for a handkerchief, and brought out both handkerchief and a tissue package. She put the package on the desk beside her and wiped her eyes.

"It would have made more sense for Dabronski to call the Rev and ask for money,'' Shirley mused.

"Oh, he did! Right there, from the annex. The Rev was out of town, but the deacon had a little book with the number in it, and he called long distance. I told him he'd have to pay for the call. Nobody's supposed to use that phone for long distance. He told me to shut up or he'd make me shut up. So I went in the other room, but I listened.''

"What did you hear?''

"He must have called a hotel, because he told somebody the Rev was at the hotel at a meeting of the something or other, and it was an emergency. Then he had to wait a long time while they found the Rev, and I kept thinking about the phone bill and what Andy was going to say. Then evidently the Rev came to the phone, because Dumb-Bronski told the Rev what he'd told me, about having the record to prove what the Rev had been up to with me, and he said he needed money right then, that day, or he'd show it to the other deacons.''

"What then?"

"Then he didn't say anything for awhile, then he said he had to have money that same day. He kind of screamed it."

"And then?"

"And then nothing. I guess the Rev told him it would have to wait until he got back. Anyhow the Deacon slammed the phone down and started cussing, then I heard him making another call."

"Local call?"

She thought about this. "I guess. It didn't take him long, like it was a number he knew real well. So somebody answered and he said to the person, 'This is Ira. I've got a picture of you and John, and I think you ought to pay me for it. Stay where you are for half an hour, I'll call you back.' Then he hung up." Diane wiped her eyes.

"You and John? He didn't say John who?"

Diane shook her head.

"What did he do then?"

"He went out and got in his car and left, and that's the last time I saw him." She wiped her eyes again. "Will I get into more trouble?"

"Honey," Shirley sighed, "you've already had all the trouble you're going to have over this, I hope. Just try to keep from getting into any more, will you?" She opened the office door and went to find J.Q. to ask him to take the girl back to the church annex.

"Are you going to tell me what's going on?" he hissed.

"The first chance I get, yes. Have you got the pictures?" she hissed back.

He handed her an envelope. "These are the ones Dabronski left there before he was killed. The woman at the drugstore had to hunt for them. Lucky they'd kept them. Normally they throw out anything unclaimed after ninety days. I hope you have better luck with them than I had. They don't tell me a damned thing. I don't know what they'll show you. I'll call from town in case you need another errand."

His face was haggard, sunken around the eyes, but his voice was steady as he summoned Diane. He was as worried about Allison as Shirley was. Where was Allison? Don't think about Allison. Shirley opened the envelope and spilled the prints onto the table along with yesterday's claim ticket. She started to go after J.Q. to give it to him then heard the truck rattling over the cattleguard and knew it was too late. He'd forgotten he'd put the claim check in with the pictures, the pictures that lay on the table making no sense. Dim. Mysterious. Ghostly prints. No flash. What in hell were they? She sat down and peered at them, turning them one way and then another, trying to decide what direction was up. One was of a storefront, with a figure at one side, with parked cars reflected in the store window. It was night. A blur resolved itself into a face lighted only from the side. Okay, a woman standing at one side of a lighted store at night.

A hooker, Shirley amended to herself, making out the tight, short skirt; the short, fluffy jacket. Fur? Or feathers? The head was turned to the left, showing the right profile, dark hair making a straight line across the ear, dark glasses closing off the eyes. She leafed through the other pictures. More of the same woman. The woman with a man, clinging to his arm, leaning her face close to his.

Well, so Dabronski had liked prostitutes, precisely as Diane had said. And he had taken a few pictures, not even porno, just street shots.

The phone rang. She tripped over her feet getting to it, panting into the mouthpiece, "Yes? McClintock."

A voice, muffled. A woman's voice? Or a man? She couldn't tell.

"You've got something I want."

Mentally she scurried. Could she equivocate? Could she give J.Q. time to pick up the pictures so she could see them first? Could she risk Allison's life?

She could not. "Botts Tempe has everything I found except the film that was in Dabronski's camera."

"I want that."

Again the quick mental survey. Could she lie, say she had them, say Botts had them, say they were being picked up? Any lie she told might get Allison killed. Even the truth might do that.

"On my way home yesterday I took the film to the drugstore at the corner of Fifth and Creek streets in Columbine. The film is supposed to come back from the processor any time now, any minute. I've got the claim check in my hand. I can tell you the number on it."

"Yes."

"Five zero four dash nine nine."

"Don't go near there. If you don't get in my way, I'll turn the girl loose."

She was sure it had been a man's voice. The phone went dead. Shirley collapsed, her face wet, her mouth opening and closing like a fish as she gulped for air that didn't seem to be available. She could not call the drugstore and tell anyone there to do anything. She could not call Botts Tempe. Explanations would take too long. J.Q. was about a fourth of the way to the church by now, on his way to take Diane home, unavailable. She herself was half an hour away from town. All she could do was pray that the pictures were what was wanted, that the kidnapper would be satisfied.

What would he do? Go for the pictures, obviously. Or send someone. Probably send someone. At least there would be no question that Shirley had kept negatives or had copies. What was in the envelope would be all there was. The key to three murders. Unless that key lay under her hand now in the other pictures. The two sets might have been taken only hours or minutes apart. Shirley had done that herself, taken pictures at a party or an event until one roll of film was completely exposed, then put in a new roll of film, taken a few exposures, put the camera in its case, and not used it again for months. The completely exposed roll of film went to Fotomat. The incomplete roll lay on a shelf for a year, until some other occasion came along. Then, when that roll was developed, someone said,

"Oh, I'd forgotten about that. These are pictures of the picnic, the party, the Smith's wedding, the flower show last spring."

Where had Dabronski been during the days before he died? A church picnic the previous weekend. According to Mabel he'd had his camera there. A clinic break-in on the Saturday; no camera there. In jail on Sunday; no camera there. Out of jail by Monday noon; demanding money from Diane during the afternoon; then from the Rev; then from some third party, unknown. And he was gone by Monday night.

She went back to the pictures. Shadowed face, glassy storefronts reflecting the street, nothing to show whether it was June or January. No trees, no flowers. Blow up the photograph looking for goose bumps maybe? Evidence of a cold wind?

Something about the photograph. Something familiar. She couldn't place it. Perhaps she had seen that particular store before, that particular window; but even if she could identify it, what help would it be? There was a clock inside. Maybe ten o'clock. Maybe ten to midnight. What difference did it make?

Why had Dabronski been so desperate for money? What had happened to him to make him desperate enough to plead with Diane? To demand from the Rev? And finally to demand from someone else?

He had been arrested, released on his own recognizance, with an appearance to be made later. . . .

Maybe he had a reason to run.

She called Botts Tempe's office on the remote phone and left word for the sheriff to call her.

When she hung up, the other phone rang, shrill as a harpy's scream. She picked it up, breathing, "Yes?"

"J.Q., Shirl. Did the person call?"

She began to cry into the phone, great gulping cries. She hadn't cried this way since Marty, young Marty . . .

"I'll be there. Quick as I can. I'll be there," he said.

Then quiet again. No phone. Nothing. A vacancy as deep and endless as the one when Marty died. When Sally died.

When Bill died. A chasm. A place one wanted to sink into, giving up consciousness, giving up life.

She knocked the package off the corner of her desk, picked it up and unwrapped it. An angel made of corn-husks with a wide skirt and frilly wings. The face was painted, and it had a tinsel halo. She propped it against the wall and went to wash her face. It had been only an hour since she'd spoken to the kidnapper or the kidnapper's associate or the kidnapper's messenger, whoever that person had been. Only an hour. Not time to get hysterical yet. Not time to give up yet.

The phone again. Botts this time. Her eyes kept leaking, but she kept her voice calm. "Botts, did you do any kind of wants or warrants check on the people you arrested for breaking into the women's clinic?"

Long silence. "They were all people from right here, Shirley. They weren't strangers."

"I have a hunch that Ira Dabronski may be wanted some-where for something, Botts. I have private information that he was trying to get money out of his acquaintances the Mon-day afternoon he was released from jail. It could be that his Monday night excursion was related to that. Trying to get money. I'm told he was fairly frantic and desperate. Like a man who wanted to get out of town before he had to appear in court."

"Are you saying blackmail?"

"I don't know. Blackmail. Extortion. I think he went up to the picnic ground to try and get money out of some-body. He had something; pictures, I think. Or he said he did."

"What pictures?"

She couldn't tell him. Not until she got Allison back. "I don't know, Botts. Honestly. Find out if he's wanted any-where, will you, but don't ask me who he went to meet. I don't know who he went up there to meet. I honestly don't know," she said, hanging up.

If Patterson had been in town, Dabronski might have ob-tained money from him. The Rev didn't get back until midnight, according to Botts. Supposedly. Who did she know who could check whether he was really on that plane and not an earlier one?

Roger had an in with the airlines. Make a note to call Roger.

She was bent over, head on her knees, shaking, when J.Q. came in.

"Come on, Shirl. Come on. For God's sake, dear love, not now. We have to keep it together here. Tell me. Tell me what's been going on."

She gulped and told him, all her suppositions, all her theories, all the perhaps and maybes.

"You think Dabronski was that anxious to get out of town?"

"It's possible he'd been convicted of something before or was wanted somewhere. For blackmail or extortion maybe. Or maybe something else. Rape, maybe, or some other sexual crime. He was the type, all full of repressions and urges warring with one another. It's more likely he had an outstanding warrant on him. He was in such a tearing hurry! He may have assumed the sheriff's office would do a check on him prior to his court appearance, and he didn't want that. He demanded money from Diane. She didn't have any to give him. She told him to tell on her and the hell with him, she wasn't going to pay him to keep quiet. He called the Rev and my guess is the Rev told him the same thing and threatened him into the bargain. So he had to get money from someone else. He called someone and said he had a picture of that someone and John. That was enough, evidently, to get him killed. Which, in turn, got Charles and Gloria killed and may end up getting Allison killed. Unless the pictures in that camera are what the killer was looking for!"

He held her tightly, rocking her as though she had been a child, as she had rocked Allison.

The phone rang. J.Q. picked it up. Monosyllables, mutters, then he was back.

"She's all right," he said. "That was the man who found her. She was in the alley behind his store. Tied up, blindfolded, but she's all right, Shirl. Let's go get her."

6

ALLISON WAS TERRIFIED and sobbing. In the emergency room at the county hospital, Shirley held her, rocked her, and listened to her cry. When Botts Tempe stuck his head around the door she shook her head at him fiercely, warning him away.

When it happened for the second time he muttered, "Damn it, Shirley, if we're going to catch the bastard I've got to know what he looked like."

Shirley summoned calm like a taxi and said in an utterly unruffled voice, "Allison doesn't know. I've asked her, and she doesn't know. It was a man, he had a mustache and dark glasses, he called her by name and said he had a package for Ms. Minging. She went over to her car, and he put something over her head. She saw him for all of twenty seconds, Botts. That's literally all she knows." She was hoping calm would be contagious. She could not bear many more of Allison's hideous, gulping sobs.

"What kind of car?"

"Alison doesn't know cars. It was dark-colored and had

four doors. Period. Probably the mustache was false; it may have been a man, as she thought, or maybe a woman.''

In her lap Allison struggled. "A man!" she insisted indignantly, forgetting to cry. "He picked me up and put me in the car, and he felt like a man.'' The sobs had stopped for the moment.

"You mean he was bigger than a woman?'' J.Q. asked.

"He was hard in the chest,'' Allison howled. "Not soft like a woman. Even Shirley is softer than a man.''

Great, Shirley thought wryly. She'd always been rather proud of her chest. Not ostentatious, but nice. At least, so Martin had always thought. And Bill. "A man,'' agreed Shirley.

The doctor came in like a hummingbird, hovering, dipping his head toward his patient, sampling, zooming away again, the nurse rushing after him.

"Can we take this child home?'' Shirley cried angrily.

In a moment the doctor came zooming back with a pill bottle in one hand, comforting pats in the other. "If she has trouble sleeping,'' he said. "Try reassurance first. Cocoa and cuddling. That's best. Use these as a last resort. She may be sick to her stomach. He used an anesthetic on her to knock her out. He didn't use much obviously. No physical harm. Not even a bruise. Mostly scared, and I don't blame you, sweetheart, not at all!'' He ruffled Allison's hair and was gone again. Outside an ambulance siren approached and wailed itself into silence, like a tired baby.

"When did he knock you out, Allie?'' asked J.Q.

"When he put me in the car. He put this stuff over my face.'' She sobbed again. "I want to go home.''

Shirley stood up, the child over her shoulder. "We're going, honey. Right now. I'm so sorry this happened. I'm so sorry we haven't figured out who's doing all these awful things so we can put a stop to it.''

"You should have called me the minute you got that note,'' growled Botts, striding along beside her as she carried Allison down the hall. It was a muted growl, for hospital use.

"You and me are going to have to talk about that, McClintock!"

She snarled at him, "I couldn't call you, damn it, Tempe. You told somebody about my finding Dabronski's film, and that's what got her taken in the first place."

"I didn't tell anyone about those pictures except my own men."

"Well, then one of your own men is in on this."

J.Q. put his hand on her arm. "This is neither the time nor the place," he said. "Sheriff Tempe, I'd suggest you give Shirley and Allison a chance to get home and get sorted out, and then if you need to know something, I'm sure either one of them would be happy to talk to you."

"Go find out who picked up the pictures at the drugstore," suggested Shirley angrily. "Whoever picked them up is in this thing up to the neck!"

Botts Tempe threw up his hands, spun around, and left them, striding off down the hospital corridor as though for an overdue appointment with the governor. Allison, still snuffling, lay across Shirley's shoulder as they followed him. When they got to the Wagoneer the sheriff's car was pulling away with squealing tires.

"He's mad," said Allison with a certain satisfaction.

"Yes, he is," agreed J.Q. "He wants to catch the person who did this, and he thinks we're not helping."

"I didn't want to tell him anything anyhow," she sniffled. "He yells. He yelled at Mommy when he came and arrested her that time."

"Did you have anything to tell him?"

"Only about when I was playing possum."

Shirley took a deep breath. "You were playing possum while the person had you tied up?"

Allison nodded, her nose making wet smears on Shirley's neck. "He had this thing over my head, like a bag, only I could breathe through it all right after I woke up. And he had me tied up, so I couldn't do anything. And I didn't want him to know I was awake, because he might, you know, put me to sleep again."

"Very sensible," said J.Q.

"So I just laid there very quiet. Like a possum. And I heard him."

"What did you hear?" Shirley asked, setting the child upright on her lap and fishing for a handkerchief. Before she found one Allison wiped her nose and eyes on her sleeve, emerging somewhat streaked.

"I heard him breathing. He breathed very hard, like he'd been running. And the car door opened. . . ."

"You were still in the car?"

"I think I was on the floor in the back. It was sort of cramped." She stopped, her chin quivering.

"And the car door opened," prompted J.Q., giving her no time to weep.

"And somebody else got in. I heard somebody say, 'Is that it?' And then they tore some paper. I thought maybe you'd paid ransom for me and the money was wrapped up."

"They didn't ask for money, sweetie. Did you hear anything else?"

"I heard one person say, 'This has to be it,' and the other one said, 'He said pictures.' And then the other one said, 'This one is all there is. This has to be it. Let the kid go.' And the car door opened and shut again, and then the car started, and we drove not very far, going around corners, and then it stopped and somebody pulled me out of the car. . . ."

"With you playing possum all this time?" asked J.Q.

"I was. And somebody put a hand on my neck, I guess to see if I was breathing, and went away. I heard the car go away, and then I started yelling."

"She was left behind the bakery on Sixth," Shirley told J.Q. "The owner heard her, came out and found her, took the bag off her head but was afraid to take the tape off her eyes and wrists for fear he'd hurt her, so he called the ambulance. That's how she ended up at the hospital."

"Only I told him to call you," said Allison. "And he promised me he would."

202

"He called," said J.Q. "He told us you'd be at the hospital, and we got there as fast as we could."

"These voices," said Shirley. "Would you say they were men's voices or women's voices or what?"

Allison shook her head sadly. "I knew you'd ask me, so I really tried to pay attention, honest I did, Shirley, but I couldn't hear! There was this thing around my head, and I was all scrunched down trying not to breathe too hard, and they were kind of whispering, like they were afraid they'd wake me up. It could have been a man and a woman or two men. I couldn't tell."

"You did very well," said J.Q. "Very well. But you're sure it was a man in the car when he grabbed you?"

"Yes, because he picked me up and held me against him, and he was just, you know, solid in front. He didn't have any boobs."

"Is that what you call them?" mused Shirley.

"That's what the boys at school call them," she said with some dignity. "Mom says breasts, and she said I'd get them pretty soon, but the kids at school call them all sorts of things. Especially the boys."

"I guess it doesn't matter what they're called so long as we know he didn't have any," J.Q. offered, his lips quivering with amusement or withheld anger or some other unidentifiable emotion. "Shirley, do you think this is the end of this thing?"

She shook her head. "It's the end of Allison's getting involved, that's for sure. It's not the end of my being involved, however. I'm going to get the . . ." She subsided, letting the anger drain away, hugging Allison until she squeaked. "Alli, love, where's your other shoe? Did we leave it in the hospital?"

"It got caught under the car seat when I was scrunched in there. I guess when he pulled me out, he didn't notice. He was kind of in a hurry."

"He must have seen that," said J.Q. "He had to."

"I didn't," Shirley said grimly. "Not until this minute. And if I didn't, then maybe he didn't either. I hope."

"You don't think it might be a good idea for you to let Botts Tempe take it from here? I mean, he is paid to catch murderers."

"Botts may do as he damned well pleases, but he'd better hurry or there will be nothing left for him to catch."

Not long after they reached home Allison fell into an exhausted sleep on the couch. Shirley covered her with a blanket and left her there. Then she and J.Q. went into the kitchen, made themselves some hot tea, and sat down at the table. Shirley had her notebook, the one she had written the questions in, and she wanted to go over them with J.Q.

"It seems like a month ago," she said. "Everything has happened too fast. There hasn't been any time to think."

"Read me the list," J.Q. said. "You must have solved some of it."

"Oh, I have. Number one was why nobody reported Dabronski missing. We know why. Because someone removed his car, his clothes, and made it look as if he'd gone of his own accord."

"Someone who knew him."

"Yes. Someone who knew where he lived, what room he had. Someone who knew him."

"What's the second question?"

"Who had the opportunity to retrieve the arrow. A lot of people had the opportunity, but very few could have known where. Since I didn't tell anyone specifically it had to be someone Botts Tempe told. Or someone the chopper pilot told, though that would be pretty farfetched. He was from Denver. The men Botts had with him weren't from Columbine. We do know it wasn't the Maxwells, either of them, but it could have been virtually anyone else provided someone told them where. Maybe that wasn't a good question. Good questions ought to lead somewhere, and this one hasn't."

"All right, what about number three?"

"That is a good question. Why didn't the murderer use a

204

gun on Charles? I call the murderer *Jones*. Why didn't Jones go on using a gun?''

"Noise?"

"Use a silencer.'' She thought for a momont. "You do have a point. The reason might have been that he killed Dabronski up in the kills, where there are gunshots all the time, but he killed the Charleses in town, where a gunshot might attract attention. Except that it doesn't explain Gloria. Put that down as a theory."

"Number four?"

"Number four was the warehouse fire. I know the answer to that one. It was arson, yes, probably connected to this case though not certainly. Number five is where did Dabronski get the $4000 he was carrying, and I've postulated the answer to that. He got it as extortion or blackmail from the person who killed him. My last question, number eight, what the claim checks were for, I know the answer to. That leaves numbers six and seven. Number six is still a good question. Why was Gloria killed?"

"Tell me again what Diane told you about that conversation she overhead. The part about 'I have a picture of you and John.' ''

"That was it. 'I have a picture of you and John, and I think you ought to pay me for it.' ''

"There are certain implications there,'' mused J.Q. "Such as that the person receiving the call isn't supposed to know John or be with John.'' He rinsed out his cup, filled it with water from the tap, and drank thirstily.

"I've been listing all the Johns I know. You, J.Q. John Fogg. John Abernathy at the newspaper.''

"How about the church? There are bound to be a few among the members.''

"Among the deacons. One at least. What did Mabel tell me? John . . . John Brown. Of Brown's Equipment.''

"Why would someone not want to be seen with him?''

"Why would someone not want to be seen with you? Or John Fogg?'' She stirred her cooling tea. It had leaves floating in it. She fished them out and dumped them in the saucer.

"Unless . . . say he was calling Charles Maxwell. Or Mike Carmichael. Suppose John Fogg was in on the fiddle at the bank. Suppose Dabronski got to know about it somehow. He was a deacon. The fiddle was over church property. We know he was a sneak. Maybe he snuck around and overheard something."

"Do you really think John Fogg is fiddling the accounts at the savings and loan?" asked J.Q., one eyebrow cocked.

"No, damn it."

"I don't either."

"Maybe it was sexual misconduct! Dabronski was calling a woman, not a man. He has seen her with someone named John, maybe in a compromising situation. I wouldn't put it past him to take pictures in the church parking lot. Maybe Diane and the Rev gave him the idea. Somebody with John Fogg. Somebody with Deacon Brown. Somebody with somebody else named John."

"Where did you put the pictures he did take? The ones of the prostitute."

Shirley returned to her office, retrieved the photos from her desk drawer, and carried them back to the kitchen where J.Q. was now making toasted sandwiches. When he had browned the bread to his satisfaction he put the assemblage on plates, fished his reading glasses out of his pocket, and perused the pictures while consuming rye bread and melted cheese with onions and green chiles.

Shirley broke off a chunk of her sandwich and nibbled at it without appetite. "J.Q., Allison said the person who took her—or maybe the other one—said something about 'There's only one.' Only one picture, do you suppose? Before I took out the film I noticed there had been ten exposures."

"Maybe only one picture that the kidnapper was interested in. Plus nine others. Nine church picnics maybe."

"So if these pictures are from the roll he took just before that one, then these might be of the same subject matter— the same as the first picture on the subsequent roll of film."

He stared at her. Her eyes had opened very wide. Her face

206

had that concentrated expression he had learned to either delight in or despair at. "What?"

"Wait. If . . . if the picture the kidnapper got is the same, more or less, as these pictures, then possibly what Dabronski said on the phone wasn't 'I've got a picture of you and John,' it was 'I've got a picture of you and *a* john.' A john. A client, a what would you say?"

"Client, I guess. But if the person being called were the hooker, what difference would that make?"

"Because maybe she's not supposed to be a hooker, J.Q.! Because she's somebody respectable. Somebody connected to this whole case. Arlette Carmichael. Gloria Maxwell. John Fogg's young wife. Somebody connected to the church somehow. Who does that look like?" She went back to the office at a dead run and returned with a magnifying glass. "Who? God, does that look like Elise Fish?"

He shook his head. "Shirley, I can't say whether the woman in this picture is either of the women I saw in that van the day they picked you up, and I don't know Elise Fish."

"This woman could be wearing a wig. She's definitely wearing a lot of makeup."

"Possibly a wig. Maybe. Damn. You need an expert on this. You need somebody who can do noses or something. All you've got is a profile. Her hair covers her ears. She's even wearing dark glasses."

"Maybe in the other picture she took her glasses off. Maybe she even had her clothes off. Who the hell knows? If this is true, though, it answers my question number seven. Where did Dabronski get X, the thing everyone was looking for? For a while there I thought X was the record folder from the women's clinic. The real X was a photograph. He got it on Colfax Avenue in Denver when he was pursuing his extracurricular activities among Denver's working girls." She sighed and sat back, finishing the last of the sandwich. "I don't know enough about the people, J.Q."

"What kind of person are you looking for?"

She thought about this. "I'm looking for a woman, or for someone maybe related to the woman, a husband or brother.

The woman is respectable, but she has a guilty secret, probably to do with prostitution. Dabronski called her and threatened her, and she showed up later—or her man did—with $4000 and a gun. Then, later, she—or her man—killed Charles Maxwell by shooting him with an arrow because she thought Charles had whatever the incriminating material was. And, later yet, the same person shot Gloria because they thought she knew where it was. In between all that this same person or persons retrieved an arrow, burned down a warehouse, searched our house, searched the Maxwell house, and later on kidnapped Allison.''

''It works out better with two people, doesn't it?''

''It really does,'' she admitted. ''Now if we just had some suspects.''

''Pretend we do. Who would you pick?''

''Arlette and Mike Carmichael. I already pretty well know he's a crook. And Mike was associated with the sale of that house to the church, so Dabronski probably knew him. He could have met Arlette, or at least seen her with Mike, enough to recognize her if he saw her . . . elsewhere.''

''Who else?''

''Elise Fish and her husband.''

''Why them?''

''Because I don't like them. Because Dabronski knew them both, and because Elise is just the type. She's got that puritanical reputation to maintain in Columbine. She'd be particularly susceptible to blackmail if it was her.''

''Do you really think it could be her?''

''Do I think she could be a prostitute? No. Not unless she's got a split personality. Maybe she's one of those multiple ones you read about. But maybe she could have been with someone named John.''

''Who else? Any possiblity?''

''John Fogg and his young wife. That's really reaching, though. I've known John for a thousand years. His new wife is too young for him, but everyone says she's a perfectly nice woman. Or maybe it isn't John's wife, it's John's niece, his sister's daughter. John doesn't have any children, and he's always been fond of his sister's kids."

"So what do you do now?"

She shook her head. "None of this feels right, J.Q. We're leaving too many things out."

"Like what?"

"Like why Patterson came out here that day. Unless . . ."

"Unless?"

"Unless he suspected that the body I'd found was Dabronski. Unless he knew something or had a hunch Dabronski had been up to no good. Then he might have come looking for verification."

"You mean, someone in the congregatation told him Dabronski was extorting money? Or trying to?"

"Or told him Dabronski wasn't what he pretended to be." She laughed harshly. "The only thing I can figure out to do that might be helpful is to go into Denver, park on Colfax Avenue, and see if we recognize anyone."

"They wouldn't be there now," he said. "Not now."

"You're right, J.Q. Whoever it was wouldn't be there now."

Shirley lay awake most of the night, unable to concentrate on anything much. Toward dawn she fell asleep and did not wake until midmorning. While she was in the shower she heard the phone ring, only twice, which probably meant J.Q. was still in the house. When she was dressed she found him and Allison in the kitchen; Allison looking tearstained but alert, J.Q. looking anything but.

"The sheriff called," he announced. "Some teenage kid picked up the pictures from the drugstore. Nobody in the drugstore ever saw him before. The kidnapper probably picked him up along the road, offered him a few bucks to pick up the pictures, then took him back where he found him."

"One strike," muttered Shirley, giving Allison a hug.

"Dabronski was wanted in North Carolina for assault and for extortion," J.Q. went on. "Evidently he used to threaten

209

women that if they didn't have sex with him, he would hurt their children. Sometimes he demanded money as well.''

''Assault?''

''On a child,'' said J.Q. ''That is, according to the sheriff.''

''Nice guy to have as a deacon of a church,'' Shirley said, dumbfounded. ''Was his name really Ira Dabronski?''

''That's the person the warrants were for. Botts Tempe says the North Carolina police were very happy to learn that he's dead.''

''One hit,'' said Shirley. ''Allison, J.Q. It's time we put an end to this thing. I'm going to town to see some people. While I'm gone, I don't want either of you out of the sight of the other except to go to the bathroom. Understand?''

''You think it might happen again?'' asked Allison, shivering.

''I do not. I simply don't want you alone. Not for more than half a minute. I don't want to have to worry about you, either one of you, understand?''

J.Q. said solemnly that he understood. After a glance at his face, so did Allison.

Shirley went into her bedroom and put on her go-to-meeting clothes. Dress boots, a warm skirt, turtlenecked sweater, and tweed jacket. Just in case the day turned cold, she took along her raincoat.

As she went out through the kitchen, J.Q. said, ''Dressed for business there, Shirley.''

''Dressed to kill,'' she said. She meant it.

Her first stop was at John Fogg's office. She did not have an appointment, but she suggested most strongly that the receptionist ask Mr. Fogg if he had time to see her. Mr. Fogg did have time.

He looked so harried when she got into his office that she felt sorry for him.

''More than just that one, huh, John?''

''I've found six so far.''

''Does he know you've found out?''

''Not yet. I've asked for some federal help to find out

210

where he's got the money hidden away. I don't want him to run before we locate the money. I think they've tapped his phone and are watching his mail."

"I'm sure Charles Maxwell was in on it."

"I know damned well he was. He was the agent for all six sales I've found so far."

"I had an idea about this, John."

"I should've known," he said bitterly. "I thought you just came by to commiserate."

"I got to thinking what I'd have been planning if I'd been Carmichael and Maxwell. Originally I thought it was a limited kind of thing, one where they'd take the extra interest for a few years and then pay the money back when the balloon payment came due. However, the more I think about it, the more I think Maxwell and Carmichael would have stayed with their jobs, stayed with the con, sold as many properties that way as they could, then, when they had a million or so in the bank, they take it and run."

"You mean, at the end of the five years . . ."

"I mean whenever they had as much as they thought they could get away with. You say you've found six. What's the total of the supposed balloon payments?"

"Million and a couple hundred thou."

"Carmichael might figure that's enough to set him up in Mexico."

"I'll alert the federal people."

"They've probably already thought of it."

"I wouldn't be too sure, Shirley. This was a new one on them."

"Are you grateful to me, John?"

"Oh, sure, sure. Nothing I like better than being told one of my loan officers is a crook."

"Grateful enough to do me a favor?"

"If I can, Shirley."

"What do you know about Reverend and Mrs. Patterson, and Dr. and Mrs. Fish?"

"You mean financially?"

"I mean anything, John. I've been away from Columbine

211

the greater part of my life. You've stayed here. I've never lived in town. You have. You were married here, your wife took part in social kinds of things before she died. Maybe your current wife does, too.''

''She does, yes. She likes the gossip. She tells me a lot of it. Mary did, too, when she was alive. I'm just not sure that I know anything helpful. You know Mrs. Patterson and Mrs. Fish are sisters.''

''I know that, yes.''

''They grew up over in Wallace, then the family moved here where the girls were in high school. Watson was their maiden name. George Watson was their father. Can't remember what his wife's name was. They were nice people, ran a little grocery store. That's why they came to Columbine, some chain bought out their store in Wallace—it was right on the highway when the new road was built—so they moved here to start another one. We held the mortgage on their store and their house, as a matter of fact.''

''The sisters don't get along. Do you know anything about that?''

He drummed his fingers on the desk, trying to remember. ''Mary told me about that. Something to do with Orrin Patterson. Handsome man now; even handsomer when he was younger. Something about Bonny coming home from Kansas City and taking Orrin away from her sister.''

''That's all it is, jealousy?''

''More to it than that, but I can't remember what.'' He furrowed his brow and scowled at his desk. ''I'll tell you who would know. My secretary. You remember Phyllis Benson?'' He went to the door and spoke softly to someone just outside. When the woman came in Shirley recognized her as a schoolmate from years ago. She had been a year or so behind John and Shirley, but she remembered Shirley when they were introduced.

''Phyl's mom and dad lived next door to the Watsons,'' said John.

''Two houses down,'' corrected Phyllis.

"Phyl, tell the story about Bonny and Elise Watson, about Bonny taking her sister's boyfriend."

Phyl looked sideways at Shirley.

"That's all right. I want Shirley to hear it."

Phyllis repeated what John had said about Bonny taking Orrin Patterson away from Elise, but then she went on, "Mrs. Watson used to talk to my mother about her daughters. According to her, Elise was furious, of course, but it wasn't just that Bonny had stolen her fiancé. It was a question of morals according to Mrs. Watson. Elise had always been a churchgoer, you know. Always been a little better than anyone else, at least in her own eyes. She was in my class in school, and if there'd been a holiness sweepstakes, she'd have won it, so of course she thought she was the best possible candidate for a minister's wife. And here came the sinful sister, making off with the reverend!"

"Sinful sister!" said John. "That's it. She'd been a model, or a dancer? Nude photos? Something like that."

"Something like that. I'm not sure Mrs. Watson ever said definitely what it was that Elise objected to so strongly. Maybe she didn't even know. I asked Elise once myself what Bonny had done that was so awful, and she wouldn't tell me. She just shut her mouth the way she did, like a rattrap, and said Bonny had no right to pass herself off as a proper minister's wife."

"Where did this sinfulness take place?"

"Oh, wherever it was Bonny had gone when they got out of school. Kansas City, I think. St. Louis maybe."

Shirley thanked them both and took herself out of the bank. Mike Carmichael was at his desk, and she waved cheerily at him as she went out the door.

Next stop was the Living Church annex where Shirley found Andy and Diane in the kitchen, wrist-deep in meatloaf. "It's for Sunday," Andy told her as she plopped globs of the aromatic mixture into one of an endless series of loaf pans. "There's a church supper."

"Could I see Diane alone for a moment?" Shirley asked,

taking the girl by the arm and drawing her out into the hall without waiting for Andy's permission.

"What now?" asked Diane. "I hope you're not going to get me into any more trouble." She straightened a stack of church papers on the table beside her then wiped her forehead with a wrist. "I guess I got myself in. It's not fair to blame you."

"No trouble. A little embarrassment maybe. I need to know some personal details. I want to know what Reverend Patterson said to you about his wife's sex life."

Diane's mouth dropped open. Shirley nodded in confirmation. "It would really help, Diane. That is, if he said anything at all."

"But you said that was just, you know, a kind of line."

"It probably was. But there may have been some truth in it, too, and I really need to know."

Diane blushed, twiddled her hair, bit her lip, finally blurted, "He said she wasn't normal. He said she couldn't get warmed up like a normal woman. He said she had to have . . . I forget. I think he said *unusual stimuli* or something like that."

"What did you think he meant?"

"At first I thought she was into . . . you know. Like in the porno books. Being whipped or something. But then when I thought it over I decided he meant something like a pearl necklace might steam her up some, or some sapphire earrings. Something like that."

"Bonny likes jewelry."

"She has a lot of it. A lot of it she bought for herself, too. She keeps it hidden from him."

"How do you know that?"

Diane laughed. "Don't try to keep secrets from the cleaning lady. When you clean a place you find all kinds of things. You find people's birth control and their guns and their dirty books. Andy and me were cleaning over at the Palace Pines place once way last winter—Bonny's regular people didn't show up or something. She had this stuff in a shoebox in her closet, down at the bottom, and I was cleaning the closet. I thought the box was empty, so I started to throw it out, but the top came off, and this stuff fell out. Pins and rings and earrings wrapped up in pieces of tissue paper. Real ones, too. She came in and saw me."

"And what did she say?"

"She laughed. She said they were her secret hoard, not to tell the Rev."

"So he didn't give them to her?"

"If he'd given them to her, they wouldn't have been secret!" She fiddled with the stack of papers again, drawing Shirley's eyes to them.

Shirley picked up the top copy and stared at it. Pictures of a church picnic. Mabel Brubacher serving pie. Reverend Patterson hugging his wife. "Diane, who took these pictures?"

"I don't know. Different people. They bring them in, and the Rev picks which ones go in the church paper."

"Can I have a copy?"

"You can have the stack. I keep dusting them, but nobody ever reads them. There's a whole year's worth there."

Shirley took the stack, putting it under her arm. "Diane, is the Rev gone a lot at night?"

"He goes out of town a lot. I don't think he's gone unless he's out of town."

"How about Bonny? Does she go out a lot at night?"

"When the Rev's gone. Sure. She goes into Denver to movies or a play. He doesn't like movies much, so she goes when he's out of town."

"How do you know?"

"I told you she says I remind her of her little sister. She tells me stuff. We talk about movies."

"Does she mostly go with someone? Or alone."

"No. She always takes somebody with her. She says it wouldn't look right, her going out alone at night. She always goes with somebody."

"Who?"

"Oh, sometimes she goes with Arlette Carmichael. Arlette's a member of the church. And she used to go with that woman who got killed, the little girl's mother, Gloria Maxwell.''

Shirley's mouth dropped open and threatened to lock in that position. "You didn't mention that before."

Diane bridled. "You didn't ask me. You got me all upset about the Rev and me but you didn't ask me anything about Gloria Maxwell."

As indeed she had not.

Her third stop was at Botts Tempe's office where she asked the deputy to show her the arrow that had killed Charles Maxwell. He, after a few obligatory disclaimers, got it out of a locked cupboard and laid it on the counter for her perusal.

"This is the way you found it," Shirley asked, fingering the crumpled vanes. "Before the doctor took it out of the body."

"I wasn't there," he said, "but the sheriff said it was all messed up. Of course, it had been taken out of the deer, so that would have messed it up some."

Shirley merely nodded, not correcting him. The head of a hunting arrow unscrewed from the shaft so the shaft could be withdrawn without destroying the vanes. Of course, not everyone knew that. The vanes on the arrow before her were broken as though they'd been put in a vise.

"What are you smiling at?" the deputy asked.

"At my own stupidity," she said. "At all the dead ends I've been exploring. At how much of Botts's time I've wasted."

She went back to her car in a daze, dumped the contents of her purse on the seat beside her, and flipped through them to find the envelope J.Q. had picked up from the drugstore. She spent several minutes staring at one of the photographs, then took the Denver phone book out of the backseat where she always kept it for just such emergencies, and spent some time going through the listings for photographic specialists.

She called Allison from a phone booth at the gas station. "Allison, sweetie, I need to know something."

"I don't know very much today, Shirley. I feel sort of tired and dumb."

"I know the feeling, love. What I want to know is, did your mom go shopping with her friend at night, mostly?"

"Mostly at night. After supper. She'd tell me she was going shopping with her friend, and I should go to bed or do my homework in my room. And not to let anybody in. You know."

"And that was when your dad was out of town, mostly."

"Yes. When he was home she didn't go out. Unless she went with him."

"Thanks, love. Put J.Q. on the phone, will you?"

"Shirley, what are you doing?"

"I'm calling you to say I'll be back sometime today. I have to go into Denver, J.Q. Take care of Allison."

"What are you up to?"

"Solving this thing, love. I'm tired of it. Tired of people doing nasty things to other people. Tired of people bothering me, bothering Allison."

"Shirley, you won't get yourself into any trouble, will you? Not without my being there."

"No trouble, J.Q. One photographer, and if everything works out, back home. Thaw out something good for supper."

She talked to herself during the fifty-mile drive to town. When she returned several hours later she talked to herself all the way back. Beside her on the seat lay a large brown envelope clipped to an invoice marked "paid."

She drove through the Palace Pines, past the Winterburn house. She stopped in Columbine to speak to Botts Tempe briefly, imperatively.

Then she went home to dinner.

"Let's have some wine," she suggested to J.Q. "You've got spaghetti made, so let's have some of that dago red you bought last month."

"Shirley, that's a Chianti classico, and only a reverse snob or a wino would say dago red."

"Right. Mark that down, Allison. You must never say dago red."

"I don't even know what it is," complained Allison, grinding away at the cheese grater.

"Right. So it should be. There is no such thing. Would you like to have some wine with us? You may have half a glass, if you like."

"Is wine good for kids?" she asked doubtfully. "Mommy always said alcohol wasn't good for kids."

"Learning to drink wine is good for kids," said Shirley. "Learning to drink in moderation, an occasional beer, wine with meals, that's good for kids. I don't think hard liquor is good for anybody quite frankly, though there are times when a Scotch does much to ameliorate the struggles of life."

"Shirley drinks Scotch when she's impossible," remarked J.Q., biting a test strand of spaghetti.

"Mommy drank," sighed Allison, taking a wet-finger taste of the grated cheese.

"Because she was lonely," Shirley said sternly. "It's important to have many interests so that when one is alone, one need not turn to alcohol or drugs or some other dangerous pastime."

"Shirley should have been a schoolteacher," said J.Q. "Or perhaps a preacher. She gets very pedantic."

"What's pedantic?"

"Teacherish," said Shirley. "Indeed I do. J.Q., is that ready? I'm starved."

They dished up the spaghetti and sauce and the cheese and the salad J.Q. had ready in the refrigerator. They drank wine. Allison drank part of her half glass though she wrinkled her nose when she tasted it. They did the dishes; they played Monopoly. About nine o'clock Allison yawned, and they told her to go on to bed.

Shirley checked to be sure she was asleep, then made a phone call.

"You're being very mysterious," muttered J.Q.

"I called Botts Tempe. He's coming out."

"Why here?"

"Why not here? I stopped by his office this afternoon on my way home. Botts couldn't see me then, and he had a dinner date he couldn't break. Once I got home I didn't intend to leave again soon. We agreed I'd call him after Allison went to bed, and he'd come out."

"Have you solved it?"

"I think so, J.Q. Only thing is, I'm not sure whether I'm glad or miserable."

Botts drank bourbon. Shirley and J.Q. stayed with the wine they'd been drinking with dinner. J.Q. built a fire in the stove and left the doors open so they could see the flames.

"So," said Botts when these preliminaries were taken care of.

"So, Botts, I'm going to tell you a story. Not one I like much. You may be able to pull it apart later on, though I don't think so.

"The story starts with this lousy economy. It starts with the oil bust, with people moving out of the state, with unemployment going up, with real-estate people unable to sell houses. A lot of people are hurting, Botts. People who were living very well but who are now going broke. No money. None at all.

"Now it's a fairly common thing for women who have been living pretty well on their husband's income to take a job if and when the husband loses his."

"Are you going somewhere with this, Shirley? Or are you just making noises?"

"Bear with me, Botts. I'll connect it all up.

"I was talking about women taking jobs. However, some women have never been trained to do anything. And they've been led by their husbands or families to believe they're not capable of doing anything. If a woman like that wants to earn a little money, or a lot, there's always one thing she can do if she's a mind to. She can turn to the so-called oldest profession. Lots of housewives and college students, so I'm told,

219

earn a little on the side. You'd know about that more than I would, Botts.''

"If you're asking me do married women and college girls turn some tricks for money, yes they do. And usually I try to scare the pants off 'em and not prosecute when it becomes a legal matter.''

"Right. Of course, Columbine's a small town. If you were well-known in this community, you wouldn't turn your tricks here. You'd go somewhere else, to the nearest city, for example. Particularly if it was only fifty miles away. Less than an hour on the highway.''

"Who are we talking about here, Shirley?''

"Well, two of the people I think we're talking about here, Sheriff, are Arlette Carmichael and Gloria Maxwell. There is at least one more person who also takes part. I don't think either Gloria or Arlette had the know-how to begin their . . . careers on their own. I think they both were initiated by someone else.''

"A pimp?''

"Not in the usual sense, no, Botts. I'll get to that in a minute. Now I was pretty slow to catch on to this, I'll admit. It isn't the kind of thing I expect to run into or know anything much about. Because of that I didn't connect up a number of facts I should have connected up early on. One: Gloria had quite a bit of money in tens and twenties hidden in her bedside table. Two: Charles was broke. They were living on their credit cards until the cards were cancelled. Three: Gloria was a drinker. She needed cash to buy liquor. Four: Gloria evidently bought stuff for Allison's birthday with cash even though she didn't buy groceries because, she said, Charles didn't give her any money. In other words she had a source of cash and needed a source of cash that Charles wasn't supposed to know about.

"Arlette wasn't quite that badly off. Mike Carmichael had his salary from the savings and loan, but according to his boss, he was in up to his ears with real-estate investments

220

that had turned sour. So I think we can be pretty sure Arlette was short of cash, too.

"Allison says her mother went 'shopping' at night with someone. I don't think the someone was Arlette, because Allison says her mother wasn't that fond of Arlette. I think it was someone else. Someone Gloria giggled about. Someone associated with the Living Church."

Botts said angrily, "Now look here, Shirley . . ."

"Botts, I can give this information to you, as the sheriff, or I can give it to the police in Columbine or to the state police. If you want to leave, I can call them."

He subsided, rumbling.

"I got this information from Gloria's sister. Gloria was associated with someone from the church. Esther thought it might be a man. I think it was a woman. Allison said the person her mother used to call was probably a woman.

"Charles Maxwell and Mike Carmichael had a scam going that was due to pay off any time. I thought for a long time that their business had some connection to the murders, but I was wrong. Their crime was unconnected to the other thing. John Fogg knows what they were up to; he's already called in the federal banking people. Mike Carmichael doesn't know he's being investigated, however, so you can't go roaring off talking to him about this. Mike thinks he's going to cash in a very large amount sometime soon, but the only thing that has to do with this case is that it explains who's responsible for the final search that took place at the Maxwell house. Carmichael did that in order to remove the incriminating files. Both he and Maxwell were living from day to day, using up every dollar's worth of credit they had in expectation of cashing in. They were trying to make a last few sales maybe. That's probably what Charles was doing on the western slope, and even after Charles was dead Mike tried to make one final sale, to me.

"I don't think Charles knew what Gloria was up to. If he had known, I think he would have stopped her, if for no other reason the fact that her being arrested for prostitution might call attention to him. Charles didn't want any publicity. Charles just wanted to take the money and run.''

"You haven't said one word about the murders!"

"I'm about to. Ira Dabronski was a twisted, warped man who had all kinds of sexual hangups. He had a record of extortive rape. He had a record of assault on a child. He read exploitation magazines. He went to prostitutes. And we find this man serving as a 'deacon' in a conservative church, paid a salary to act as a kind of servant-chauffeur for the minister of that church and that man's wife.''

"How much of this is just conjecture?''

"Little or none. Ira went to prostitutes. We have a witness to that. Ira was interested in kinky sex. We have a witness to that. Ira was arrested for an entirely unrelated offense—except that this offense also has overtones of sexual dominance and rape—and a hearing date was set. People who rape women and get them pregnant or rape them by forcing them to continue pregnancy are the same kind of people, at least in my opinion. Ira knew there was a warrant for his arrest in North Carolina, and he was afraid that warrant would come to light if he were tried. He needed money to leave town.

''He tried to blackmail a young woman who had an abortion at the women's clinic. Ira saw her patient record when he invaded the clinic, and he convinced the young woman that he actually had that record.''

"I didn't know that!''

"No, and I'm not going to tell you who she is until I have your word you're going to treat her gently, Botts. Her part in this isn't relevant except to show what Dabronski was trying to do. She didn't pay him anything. However, what happened next is relevant, and I don't want you losing your temper.''

Botts took a long drink and simmered.

"Ira then called Reverend Patterson and demanded money from him on the grounds that the reverend had caused the young woman's pregnancy. Botts, don't say a damned word, I have a witness, and I don't want you yelling at me."

"You have a witness?"

"I do. I have the girl herself. The reverend, to put it vulgarly, wasn't getting any in the home pasture so he grazed across the fence."

Silence.

"Can I get you a refill?" J.Q. asked the sheriff.

"Yeah," Botts grunted. "I guess I need it."

"Can I go on?" asked Shirley.

"Go on."

"The reverend was in Kansas City when Dabronski called him. He told Dabronski he'd have to wait until he, the reverend, got home on the following day. This happened on Monday afternoon, Botts. Right after Dabronski got out of jail."

"And the reverend was out of town."

"He was."

"Well, all right then."

"So Ira then called another person and said, 'I have some pictures of you and a john, and I think you ought to pay me for them. I'll call you back.' We have a witness to that phone call."

Botts did not comment. He took a swallow of his drink and stared into the fire.

"So Ira Dabornski called his victim back and arranged to meet her at the picnic ground at Redstone Point. She paid him four thousand dollars, and she probably expected to get the pictures in return. Then—then something went wrong. Maybe he suggested that the woman have sex with him, there, right then. That was his pattern, and I think it could have happened. Maybe he told her she would have to pay more later. Whatever he did he infuriated her, and she shot him. She wasn't a good shot. It was probably the first time she had ever fired a gun. She didn't kill him. He staggered off into the darkness and the rain, and so far as *she* knew he had the pictures with him."

More silence. The fire crackled, spitting sparks out onto

223

the hearth. J.Q. poked at it, making a shower of falling coals.

"She left. She drove away. She left his car there, Botts."

"Do you know who she is?"

"I think I know who she is, yes. Shall I tell the rest of the story?"

"Tell it."

"She went and fetched her husband. She told him what had happened. He came back with her to the mountain-side. He searched Dabronski's car, and then he ditched it. He went to Dabronski's room and searched that. Then he packed Dabronski's things, everything he could find, and took it away. Then he went home to his wife and probably spent the rest of the night hearing all about her turning a few tricks on Colfax Avenue with some other Columbine housewives."

"I suppose you have a witness."

"I have what amounts to a witness, Botts. I've got some pictures of the woman in question."

"Then what?"

"And then nothing. The murderess may have settled down and behaved herself for a while. Not permanently, just for a while. Everyone assumed Dabronski had gone back to North Carolina. Nothing happened. Not for months. And then came October, and Shirley McClintock found some bones in the mountains. Now so far as the murderer and her husband knew, the pictures were with the body. They hadn't been in the car. They hadn't been in the room. They must be with the body. And, possibly, Shirley McClintock had found them."

"So the murderer searched your house."

"Or her husband did."

"Her husband did," said J.Q.

"And you know who he is?"

"So do you, Botts. He is the man you told exactly where to find that arrow. I didn't tell anyone exactly where except the helicopter pilot who flew me there. The pilot was from Denver and unconnected with the case. Your men paid no

224

attention, and they were unconnected with the case. But you knew exactly where we were, and you must have told someone, because that is the only way he could have found the arrow that led him to Maxwell's house when he didn't find what he was looking for at my house.''

"I didn't tell . . .''

"You did. Someone was very interested and sympathetic. Someone who wanted to know all the details. All through this case this same sympathetic person has wanted to know all the details. I'll bet he's dropped in on you at least once a day or called you. You never thought twice about it, Botts. You just told him anything he wanted to know.''

He groaned. "Patterson.''

"Right.''

"He's never shot a bow in his life! I checked that!''

"Well, there I got a little misled. I thought we were looking for a bowshooter, but Patterson didn't need a bow. He had the arrow in his hand when he went to Maxwell's house. Oh, he was probably very angry. He thought Maxwell might have taken the pictures. He knew that Gloria Maxwell had been part of the prostitution business. He was angry and frustrated, and he's a tremendously powerful man. He confronted Charles Maxwell when Charles found him searching his house. Charles was drunk, loud; the Rev wanted to shut him up. The arrow was in his hand, and it probably happened so fast he didn't even know he'd done it until it was too late. When I looked at the arrow I knew someone had gripped it around the vanes, gripped it hard enough to break that tough polymer and twist it like so much tissue paper.''

"He stabbed him with it?''

"I believe so, yes.''

"Why did he kill Maxwell's wife?''

"Patterson didn't. The afternoon I took Gloria home from the jail she called someone, she said, to come help her because she didn't have a car. Who would she have called? The person who always drove her places. Bonny. Bonny was her buddy. And Bonny was the one who killed her. Maybe Bonny said she didn't want to help Gloria, and then Gloria may have told Bonny she had to help her or she'd tell on her. That was Gloria's style. Childish. 'I'll tell on you.' She never got the chance to tell on anyone.''

"How do you know?''

"I should have known days ago. There was an oil stain on the floor of the Maxwell garage. It hadn't been there before Gloria was killed. When Gloria called her Bonny probably told Gloria to open the garage door. She drove in, shut the door, shot Gloria, waited until no one was around, then drove out again. We even know exactly when it happened. It happened during the thirty minutes between the time the neighbor saw Gloria coming out the side door and the time that same neighbor went through her house looking for her. The neighbor thought she heard a car. I saw the oil stain on the garage floor when I went there later, at your request, Botts. I stepped in it. I even wiped my feet before I came back into the house, but it didn't connect. You expect to see oil stains in a garage. You don't find them remarkable. Only later I remembered the floor had been absolutely clean the first time I saw it. So I started thinking about oil stains. The car Patterson drove out to my place leaves oil stains like a horse leaves shit. There was an oil stain beside the road where the car was parked when Allison was grabbed.''

"But Bonny Patterson drives a little red car.''

"Not when she's trying to be inconspicuous she doesn't. Then she drives her husband's car. She was driving her husband's car the day the furniture warehouse burned down. Of course, when she goes into town on one of her extracurricular expeditions—then she drives the Porsche.''

Shirley took the brown envelope from the floor beside her, removed several photographs, and laid them on the table where Botts was sitting. "I've had these blown way, way up. The reflections in the window, Botts. See the car parked there? Its angle parked at the curb. You can't see that it's red, but you can see it's a Porsche. You can see the little rally emblems on the door and the little angel hanging from the rearview mirror. You can see the license plate. I drove out to Palace Pines today. The car was parked in the driveway of the Patterson house. Same little rally emblems. Same little angel. Same license number. My witness gave that little angel to Bonny. It's handmade. No two alike. She can identify it.

"Now look at the woman in the picture. I had them blow her way up, too, so you could see the distinguishing mark." She took another picture from the envelope. "This is an enlargement from a picture printed in the church paper. Different hair. Different glasses. Different makeup. Same mole behind the ear, Botts."

Another lengthy, painful silence. "I can't believe Patterson would kidnap a child."

Shirley shook her head. "I don't think so either. So who did you tell about the film? Patterson?"

He shook his head miserably. "She called. She said the reverend wanted to know if there was anything new."

"I don't think Patterson was involved in the kidnapping. I think Bonny got somebody else to help her do that. I don't think Patterson even knows about it."

"Why do you think that?" J.Q. asked curiously.

"He's a big man," she said. "A very big man. I think if Allison had been handled by a man that size, she'd have realized it. She'd have said something. She didn't even notice the size of the man who grabbed her, just that he felt hard in the chest. I don't think it was Patterson."

Botts put his head in his hands and moaned. "Oh, my God, what are people going to say?"

Shirley gave him a mirthless grin. "Elise Fish is going to say the reverend should have known better. Presumably he knew what his wife was—or had been—when he fell in love with her. According to the story I get she was quite an experienced woman when he married her. She was the only one among the housewives who had the know-how, Botts. She was the one who taught Gloria Maxwell and Arlette."

"How'm I going to prove all this?"

"I suggest you start by looking for Allison's shoe. You'll probably find it under the back seat of Patterson's Mercedes. Then, if you can do it without alerting Carmichael, I'd question Arlette. I'll give you the pictures. I'll give you the name of my witness, but you've got to treat her well. I won't have you yelling at her. I don't know where the reverend put the suitcase full of Dabronski's clothes, but maybe you can find that if you go looking. And I have no doubt that Bonny still has the gun."

"I heard voices," said a small voice from the hall. "Is something the matter?"

"Not a thing, Allison," said Shirley. "The sheriff just dropped by to say hello. He's leaving now."

The week before Christmas Shirley announced that she had something wonderful to celebrate. She held up a multi-paged legal document, showing Allison and J.Q. the signatures of Esther and Lawrence Brentwood, and invited them to sing a few brisk bars of the "Alleluia Chorus" with her.

"Does it say they don't want me?" Allison asked with great satisfaction. "Does it really?"

"More or less. It says that in consideration of the fact your mother placed you in my care, they are going to leave you here until you are eighteen years of age or until I beat you or until I fall dead of old age."

"Shirley had to sign over her soul," muttered J.Q.

"I am to make no claims upon them," assented Shirley. "I am to assume total responsibility for you. They do not wish to be held responsible for any future aggravation. I am more than willing to do so."

"Within reason," said J.Q.

"Within reason," Shirley agreed.

"So long as I get good grades and don't take up dope or have sex before I'm eighteen," said Allison. "J.Q. told me those were the rules."

Shirley gulped. Well, J.Q. had raised two daughters who

were now respectable matrons. Presumably he knew what he was doing. "I am highly gratified," she said.

"I'm going out to the barn and tell Beauregard," Allison announced. "He'll be very happy to know about this. I think I'll celebrate it, too, along with you, when I get back."

When she was gone J.Q. asked, "Do you think she knows about her mother?"

"I don't think so, J.Q. Botts never mentioned it to anyone except the district attorney, and he says he may not have to bring that up in the trial. The fact that Bonny was blackmailed with those pictures is enough. The fact that Gloria knew about Bonny's prostitution is enough. They don't have to have testimony that Gloria took part in it. We don't have any real proof that she did."

"The gun ties Bonny, does it?"

"Very firmly. The gun they found in Bonny's closet in the shoebox with her jewel hoard is the same gun that killed Gloria and is probably the same one that killed the deacon. The oil on the floor in the Maxwell garage matches the oil from the Mercedes. Allison's shoe was under the rear seat. And, of course, they found Dabronski's clothing where the reverend had stashed it, in a crawl space behind the organ pipes at the church."

"What about Patterson?"

"Change of venue probably. They aren't even going to charge him with murder. Not first-degree anyhow. And I guess that's probably right. He didn't go there planning to kill Maxwell."

"I should have known it was him right at the first."

"Why, J.Q.?"

"That day he came out here to see you? He had to go to the bathroom. He came in the house, nodded at me, and went right to it. He knew right where it was, even though he had to cross the living room and go down that back hall."

"He'd been here before!"

"That's how I knew he did the search. And they've never found out who helped Bonny kidnap Allison?"

"Never have. Possibly someone long gone. When it comes to trial Bonny may tell them. I think it was probably her pimp from Denver. She had to have someone there in case she or the other women got arrested or ran into trouble. Her experiences in Kansas City—where, by the way, she had several arrests for prostitution—would have taught her that."

"Allison doesn't say much about it."

"When I told her it was Mrs. Patterson, she wanted to know why. I told her Mrs. Patterson had a secret, and she was afraid Gloria was going to tell it, so she killed her. I said it was important never to do anything you had to keep secret and never to go digging into other peoples' secrets and if you did find out something dreadful by accident, you should go tell a lot of people right away." Shirley laughed, tears at the corners of her eyes.

"Nice kid,'² he said. "Getting good at math."

"Nice kid," Shirley agreed. "Oh, J.Q., I hope I'm not being selfish. I'd hate to be doing the wrong thing. . . ."

He gave her a long, level look. "Back a few months ago, I used to get kind of nervous when I saw you going off with a gun on your hip, Shirley."

"I've always carried a gun on the ranch," she objected.

"I know you have. Loaded for snakes. Or wild dogs. You know what I mean."

She started to lie then decided not to. She flushed instead, being well aware of what he meant. "I wasn't doing too well there for a while, J.Q."

"All I want to say is, you and Allison, the two of you probably saved each others' lives. And I'm very grateful for that, both ends of it. So you can forget what I told you once about not getting used to having her around."

Shirley hugged him. "I remember. And I did try, J.Q., but I couldn't help it."

"That's the trouble with love," he said. "You do get real used to having people around."

"Why, J.Q." It was the closest he had ever come to saying
. . . or had he said?

"Merry Christmas, Shirley," he did say, burying his nose
in the *Wall Street Journal*.

"Merry Christmas, J.Q."

About the Author

B.J. Oliphant lives on a ranch in Colorado. She will be writing more books for Fawcett, Gold Medal.

mood·y (moo′dē), *adj.*, **mood·i·er, mood·i·est**   1. given to gloomy or sullen moods.   2. exhibiting sharply varying moods.   3. one of the best authors of the Twentieth century; as in

Susan Moody.

For example: